ISBN:
978-1-9160503-5-8

Copyright © 2019 by Space Monkey Creations Ltd

Published by

Space Monkey
Creations Ltd

www.spacemonkeycreations.com

The Traveller

Chuck Thompson

Dedicated

to

Travellers all over the World and beyond

Prologue

Walking across the hot sand, boots dragging through the arid dust, the still air not helping, each dune seemingly bigger than the last and the temperature ever rising, the question lingered heavy and unrelenting like my body odour: how did this happen?

Wales
1

Llanelli

1

After World War II the Big Brains of the West – the same great minds who had imagined such dark ideas as 'Game Theory,' which involved concepts such as the Nash equilibrium, a strategy whereby each person fucks over the other to win – turned their sights on the world leaders they had once strategised for. The fifties saw the end of patriotism, particularly among the politicians and bureaucrats of leading nations as well as the beginning of the end of the British Empire. 'Public Choice Theory' was born and showed that those who had once served and governed empires now did little more than perform a series of self-interested acts. The politicians and bureaucrats of the West continued to speak like public servants, but in reality they performed acts of selfish acquisition to build their own personal wealth at the expense of society as a whole. This was due in part to there being no agreed version of the 'public good.' Patriotism of the masses and their leaders was dead – only the individual and their ambitions survived.

The year of 1979 saw several key events take

place in the UK. It was the year that Margaret Thatcher came to power as the British Prime Minister and promised to build a society based on the dreams of individual freedom – a continuation of 'Public Choice Theory'. Her decision to use the strategists of the Cold War era, the same people who had invented 'Game Theory', gave rise to what became labelled as Systems Management – a process that removed human values and emotions from the equation, be it politics, law or how you ran your company, as these values were believed to corrupt the systems they governed. People were replaced by mathematically defined targets and incentives. Patriotism and duty were replaced by mathematically deduced rational outcomes and objectives. These targets were all that mattered.

This same system was first used during the Vietnam War in order to try to prove to the public that the war was being won. It attempted to show that America was winning based solely on numbers – specifically the number of dead Vietnamese. Soldiers were given targets to reach, a set number of enemy combatants to kill each and every day in order to reach their quota to satisfy their leaders back in Washington. The result was often the slaughter of innocent people in order to meet 'kill board' numbers to earn an extra case of beer or day off, including the My Lai massacre and the atrocities committed against civilians in the Mekong Delta by General Julian Ewell's 9th Infantry Division in 1968, AKA the 'Butcher of the Delta'.

In the 80s Thatcher privatised almost everything and ran the country based on target quotas. The old ruling elite of expert people were replaced by a system whereby maths gave you targets and then you were free to reach that objective by any means necessary – just like those American soldiers in the jungles of Vietnam who operated on a 'kill anything that moves' policy. Even Adam Smith, the high priest of capitalism, wouldn't have seen it coming. A modern Western world governed by numbers with individuals free to achieve targets by any and all means at their disposal, with zero regard for humanity.

Along with Thatcher and her 'Systems Management' had come Dr Robert Spitzer's 'New Diagnostic System'. A scheme whereby a lay interviewer – a computer – asked a series of yes/no questions and then the person's answers, or data, were crunched and then used to diagnose that individual as being sane or having some kind of mental health issue, such as depression or Attention Deficit Hyperactivity Disorder or social anxiety or PTSD. The system diagnosed 50% of participants as having some form of psychological problem. It could not tell you why you suffered from this issue (or issues), just that you did. No clinical judgement required. The psychiatrists who saw the data believed there was a hidden epidemic in society and that people everywhere were secretly living with mental disorders. Soon the general public, your everyday average man and woman, began to diagnose themselves as crazy. This in turn gave rise to a new era known as the Prozac Age. Drug companies developed a medication that would turn complicated beings into simple and easily managed creatures.

Years later, Spitzer would acknowledge that his test had actually wrongly diagnosed regular human feelings and experiences as mental disorders, but of course it was too late to stop the pharmaceutical giants by then as they too had targets and quotas to meet. Even John Nash, who spent years in a mental institute, would in later life acknowledge that his contributions to 'Game Theory' were as a result of him being a paranoid schizophrenic.

The 1980s and its obsession with systems and theories created a Brave New World. A world with selfish leaders spouting doublespeak, citizens numbed by pharmaceuticals and targets that must be met regardless of the price humanity paid.

Llanelli

2

In 1972 the Llanelli Scarlets beat the New Zealand All Blacks 9 points to 3. Several decades later it's still the town's crowning achievement – its 15 minutes of fame. Whether you're interested in rugger or not, you'll be told about it at some point if you're unfortunate enough to spend any amount of time in the purgatory that sits on the south-west coast of England's garden.

Growing up in the eighties, damn near every parent dreamt of their son playing rugby for the Scarlets and then eventually Wales. And, of course, one day repeating that glorious moment in Welsh history when arguably the greatest team in the world was defeated by the Celtic underdogs. That one time when we were thought of as more than a nation of singing drunks covered in tattoos with scarred knuckles from constantly fighting.

Those sons, on the other hand, had different aspirations. There were few from my generation who gave that much of a fuck about the sport that they would ever devote time and effort into becoming professional players. Of course there were some, but a few of us had different dreams and most none at all.

It was the dawn of a new age and the technology of the nineties was changing everything for the better as far as most of us were concerned. Over our lifetime we would see the rotary-dial phone in the hallway of our parents' homes evolve into the smartphone carried by everyone everywhere. Computer power went from science fiction on a library shelf to your bedroom desk to your pocket with high speed fibre optic connection to the entire fucking planet. The Information Age was upon us and the game of rugby could go fuck itself.

In schools across the land kids had been forced to scrum with other lads and then shower with them afterwards. Is it any wonder our teenage years would see us turn to hardcore pornography and drugs for comfort and escape? Is it any wonder that so many of us would go on to spend long stretches in prisons, repeating their childhood actions of rucking with other males and then showering with them?

Alcohol had been the crutch of our parents and ancestors in the valleys, but for our generation there were also drugs. Drugs of any and all kinds, for any and all pursuit of pleasure and/or pain. Sure, in other parts of the world they'd had their psychedelic revolution decades earlier, but for us in our small coastal town it came at the end of the twentieth century. For us, it happened in warehouses and fields located in the arse-end of nowhere to deafening beats, blips, bleeps and dancing. The rave culture in the UK truly introduced many of us to the new concept of mixing drugs with external stimuli such as music and physical pursuit, i.e. dancing.

Popping pills, blowing whistles and waving glow sticks soon made way for blazing bud and aimlessly cruising around in cars. The rave culture was eventually hijacked by the gangsters due to the fat stacks being made flogging pills and powders to the ravers. For my generation, marijuana was where it was at. No need to get heavy about anything or with anyone, just spark up and go for a drive. By the time we started smoking, low-grade soap bar hash was abundant and available at decent prices – green buds were still something of a rarity.

The hippies of London's swinging sixties had hung out in forests or lounged around on Middle Eastern-style rugs and beanbags in flats to get stoned, drop acid, be with nature and talk shit about 'the Man'. We sat in front of screens, be they television, computer or wind. The flower-power kids of our parents' generation had swung to The Beatles, we grooved to Pantera and learned how Knowledge Reigns Supreme Over Nearly Everyone.

Our forefathers had sweated in tinplate factories or had their lungs filled with coal dust in quarries, and so a cold beer would help to cool a man down at the end of the day. Many would start the day with one as well. Alcohol was their thing, and still is, but for our generation it was merely a diversion on the way to better substances. We all started out with a drink from the off-license, but hard drugs were always the final destination. Our parents took a sip and then never moved past it. We slugged back the bottle and then went looking for something harder. Something to kill the monotony. Something more exciting than slavery, a sports team and a hangover. Orwell was right when he said that, "So long as they (the Proles) continued to work and breed, their other activities were without importance. Left to themselves, like cattle turned loose upon the plains of Argentina, they had reverted to a style of life that appeared to be natural to them, a sort of ancestral pattern... Heavy physical work, the care of the home and children, petty quarrels with neighbours, films, football, beer and above all, gambling filled up the horizon of their minds. To keep them in control was not difficult." But then he had died before my generation were even born, so how could he know about our departure from the herd?

We stared blankly at blackboards, bored out of our brains with the slave mentality being forced onto us at school between punishing games of rugger. Then we had a little freedom. There were no jobs, no factories, no money or career prospects. But there was now a little freedom. The Information Age and drugs had brought with them freedom of mind and knowledge. If you were the right kind of person, you acquired the right kind of knowledge and used it. You escaped from your local town for local people with local thinking. Of course, none of us knew this at the time, it was something that developed over the years. We pioneered forth, high on drugs and with a burning desire to not end up like our parents. We didn't want the heavy work, petty quarrels or gambling.

Jagger had told us about Mother's Little Helper, and Frey had warned us of that most infamous of hotels. Our generation was far from the first to fuck about with drugs and loose ourselves in music that fitted our enhanced mood, but we were the first to be conscious of the pitfalls and dangers that had taken so many before us. We usually learned from their mistakes and altered our dosage accordingly. No need to end your days laying in a motel bath with your last meal floating all around you. Control your dosage accordingly, for knowledge is power and self-control is liberating.

Not everyone thought like this, and of course there were many who followed in the footsteps of the players before them. Stomping that same old turf of trying to do well in school, only to wind up working a shit job in your shit hometown, marrying a local girl and then settling down to a shit game of musical chairs with a mortgage and several children to raise and push through the same system that churned you out.

But there were us few who had our minds expanded by information and weed. Both were just as important and enhancing as the other. A necessary cocktail of nature and technology – yin and yang. But not everyone took this path and not all who did survived.

Llanelli

3

It started out innocent enough. I'd buy a little puff and then the others would chip in and share it at the weekend. Soon, it grew to an operation that involved driving to various other towns and cities, where various lovable rogues sold larger quantities.

Soap bar hash was easy enough to conceal. It was damn near odourless and solid enough to be hidden under and in things without worry of it being contaminated, ruined or destroyed. A brick was not a hard thing to hide in a car or on a motorbike. If you were lazy or overly confident, you could have it in bags in the boot or even slipped down the back of the seats. If you were smarter you did like the professional smugglers and hid it behind panels, under the lining of the seats or in other places where a brick can slide into discreetly unnoticed by beady black eyes.

Back in the 90s, pigs weren't really sniffing around for it. If you got pulled they wanted to smell booze on your breath. They assumed the red and heavy panda eyes were the result of whisky not weed. This was fine by us.

"Sure officer, I'll breath into your little gadget.

Nothing to hide here."

You can't help but be delighted at the sadness on the swine's chops when the breathalyser read zero. They'd interrogate you a little on the side of the road, but eventually they would have to give up. If you play along with their little game and win, there is little that most of them will or can do. Sure, some of them get the hump, but they're mostly looking for that easy win. A piggy doesn't want to have to work for his meal. They won't even use their natural-born five senses a lot of the time. I've been stood at the rear of my ride, a pair of piggies before me, while having to tell them the make, model and license number of the car that they are stood next to. I even asked a piggy once why she didn't just turn her head 45 degrees to read this information for herself. Her reply was less than cordial, polite, witty, professional or called for. She asked if I was making trouble and wanted to go to the cells for the night. As I didn't fancy a night in the pen surrounded by wailing swine and drunken degenerates, and because I also had an ounce tucked in my sock, I played humble and told her what she wanted to hear.

At those times, when you had close calls with the law you would often wonder why on Earth there was all that fuss, drama and bullshit over the chance that you may have a little bit of a plant in your possession. You had to ask yourself at least once, why was cannabis illegal?

It all went back to the first half of the twentieth century, and specifically a man named William

Randolph Hearst Sr. Mainly because of this cunt, it officially became illegal in the US following the introduction of the Marihuana Tax Act of 1937, and sure enough the rest of the world followed suit.

Hearst was the inspiration for the protagonist of Orson Welles' movie Citizen Kane. He was an American businessman and newspaper publisher who unsuccessfully ran for president as a member of the Democrats. Hearst built America's biggest newspaper chain and media company before eventually fucking it all up due to his poor money management, and in the end he had to liquidate most of his assets. He built his newspaper empire using what is known in the industry as 'Yellow journalism'. This is when there is little to no research done on a story, and you instead use eye-catching headlines and sensationalism to get people reading your stories and buying your papers – known today as just plain, old regular journalism. For Hearst all that mattered was big sales and big profits. Later, he would use his newspapers for propaganda, but still to achieve the same monetary goals.

For thousands of years, civilizations have been farming and using hemp for all manner of different things. It was the earliest plant cultivated for textile fibre. Hemp is an unbelievably versatile plant. In the 1500s, Henry VIII forced farmers to grow it for the British Navy, which was one of the biggest contributing factors to the Empire becoming as powerful as it did. Other Navies were still using cotton for their sails, which couldn't stand up to the harsh conditions out at sea and the erosive power of wind and saltwater. Hemp sails on the other hand could cope admirably. Traditional ships would need to take multiple spare sails, ropes and other supplies because they knew that the cotton wouldn't last long under the difficult conditions. The British started using hemp, and then suddenly had more space on their ships for things that gave them an advantage out at sea, plus less time was wasted changing sails and most importantly less weight was carried which allowed them to sail faster. *Rule Britannia! Britannia rule the waves* indeed. The word 'canvas' even derives from the name cannabis because it was used so much for so long to make the material, which was used for sails among other things.

Over time, cotton became the go-to textile due to the ease by which it could be farmed and handled – in comparison hemp was a very difficult plant to process for its fibres. Then in 1917 a man by the name of George W. Schlichten invented a new machine in America called the Decorticator, which made the processing of hemp fibres even easier than cotton fibres. Everyone assumed that hemp was about to make a comeback and become a multibillion-dollar industry. Unfortunately, and very mysteriously, both Mr. Schlichten and his new machine disappeared along with damn near all records of his new invention.

Along with the sudden disappearance of the Decorticator and its inventor was the propaganda spread via Hearst and his papers. It was Hearst that started using the term 'marihuana' and its variant spelling 'marijuana' to refer to cannabis. Marijuana is actually a wild Mexican tobacco, not hemp. Between Hearst, who had his own forests to make paper and sell timber that could have been replaced by hemp, and other companies such as DuPont who had money sunk into plastic fibres and other synthetic textiles, cannabis became demonised and illegal by associating it with non-whites. The reason Hearst used the name of a Mexican tobacco to start referring to cannabis is because he wanted the American public to associate it with Mexican people, whereby he could fan the flames of ignorance and incite the racial prejudices of the time to inspire the good white Americans to get on board the idea that marijuana should be illegal, which meant that hemp would also be illegal to farm and process. Hearst's papers started spreading the lies that black people were committing heinous crimes on decent God fearing white Americans while high on the devil's lettuce. If they weren't high then maybe there would be a chance that these dark fellows wouldn't rape our innocent white daughters and perform all manner of other nasty crimes on American citizens.

The truth is that anything that can be made from a hydrocarbon (fossil fuel) can be made from carbohydrate (hemp). This is just too big a competitor to too many other industries. And at the end of the day, cash is king.

As the months rolled on the bricks increased in quantity. It was starting to look like a viable fulltime income could be earned just selling soap. This was not what I had wanted for myself. I knew that there were bigger adventures to be had than merely picking up puff a few miles down the road and then bringing it back to sell to familiar faces. I had now passed enough courses and collected enough certificates and qualifications to go to university. I had opened a lot of doors for myself all over the country. But for a stoner from south-west Wales, it seemed only logical that the place of higher learning I attend be situated in the capital. Not the capital of Wales, no, no young sir – that would not be a big enough adventure. London was calling and I answered willingly.

England
1

London

1

My first night in the big smoke started pretty much as I would end up going on for the best part of four years. Two friends from my hometown, the Actor and the Mechanic, had taken me to Middlesex university in north-west London and then decided to join me for a drink in the uni bar before making the drive all the way back to Llanelli. Outside the toilets I met Boggart, we instantly hit it off and he introduced me to the guys he was sharing his flat with. Meeting strangers by toilets had never been something I'd experienced before, this being an activity usually done by the more promiscuous and pink of my gender, but this encounter turned into a long-term friendship with a fellow fiend. I was yet to meet my new flatmates and was happy to get to know some fellow students. My hometown friends wished me luck and left while I got acquainted with Boggart and the others. The night ended with us in Boggart's flat and about 20 other random students we had met at the bar, all drinking and smoking some of the soap bar that I'd brought with me. This became a typical evening for us, hit a pub or bar and then stay up until late into the night getting high and pouring more booze down our throats.

The following day I met my new flatmates. One dude was a German ex-officer in their Navy, who had spent several years on submarines. He was good looking, funny, loved dark rum and was a complete sadomasochist who often wore tight black leather trousers. Next was the Pikey, an English fella from Essex-way who was like a refugee from the sixties. He believed that protesting the government with placards could change the world and that the Beatles had all the answers. The fourth occupant of our flat was only seen twice. On the second night he came in to say hello to the three of us while we all got drunk and smoked soap in my room. He didn't join in or make much effort to get to know us. A few days later he asked us to return his flat key to admin for him as he said he was leaving for a different life. None of us cared, he was twitchy and had a terrible problem with his body odour. We took the key, said goodbye and continued to smoke it up. Like all students given this opportunity, we kept the key and said nothing to the university about his departure. This was now a spare room for us to party in so that our rooms wouldn't get too trashed.

Inevitably, the entire flat would get pretty fucked up. We would begin with drinking and smoking in our spare room, but most nights the number of people who came to our place to hang out and get fucked up swelled beyond the small box rooms we were given as bedrooms. Soon, all the rooms would be open and filled to capacity, music blaring from various sound systems, and even the shower base would be used as a place to sit and enjoy a drink and smoke. It was only a matter of months before the carpet, walls and ceiling were stained with alcohol and God-knows-what. The kitchen door became ventilated after several nights of the ex-sailor teaching us how to throw knives – which the Pikey and I became pretty good at even while inebriated – as well as how to disarm an attacker holding a pistol. Both useful life skills. The hall mirror was cracked after someone staggered into it and the curtains were removed due to various drunks reaching out for something or someone to save them from falling out of the third-story window. Fortunately, none did – they just slid down the pane leaving various fluids behind that gave them a strange psychedelic stained-glass effect over time.

The first year in London was debauchery personified, and it peaked during that final weekend after all of our assignments had been handed in at the end of the first academic calendar. The work was handed in at 12 noon and then we went straight to the bar. The drinking continued throughout the day, evening and well into the night. By sunrise the next day there were only four of us left still drinking beer and smoking weed, but then both ran out. The Pikey and I went on a beer run to the local off-license, and on the way back discussed an earlier conversation we'd had in the night about our mutual desire to try acid. For many months I had been scoring high-grade ganja from a guy who lived in a flat below me, who was a complete fiend and very knowledgeable about his products. It just so happened that I noticed his bedroom window was open on the way back from the beer run. We approached to hear music and revelry within, and we were in luck. The guy had told me weeks earlier that he had some great acid direct from Amsterdam due to arrive in the post roundabout now, and that the proper way to take it would be to have a good night's sleep before walking to a picturesque park to drop the advertised dose of 220 µg of lysergic acid diethylamide and let it gently wash over you like a warm summer breeze. The Pikey and I scored a couple of tabs along with some fine Black Gold hashish and returned to our other two friends. One of the girls decided that being awake and consuming alcohol, weed, MDMA and speed for almost a full 24 hours was enough. Another drink or two to let the speed wear-off and then it would be time to crash. Me and my other two companions decided it would be better to split the acid three ways and then ride the rest of the day out on a trip.

Good acid doesn't come on immediately, and after a couple of hours the Pikey and I were grumbling about how my dealer's gear may not be as good as his sales pitch. Then the giggling began. We didn't notice it at first, but our friend who hadn't dropped did. She couldn't understand what was so funny about her stuffed dolphin, but to us it was eye-wateringly hilarious. The simple act of moving the cuddly toy through the air in front of us, like it was swimming in the ocean, was enough to cause loud laughter and shrill screams of enjoyment. Our third tripper made the call that more beer was needed and that we should let the girl whose room we were in get some rest.

The campus was situated just off of White Hart Lane in Tottenham, while the supermarket was located in Edmonton. A morning walk to the shop, which would have usually taken 20 minutes, occupied the next several hours as we laughed and screamed and lost our way. After eventually purchasing half a dozen cans of lager from a bewildered till girl we proceeded to sit in the middle of the car park and laugh hysterically while trying to pour the beer into our mouths. By now our fine motor skills were starting to degenerate rapidly, having already lost our gross motor skills after leaving the supermarket; hence the sitting in the middle of the car park on dirty concrete with litter strewn all around. After some noise from the customers, a security guard and the manager we eventually made it to our feet and moved along as requested. Charlie Brown, our female companion, made another great decision, "We should go for a random bus ride."

The Pikey and I concurred, as we knew the supermarket manager had phoned the police by this point and figured a big, red double-decker bus would make the perfect getaway vehicle. Our escape was slightly delayed by my inability to feel any of my own body at this point. The bus driver grimaced at me while I fumbled around trying to get my hand into my pocket to retrieve the money to pay my fare. There was no feeling in any part of my body, it was completely numb, and by now my vision had gone way past seeing double and was constantly spinning so that everything blurred not only at the edges, but also at its centre. Eventually, I managed to throw enough coins at the disgruntled driver to suffice in me joining my companions on the upper deck of the bus. We sat for what felt like hours on some occasions and then mere minutes at others, talking shit that entertained some of the passengers and offended many others. After some complaints we were ejected at the top of 'Ally Pally', having transferred busses at some point, possibly even several points. We sat atop the hill, which offers a spectacular view over North London in the summer sun, talking bollocks and giggling at anything and anyone that passed by for most of the afternoon. Colours shifted and blurred, the sky changed into a purple jelly in an orange ocean speared by yellow rays, dogs cracked jokes with us as their owners took them for a stroll and nature kept us safe from the authorities.

When we returned to the uni's halls of residence Charlie Brown decided she could still make her date with her boyfriend, despite having been awake and off her face for 36 hours by now. She left us to our own devices.

The Pikey and I tried to continue the party back at our flat, but by now our bodies were starting to give in to a lack of sustenance and sleep. We parted company after a few hours and the sunny afternoon turned into a dark evening of music that sounded like white noise, sleep that resulted in waking up suddenly due to the feeling of having my face pressed against the ceiling and terrifying trips to the toilet where my penis appeared to have shrunk to the size of a peanut, which had already been chewed by an angry ape.

Somewhere amidst the cries and wails there was a memory of our German flatmate coming to see if the Pikey and I were ready to help him get to the airport as promised weeks earlier. We had lived together for a whole academic year and had a lot of fun. The three of us agreed that it would only be right if we accompanied the ex-sailor to Heathrow for a fond farewell. Unfortunately we had not taken into account the love of alcohol and drugs that the Pikey and I shared, which had now rendered us feeble and fucked up on my filthy bedroom floor. It was not a fond farewell, more of a 'fuck you guys for letting me down'. The German shook his head in disgust at his British flatmates, who now sprawled about in clothes we'd been wearing for two days in an unusually hot British summer. The two of us made some feeble attempt at an apology and said something along the lines of "let's keep in touch," which of course never happened. Eventually the acid wore off enough, and our bodies and minds calmed down enough so that we were able to sleep. A long, deep slumber brought on by excess and exhaustion ended our first year of university in London.

France

Calais

It could have been the desire to travel, a need for a celebration to commemorate completing our first year or just the absolute mind-numbing boredom of being forced to watch the movie Titanic, we weren't sure. It never ceases to amaze me both how awful the film is and how much people love it. It was this movie that first made me realise unquestionably that the Oscars was a complete and utter farce. Star Wars: Episode IV – A New Hope made 20 years before had far better special effects, and yet the sinking boat managed to float away with damn near every one of those little gold statues at the ceremony. Further evidence of the rigged Oscars came by way of what has been dubbed the 'black Oscars', the night the academy gave leading actor, leading actress and a lifetime achievement award to black Americans as if it could make up for decades of being an almost all white celebration of Hollywood – what bullshit.

What we were sure about was that something big needed to be done. Tripping on acid for the best part of two days had not been a sufficient enough way to end the year of debauchery. Maybe it was the ship on the small screen that subconsciously prompted me to suggest aloud, "We should go to France."

"What?" enquired the Pikey at my side.

"You got your passport here with you?"

"Well, yeah..."

"Fuck it then, let's just go dude." I sat up on the bed we were all chilling on. With me was the Pikey and the Pop Star, who at the time of my suggestion was taking a piss. We had been getting high in the Pop Star's room in the halls of residence due to his persistence that we watch the movie that had won more Oscars than any other in history – we were after all film students. The Pikey and I had avoided the movie in the cinema and for several years since its 1997 release. We both loved James Cameron's earlier movies and were indeed huge fans of his, but a love story where you already know the ending held no appeal. The Pop Star had badgered us for months and then caught us when we were weak and vulnerable recovering from the two-day binge we'd just got over. The Pikey and I both hoped there was still enough acid left in our systems to make the movie somewhat entertaining, but that never happened.

When the Pop Star returned to his room the Pikey and I were on our feet with the movie paused, and we had wide mischievous grins on our faces.

"What's going on?" he enquired, handing us cans of beer.

"We're going to France!" I answered.

"You what?"

"Come on, man. It'll be great! A real adventure," the Pikey said with a little jig.

"You want me to go to?!" the Pop Star shrieked.

"We're all going," I clarified.

There weren't that many of our group left on the campus. Some had already departed for their hometowns to visit family and friends now that the academic year was over. There were however still some stragglers who the Pikey and I promptly rounded up and coerced and eventually shanghaied into joining us on a boat trip to France that would begin immediately.

Our small band of merry travellers used London's public transport to get to Victoria coach station where we managed to catch the last big white box on wheels to Dover that night. Completely unplanned and unprepared we nonetheless managed to purchase a ticket and get on board a ferry across the Channel to Calais. On the ship we spent our time between the various bars, where we pounded booze, played drinking games and hammered the arcade games, and the deck where we smoked some of the gear we'd smuggled along for the trip. Our fellow fiend, Charlie Brown, had helped tremendously with getting a giant lump of hashish onto the ferry. As the Pikey and I shared a spliff with her out on the windy moonlit deck we enquired where she had hidden it when going through customs, to which she smiled and passed the joint saying, "Use your imaginations boys."

When we docked at Calais none of us had any idea where to go. Not one of us had actually been there on foot, only passed through en route to other cities or countries. We had no idea if there was anything to do at the famous port, other than hope we could find transport to another more famous city. Paris is almost 300km from Calais, and none of us knew of any other places in France worth visiting, save for Nice which I knew to be at the other end of the country and 1200km away from where we stood.

"Fuck it! There's got to be a boozer somewhere round here," the Pikey stated somewhat optimistically.

"Yeah," several of us nodded in agreement. But not everyone agreed.

"So we're just going to start walking around in the middle of the fucking night in the hopes that we're going to find a pub that's open?" asked the Jeweller. She said it in that way where we were clearly meant to understand how dumb an idea she thought this was. The Pikey and I both smiled widely and nodded our heads enthusiastically.

"Yep, that's pretty much the plan," I said.

"You're fucking idiots," the Jeweller informed us.

"She's got a point," seconded the Pop Star.

"Well, it's either that or sit here at the docks all night. There aren't any more ships back to England until the morning," the MC informed us.

"I don't believe this," sighed a disappointed Jeweller.

"That settles it. Let's bang up a couple of Js here for the walk and then get going," I said with a smile and a nod.

The Pikey and I rolled the joints and then we headed off into the night. We followed the signs toward Calais city centre and stuck to main roads.

After about 20 minutes of what looked like empty suburban streets we saw a lone skinny man carrying a small leather holdall and strolling along casually. The Pikey and I decided to approach him and ask if we were headed in the right direction for civilisation and somewhere to get a drink. He spoke fluent English and said that as luck had it he was headed to an all-night bar not 10 more minutes away on foot.

"You and your friends are welcome to join me," he said with a smile.

"Cheers. We'll let the others know," the Pikey informed him as he returned the smile.

We joined our friends who had hung back with the smouldering spliffs for fear of the lone stranger being some sort of psychopath or plain clothes gendarmerie bacon. I told them we were going to follow him to a 24-hour boozer and that he seemed decent enough. The females among our group were not convinced. The Pikey and I said that we would walk ahead with the stranger, and that they could follow from a distance and they tentatively agreed.

As the Pikey and I walked along the deserted streets there was no small talk with our new companion, who seemed a little on edge. We figured that he was probably just as nervous as our friends, considering he was alone and we were a group of eight, all drunk and stoned. It wasn't until we heard the thumping music and saw the neon sign for the bar that the Pikey noticed something illuminated by one of the streetlamps: blood.

My friend tapped my elbow discreetly and

nodded down at the bag in the stranger's hand. As we walked between lamps there was nothing that looked out of the ordinary, but then as we stepped directly under the yellow bulb I spotted what my buddy was now wide eyed and quietly freaking out about. From the zipped bag dripped thick droplets of blood, black as we moved beyond the reach of the street lights, and while it may have been my high imagination there appeared to be a round object in the bag resembling the size and shape of a human head. As we neared the bar the stranger turned and smiled at us, "Here it is," he said with a gesture toward the corner building and open door flanked by two white gorillas dressed in black bomber jackets.

"Nice," I said with a nervous smile.

"We'll catch up with you, we're gonna just wait for our friends," the Pikey followed up.

"I'll see you inside," the stranger said as he and his suspicious baggage walked directly into the sound of music and loud chatter.

"This doesn't look too bad," Charlie Brown said with an approving nod as her and the others caught up with us.

"Keep walking!" the Pikey and I said in unison as we headed for the nearest street leading in another direction away from both the bar and the port.

"What? Why?!" asked the Pop Star as we all hurried away.

Back en route to the city centre, the Pikey and I informed our friends of the suspicious bag only to be met with jeers and comments of how off our tits we must be in order to dream up such nonsense. For the sake of not wanting to ruin the trip the Pikey and I both agreed that it must have been our imaginations, while constantly checking over our shoulders for the remainder of the walk into Calais proper.

The next bar we found was decent enough. Small and covered in blue and pink neon, it had a kind of 80s vibe to it. We hadn't been drinking long when we were approached by three rough-looking fellas, who turned out to be both English and smugglers on their way home from Amsterdam. They joined us at our table and we all hit it off immediately, even more so when they discovered we had good hashish with us and they had strong speed with them.

At closing time we ended up back at one of the smuggler's hotel rooms with more alcohol, some strong spliffs and a mound of speed on the table. We partied on for a few more hours until things took a turn from the depraved to the dark and downright dangerous.

Between bumps and biffs the smugglers decided to show us something else illegal that they had: Tasers. The smugglers quickly went from jovial and welcoming to mean and threatening. It was at this point they informed us they had brought us back to their hotel in order to fuck us and produced three pairs of handcuffs from one of their backpacks. We naturally assumed that the three big men with Tasers had plans on raping the females in our group, but then they turned to the Pikey and announced that he was going to be their first victim. The females were shocked but visibly relieved, and the Pop Star and Pikey shrieked with horror. I laughed a little. I couldn't help myself. The Pikey had always prided himself on how much the ladies loved him, and now here we were trapped in a hotel room with three gay rapists who all had eyes for him. It was too much for my warped little mind to take when so drunk and fucked up on drugs. It was also too much for the Pikey to take too. The fear quickly got the better of him and he proceeded to projectile vomit over the three would-be rapists stood directly before him, which prompted the Pop Star and one of the girls to vomit as well. It wasn't long before the smugglers and their room were dripping in Exorcist-style vomit mixed with a lot of alcohol. Those of us not painting the room and rapists in vomit saw our opportunity to escape and quickly grabbed those in our party with the weaker stomachs and ran for it.

Outside some of us laughed, some vomited some more and others cried. After we had all calmed down we managed to find another 24-hour establishment that served breakfast and beer as the sun began to rise in the east, and we all agreed it was time to travel back to London.

England
2

London

2

I'd first started working in pubs when I was 14. It had started off as simply going to the working man's club in the rough end of town after school because that's where my mother worked. I'd sit in the cramped back office and do my homework, watch TV on an old set that had a battered bunny ear antenna attached to the top that you had to move around to pick up a signal and wait until her shift had finished at midnight. This developed into shooting pool and trying to play snooker, which in turn moved on to collecting glasses around the bar just to help out. It wasn't long before I was learning how to pull a pint as well as how to drink one.

So when the Scot threw me in at the deep end by giving me a trial at the local sports bar on a Friday night not long after the turn of the century in London, there were no issues. I'd been tending bars for years by that point and knew how to hustle. The sports bar sat on a busy crossroads between Wood Green and Palmers Green in North London and had a bit of a dodgy reputation. Having only been in the capital for a little less than a year I had been oblivious to the bar's notoriety until one day at university when a friend blurted out, "You got a job where?!" at the mention of the bar's name. He then proceeded to tell me in lurid detail that if it was weapons, drugs, violence or any other kind of criminality I was interested in, then this bar had everything I could ever desire.

The Scot always maintained that the sports bar was like kindergarten compared to the pubs he'd worked in South London, but for me it was a real eye-opener. My first Saturday night confirmed the rumours. Two six foot plus men with black skin and gold teeth had insisted that they didn't have to pay me for the double Hennessy they just threw back because they had just helped out the manager and he was personally thanking them by throwing a drink each their way. I called bullshit and insisted they pay, but after a little back and forth they told me to speak to the Scottish manager outside, which is where they were headed. Not convinced by their tale I followed them away from the bar and out to the car park, where I saw what can only be described as something like a scene from a crime movie. There were flashing blue and red lights everywhere from the multiple police cars and ambulances. Blue and white tape was already in place, cordoning off an area of the car park next to the entrance that was now glistening crimson. There was crying, screaming and yelling from multiple directions, as well as police barking orders at the drunk patrons of the bar. The manager confirmed the story given by gold teeth and I was sent back inside to keep working.

It later turned out that one of the bouncers had been targeted by a young dealer who had been ejected from another bar weeks earlier by the less-than-polite mountain of muscle in a black bomber jacket. The young man had picked this night to pull up on a scooter, slash a blade down the bouncer's face, cutting all of the nerves and muscles that would result in the right side of his face drooping for the rest of his life, before sticking the blade into the giant man's stomach several times. The second bouncer, who had tried to help his comrade, got six inches of steel in the liver for his troubles. The two doormen survived, but not without permanent scars, thanks to the two Hennessy drinkers rushing to their aid and phoning an ambulance. The youth got away, or at least he never got arrested for his crime.

The weekends rolled on, and the violence continued apace. Working in the sports bar gave my nights a very different vibe compared to what I'd been used to. For the last year I had done nothing but be a full-time student/stoner at university, which meant I had spent a year partying with happy youngsters just looking to have fun. The university had made a critical mistake early on by telling me that none of the grades I achieved in the first year counted towards the final degree. For the first year you just had to turn up on occasions and hand something slightly resembling an essay in, and that's pretty much it. This resulted in the best part of 12 months being spent getting drunk and taking drugs while exploring the UK's capital. My time at the sports bar involved ducking bottles, dodging pool cues thrown like a javelin and trying not to get killed or at the very least seriously injured.

London

3

The second year in London brought with it commitments to hand work in on time in order to pass the courses, and also a necessity to earn in order to pay bills for my accommodation and the continuation of the hedonistic lifestyle I was accustomed to.

The sports bar paid well enough to make up for what the student loan couldn't cover. My savings were long gone by this point, having been made substantially smaller in the month leading up to leaving for London by way of not being able to sell my car.

My beautiful and powerful Sierra Cosworth would have made a sizeable difference to my cash flow in London, but unfortunately I'd written it off racing at a 100+ with my friend the Actor. The Sierra had mounted a roundabout at triple figures, launching into the air with all four wheels off the ground and came crashing and scraping down along the barrier that runs the side of the bridge over the River Loughor, not far from Llygad Llwchwr caves. If it had been a lighter car it would have cleared the barrier and landed in the rapid currents of the water below, but fortunately for yours truly it landed short of those murky depths late on a Friday night. Unfortunately, the car was totalled and unsellable, leaving me with less money to take to university that I had planned on.

The management and staff at the sports bar would always stick around for a few drinks after a busy shift on the weekend, which was tame and civilised compared to my drinking habits with university friends.

Shifts at the sports bar were followed by a short walk home to my new house in one of the Greek areas of North London and all the unknown debauchery therein. Six of us from uni had decided to move in together during the summer following our first year. Three guys and three girls. But that first summer, one of the guys and one of the girls had gone back to their hometowns for jobs. The four of us that remained in London were by far the least responsible.

That first summer there should have only been four of us living in the six-bedroom house, but that number quickly jumped into double digits before the first month was up. It started with a couple of friends needing a place to crash while they sorted out their own houses, but then friends of friends turned up and then acquaintances of friends of friends of friends of complete fucking strangers started showing up to what quickly became known as the party house. On occasion you could walk in after a long and busy shift at the sports bar to find 20 random strangers in your home with decks hooked up to giant speakers blasting music loud enough to wake the entire neighbourhood and the distinctive mix of chemicals and burning plastic smell of crack wafting in the air. The only thing to do was to establish yourself as one of the true tenants of the house and demand free drink and drugs from any and all who crossed your path, which is not a bad deal really.

The first summer at that house set a strange tone, which would be continued for another two years. Violence and shady dealings at the sports bar, loud drug-fuelled parties at home and the occasional lecture and seminar on the art of film making at university.

It was at the sports bar where I met the Prisoner. He was a cockney who had been in and out of jail all of his adult life. Now approaching his fifties, he was experienced and wiser but no less a criminal. His main income was from dealing cocaine, which would soon become my white mistress, the green lady being my first love. As the infamous Howard Marks once wrote, 'You start off dealing simply because you end up buying more than you can consume yourself. You don't plan to be a dealer, it's not something you set out to do, it simply just happens because your friends want some and you've got some spare. Nothing criminally minded about it. It just happens.' The Prisoner would often inform me that he knew I'd never served time because of my lack of ingenuity. It was first brought up when I informed him that we needed to go to a shop to buy some skins as we'd run out and wanted to continue getting stoned. He said we should save ourselves the trip to the 24-hour garage and just use toilet paper, like they do behind bars. I said I'd rather make the trip, which was met by jeers about how soft I was and how I'd never make a decent prisoner. I still consider that to be a compliment.

Through the Prisoner I met the Greek. He was someone not to be fucked with. He was a supplier to most of North London's dealers and had a reputation for favouring a pump-action shotgun with a cut-down shoulder stock. Only weeks before I was formally introduced to him, the Greek had gone on a mini-rampage down a quiet close somewhere out in the suburbs where a rival coke supplier lived. He had apparently stopped his car at the entrance of the close, whipped out his beloved pump action and proceeded to unload it into the rival's car and front of his house while walking forwards like someone out of a fucking cowboy movie, minus the Stetson but with the addition of lots and lots of steroids. For reasons unknown, the Greek took an instant dislike to me. When first introduced to each other he stared coldly at me while downing his Virgin Mary and then turned and walked away. The Prisoner and I were both confused, but neither of us really cared that much. The Prisoner and I got on great, and he was an old friend, ex-celly and current business partner of the Greek, so he assured me there was no need to fear being woken up by the sounds of a shotgun being racked outside my bedroom door any time soon.

It wasn't long before the Greek's cocaine was

making its way up the nostrils of my fellow
students. It went from Greek, to Prisoner, to yours
truly and then onwards to a whole host of
degenerate students. Thanks to the Greek, many an
assignment got finished on time as students pulled
all-nighters in front of their laptops, furiously
tapping away for long bursts in between cheeky
lines. An expensive way to write essays, but a
productive one. You can produce some compelling
theories when flying high on quality coke. There
were some students who still used speed for all-
night essay writing, but the professionals knew that
cocaine is where the truly weird theories were
found. Well, cocaine lines and green spliffs if you're
a true professional; cocaine was mainly for those
paranoid that they wouldn't get their shit finished
on time.

For the best part of two years I was a conduit of
cocaine from the rough end of North London to the
four corners of academia. I wasn't the only one, not
by a long shot, just another cog in the machine.
Just another junkie helping his fellow students to
excel and live their best lives. Just another example
of Britain's fine academic system at work.

At school a gem of wisdom had been bestowed
on me by the careers adviser – I was not to pick a
trade but receive an education. There's no money to
be made and no future to be had in learning
plumbing, carpentry or the like. Get into university,
get into double-digit debt and earn yourself a piece
of paper that no employer in the land will ever give
a rat's arse about – that's what you need to do, boy.

Upon completing my BA in film studies, no employer in my field in London would look twice at me because I lacked experience. In my hometown, no employer in any fucking field would get further than the interview stage with me because I was overqualified. The only thing my BA was good for was getting back into university to do an MA and rack up more debt. By the time I'd finished my Masters in film studies, old school friends who had ignored the careers adviser and got themselves a trade were now married and living under their own roof, supporting a family and having summer holidays in Europe and beyond, all paid for by the money they earned doing their trade. I was jobless, broke and depressed. Thankfully, I'd gotten more out of my university education than just a useless piece of paper – I had gotten interesting life experience as well as knowledge, skills and hands-on know-how in an entirely different kind of trade.

Drugs pays well if you do it right. The problem with drugs trade is some of the psychopaths who operate in that world, such as the Greek. It only took a couple of years for him to tire of putting up with my presence and the Prisoner was told to part ways with me in no uncertain terms. This came at the right time as I was moving onwards and upwards anyway. The Prisoner and I parted company amicably over a few grams and half a dozen pints apiece. We never did learn why the Greek hated me, and the Prisoner and I knew better than to pry too deeply on the matter with the pump-action obsessed killer. I had gained knowledge and experience, and that was what truly mattered.

Holland
1

Amsterdam

1

There had been talk of going to Amsterdam for a couple of years. Almost everyone I knew smoked weed, and almost everyone I knew wanted to go to Amsterdam for the experience of buying and smoking it legally. It was a common subject of conversation, particularly the days when weed was dropping in quality and/or availability around London.

I'd been regularly using a coach service to travel back and forth between London and Swansea, and one day I saw an advert offering an insanely cheap deal for a long weekend in Amsterdam. You leave Victoria coach station early Friday morning and return Sunday night – perfect for a first visit. I took the details and spread the word that we were finally going to our personal Mecca by coach.

From Victoria the coach travelled to Dover. There it crossed the channel via the tunnel to Calais. We then drove through France and Belgium and into Holland. At this time access to the internet was not easy or common, so booking a hotel or hostel in advance was difficult. The decision was made to sort accommodation out upon arrival.

People grew excited and spoke in fevered tones about the stories they'd heard. The talk continued. There was no action, only more talk. I took the initiative and booked my ticket, instructing others to follow as and when they could. The main problems when trying to organise a large party of people, mostly students, to take a trip together are money and timing. The timing wasn't an issue as the coach offer was only available for one weekend in December. As for money, each of us had different funds and different expenses.

The morning of the departure there was a grand total of one lone traveller. I stood on my own at Victoria coach station, small bag on my back and a cigarette clamped between my fingers. I smoked and pondered the responsibility of traveling to Amsterdam for the first time, alone and pretty much unplanned. No preparation had been made other than packing a small backpack and getting my arse to the coach station on time. I stood before the row of giant metal boxes with wheels attached and pondered how irresponsible I was being. My attention was pulled toward several cops walking in a line and fooling around, pranking on one another by trying to trip each other up and knock their helmets off their heads. They were well out of ear shot so I wasn't concerned when I heard a voice behind me say, "Bumboclaat p'olis." The voice had a thick Caribbean twang, "Dat where me rasclat tax money go?" He sucked his teeth, "So dem can play like fool?"

I turned to see a slim black man dressed in baggy

dark greens and sporting a giant wool hat over huge dreadlocks. His beard had traces of grey that hinted at his age and his eyes had a calm and wisdom that immediately put you at ease around him. The Rasta smiled at me. "Fuck da police," he took a puff on his rollie. I smiled back at his glinting gold tooth that twinkled under the strip lights like the rest of his gaudy jewellery. There were a multitude of gold chains around his neck, rings on his fingers and bracelets around his wrists. And the vast majority of his gold bore ganja leaves, also in gold of course.

"Where you headed?" I asked, almost 100% sure I was going to hear my own destination.

"Amsterdam, man," he replied with another easy smile.

The Rasta and I got to know each other. He had been to Amsterdam many times and filled me in on the names of various coffee shops and hotels that he liked and recommended. He knew nothing about hostels as he was a working man, not a student like me, and advised me to stick with hotels despite the price difference. He informed me that hostels were notorious for people being robbed at knife point or your stuff being stolen while you were out, and that being on your own was like having a giant target painted on your back. The Rasta was a bus driver in London, but was originally from an island in the Caribbean. We sat separately on the coach as we both planned to sleep for as much of the journey as possible.

During a pit stop at Dover, the Rasta and I got talking to two Scousers who were also visiting the fabled city for the first time. The four of us smoked cigarettes and listened to the Rasta tell us about the best coffee shops and how to handle the street hustlers. While weed and shrooms were legal in Holland, other drugs were not. The Rasta explained that there were many bad people selling bad things on the streets of the Red Light district and that buying their products almost always resulted in a visit to the hospital or death. I'd heard many stories in the past about the street hustlers peddling fake cocaine and pills that were really just chemicals that were toxic to the human body to the point of causing death or injury. I'd also heard that the street hustlers preyed on tourists so they could rob them and would often get violent with foreigners that refused to buy their lethal wraps. As it transpired, the Scousers had also heard such tales and ran them past the Rasta. Our dreadlocked sage explained that as long as you were polite but firm when telling them you weren't interested in buying their gear all would be, "Cool man."

At Sloterdijk coach station I followed the Rasta to Amsterdam Centraal station by train, the hub for stoner tourists. It is impossible to describe to anyone who has not visited Amsterdam the joy you feel as a stoner walking out of a city's main train station to be hit in the face with the pungent perfume of skunk. It is the first thing that you notice when you step out into the street. The sweet, sweet smell of skunk. Once there we parted ways. The Rasta had previously explained to me that he had a room in a very nice hotel in the centre of the city and that it would be fully booked. He advised me to find shelter elsewhere. Instead, I chose to go to where he pointed to when explaining where the bulk of the coffee shops were in De Wallen, otherwise known as the Red Light district.

Amsterdam

2

I dragged my extremely heavy feet along the almost iced-over pavement. I have no idea how much I smoked or what strains I'd tried. I was absurdly high and very happy. The night was cold and the wind sharp, but I was in my element. The church bells of Oude Kerk chimed 2.00 am and the main drag was now empty and the coffee shops all closed. I had left it a little late to try to organise a room for the night. I somehow wound up at the reception of a fancy hotel-boat that was moored at a canal near Centraal train station. My battered credit card had somehow managed to get me a room for two nights and my blatant lack of belonging in such an establishment had been overlooked. I sprawled on the bed rolling another joint while chuckling at a flashback of a conversation had earlier in the night at the Grasshopper with the budtender. I'd enquired about the leniency of hotels when it came to smoking weed in their rooms and was met with the answer, "Hey, this is Amsterdam man!" followed by a joyous laugh.

Growing up in Wales, the subject of sleeping

with a prostitute had always been talked about with negative connotations as a sign of desperation. Working in London, the subject of sleeping with a prostitute had always been talked about on Fridays. Most of the Londoners I'd known considered paying to fuck a brass as no different to having a wank. Single or married was irrelevant. Fucking a prostitute was not cheating, it was just stress relief. I'd never done it. Countless offers had been made, even offers to cover the cost by mates egging me on, but it had never appealed. Then in the narrow allies, flanked by red lights and glass doors, a step was taken. A new experience was had. A trip down the dark end of the street was made.

The next day I walked the narrow alleys, women on display either side of me, ignoring the taps on the glass followed by a suggestive smile should you happen to glance over at them. Hasty steps were taken along the curve where all of the big black girls sell themselves and the Writer christened 'Congo alley', as they don't tap on the glass with a ring and smile; they scream at you from an open door "Hey, you! Come fuck me! Yeah, you boy! Now!" This was said with loud and aggressive bellows, and then followed by the sound of sucked teeth and swearing as they went back into the warmth of their room alone. Across the main canals was where the extremely expensive prostitutes work, a place that the legend and fiend D. Lynch labelled 'value alley'. Flanked by dozens of windows all housing gorgeous women of damn near every colour, size and race you could possibly wish for, it occurred to me that if

I was ever going to fuck a prostitute then this was the right time and place. When I did eventually take that step through the narrow door and into the red light it was with a cute little brunette who appeared older than me but much smaller. She had a perfect figure eight body and naughty smile, which she kept on her face while informing me, "€50 suck and fuck." The room was barely lit and housed very little. A mattress on a concrete bed that was part of one of the walls, a sink, mirror and wardrobe. There was another small door that remained closed that presumably led to a bathroom or possibly another way in and out of the tiny room. In Amsterdam €50 gets you oral and vaginal sex with a condom on, but only if you can cum in 20 minutes or less. If you need more than 20 minutes you have to pay for it. Although I never asked for it, I think I was technically due some change.

Afterwards, I sat and drank a cold beer in a very touristy pub on Oude Zijdsachterburgwal in the heart of the Red Light district next to one of the canals. I pondered the experience and searched for comparisons between paying to fuck a prostitute, being with someone you're in a relationship with and fucking a stranger you met at a club for one night. I felt the cold patch of cum against my crotch that had leaked out and stuck to my underwear and then rubbed against me as I moved on the bar stool and realised that in all three scenarios the outcome was the same sticky mess. I finished the beer and headed out to find another coffee shop.

In the UK it is very common to mix tobacco with

your weed to make it last longer. But in Amsterdam there is no need to make it last longer. In Amsterdam you want to get through each beautiful, full flavoured, exotic baggie as quick as possible in order to try the next gorgeous head-kicking strain. At least 2 grams at a time, no tobacco, with at least another gram of hash mixed in. Each flavour was as beautiful or more beautiful than the last and each flavour got me that little bit higher. While I tried to sample a strain individually at first in order to truly appreciate each one, it wasn't long before I was rolling thick cocktails and not giving a toss if I was mixing indicas with sativas with hybrids. It all got me high, it all tasted amazing and so it all got rolled and smoked as quickly as possible.

By the end of my first full day in Amsterdam I had toured most of the coffee shops located in De Wallen and got through as many different strains of weed and lumps of hash as humanly possible. I floated back to the hotel through the crisp cold air. The streetlights glistened against the pitch black backdrop of the night sky as a drunk American approached me, his breath stinking of alcohol. "Can you change a note there for us brother?" he asked, possibly not for the first time. "I need some change for the car park," he informed me as he pointed off randomly into the distance. I looked around the empty street and then back at the dirty and shabbily dressed man before me. He was short and sported a scruffy beard and unkempt hair under a battered baseball cap. "Do you have change?" The stench of alcohol cut through the cold, carried on a thick American twang.

"Sure," I said, as I rummaged through my pocket to retrieve my cents and Euros. I cupped the pile of change I'd accumulated over the day in both hands and struggled to focus my vision on the coins before me. The American suddenly gripped both of my wrists with both of his hands.

"Give me your fucking money!"

He was no longer American. His accent was obviously European, but I couldn't be sure that he was Dutch yet. "Now, English! Fucking money now!" He shook my wrists a little, which made me realise that from this position even if I really did want to give him my coins and tried, I couldn't actually do it while he held my wrists. And he couldn't accept my money from this position because he was holding both of my arms. This master criminal had obviously not thought this all the way through, but there was something else on my mind.

"I'm not English, I'm Welsh you twat!"

"What?"

"Welsh motherfucker, not English!"

I tried to make him understand but unfortunately like so many others from outside of the UK he was unaware of the difference between English, Welsh, Scottish and Irish. Sure, we're all British, but we're not all bloody English.

"You English, give me fucking money!"

"How, cunt?"

The robber was stumped. He stared at his hands gripping my wrists and pondered the situation.

Feeling no immediate threat I decided to wait and see what ingenious move he would pull next. Unfortunately, I never got to see how the super villain before me would solve this riddle as a police car pulled to a halt at the curb next to us and two giant Arian soldiers got out, fully kitted out with black leather, batons and handguns. They spoke at us in Dutch and the would-be robber relinquished his grip on my wrists and took a step back. One giant blond approached the robber and the other approached me. The robber and the blond were now exchanging words. I, on the other hand, was staring dumbly and stoned at my policeman as he spat foreign words at me. I shrugged my shoulders and said, "*English.*" He nodded his head.

"You are American, yes? Tourist, yes?" They weren't so much questions as orders.

"Yes," I replied and nodded my head.

"I see," said the cop. Then the two Arian beasts exchanged some words and there was further head nodding and more words were had. "Okay America. You go to hotel now and enjoy time in Amsterdam." He waved me on my way and turned without bothering to see if there would be any response from me. As I began to walk away I couldn't help but smile at my would-be American robber, although whether or not he saw me smile I can't be sure. It's hard to see if someone is smiling at you from a distance as two six-foot-plus brick-shit-houses kick and stomp you up and down a deserted high street late on a winter's eve in Amsterdam.

Amsterdam

3

I got to the coach station early as I had no real times to go by and I wanted to make sure I left early enough so that I wouldn't miss the damn bus. I finished my multiple bags of weed sitting alone in the car park, trying to remember as much of the weekend as I could. There had been a lot of walking. The canal ring near the centre has multiple little streets filled with some of the most eccentric architecture in Europe. You can walk for hours in Amsterdam, stoned and drinking in the curiously designed urban surroundings. It's a beautiful city spoiled by the hordes of tourists that cover its cobbles in litter and piss. Most of the drinkers and smokers pay little to no attention to the splendour that is central Amsterdam. Some of the buildings there are parts of history that have survived the trial and tribulations of time and man.

The Jolly Joker had been recommended to me at some point in my past and had proved to be a truly great spot to stop and smoke. The coffee shop is situated on a corner in the Red Light district, or at least right on the border of it. The corner structure affords both walls to be giant windows offering an almost 180-degree view of the surroundings. Inside is a counter, tables and chairs, and an upstairs seating area with a mezzanine overlooking the ground floor and offering a great view out of the windows. A lot of time had been spent sitting on the balcony people watching and getting extremely high.

When the Rasta turned up at the coach station we exchanged pleasantries and then got on the bus to sleep during the return journey. Once back at the coach station in Victoria I exchanged phone numbers with him, who as it turned out was a full-time bus driver and part-time weed dealer in West London for some Yardies.

England
3

London

4

A few days later I called up the Rasta and he gave
me directions to his flat in Ladbroke Grove, which
was quite a journey from where I was living in
North London. I listened to music on the tube as I
thought about the trend I was following of going
headfirst into potentially dangerous situations
without informing anyone about where I was or
where I was going or who I was meeting and so on.

A short bus ride ended my journey to the block
of flats where the Rasta lived. I buzzed and
announced my arrival. The place was a two-storey
box flat, well-furnished and very homely. This was
thanks to the Rasta's woman, a big blonde with a
northerner's accent. She let me in and directed me
to the very small kitchen that housed all of the
usual mod-cons, as well as a small table in the
corner with two chairs occupied by the Rasta and
another dreadlocked man in his fifties, then she
disappeared into another room. Around the kitchen
stood several other dreadlocked and very high men
of various ages. I, the only cracker in the box,
stepped into the thick and pungent smoke. All
turned and smiled at me, so I smiled back, "All

right?" I said with the traditional Welsh greeting. "Yas man," came the Rasta's thick accented welcome, "how are you my brother?" He nodded and beckoned me to him. "Come, come. Relax." I managed to find an empty spot of floor in the corner to occupy. The Rasta finished his conversation with the older dread at the table with him and then turned to face me. He was extremely high. His red-raw eyes were almost closed and his English was barely recognisable, "Wha' ya' come ya' far man?" he asked as he reached down the side of his chair. I was confused by the question. He already knew I'd come to buy weed. He produced a big and sharp-looking machete from the side of his chair and held it tightly as he asked me, "Wha' ya' wan' man? Te' me."

The thoughts I'd had earlier on the journey, the ones about danger and not telling anybody where I was, now flooded my mind and were screaming nouns and descriptors at me. I was an idiot, a twat, a moron – and fucked. I stared at the machete and wondered where my body parts would be found. More adjectives now – imminent death, painful, severed and decapitated were just a few. Would my body ever be found? Would my death be slow and painful as he hacked away randomly at my flesh? Would all the other dreads join in? Would there be rape? The Rasta laughed. I feared he could read my face and mind. Was I already very high and paranoid from the thick blanket of ganja smoke that wrapped us and filled the kitchen like a giant ball of cotton from some alien horror movie?

"My bad, man," he chuckled, "ya' dun' even know me weed ye'." He shook his head as he turned back to the table and placed the machete down, cursing himself out the whole time for not being a better host and salesman. He retrieved two bundles of weed, one very dark in colour and the other pure green skunk. He proceeded to inform me that both were high quality, but the darker one was weaker and therefor cheaper. The more expensive one, he assured me, would knock my head off, but the darker one was not to be taken lightly either. He could see that I was confused and lost as I didn't know what either strain actually was or the effects they may have on me. Instinct told me to just go for the strongest one, which is always the right choice in these situations – don't fuck around, you want to get high, right? The Rasta handed me some papers and a bud of the darker weed. "Roll one an' try man. Only way to be sure, righ'?" He smiled and nodded.

"Cheers dude," I said politely as I accepted the weed and papers.

It was like nothing I had seen before or since. It reminded me of Thai stick, but it was a bigger plant. The smell was what was most unique about it. It smelled like chocolate dirt. It was a nice smell, verging on sweet but not quite there. It was a little dry and very compressed, with some very big black seeds inside the nugget. I rolled and started to smoke a little before conforming to traditional etiquette and offering the joint to the guy next to me, who declined.

"Nah man, is your join', ya smoke it," the Rasta informed me. I then noticed that everyone in the room was indeed rolling and smoking their own joints. Nobody was passing. Time ticked by, but how much of it I had no idea. I was leaning against the kitchen unit staring at my half-smoked spliff and trying to remember if I had smoked any of it or needed to pass it to someone. I was very high. I can't completely give credit to the pure weed spliff I was smoking as the small boxroom kitchen was completely hot-boxed out from all of our combined efforts.

Some time later I managed to let the Rasta know that the darker weed was more than sufficient for me and bought a half ounce from him. The Rasta was good enough to arrange a lift home for me with one of the younger dreads in the room, who just happened to be living in North London and heading in that direction as well. I thanked the Rasta and said my goodbyes to the other dreads, who all warmly wished me safe smoking. I have vague memories of sitting in a car, congested streets, some headlights and then being asleep in my bed. Needless to say, my relationship with the Rasta blossomed from that point onwards.

London

5

The weeks rolled on and I continued to buy from the Rasta on a weekly basis. Every Sunday I made the trip west and spent a few hours sitting in the box-kitchen smoking weed and chatting shit. I'd developed friendships with several dealers over the years – I always preferred it that way. Buying off strangers is a risk, and buying from a dealer regularly doesn't mean you're always getting regular deals.

The Rasta shared many things with me about himself, including the growing and selling operation he once had on the island he was originally from. He told me how he had started a plot deep in the bush so that the police and other dealers wouldn't find it. He grew a large number of plants over a sizeable area of land surrounded and partly sheltered by wild bush. He had to hack his way through the thick growth each time he went back to check on it or do some cropping. He explained that while cannabis is illegal in Jamaica and the rest of the Caribbean, he's a Rasta and believed that it opened his mind to the truth. One truth being that the weed was made illegal by the rules and regulations of Babylon – the authorities – to persecute the Rastafari.

Rastafari is an Abrahamic religion, meaning that it belongs to a group of religious faiths of Semitic origins that descended from the practices of the ancient Israelites and the worship of the God of Abraham; that means it is derived from Old Testament bullshit rather than that concocted by King James. Rastafari developed in Jamaica in the 1930s and never really adopted any kind of hierarchical structure with a central authority figure like the Catholics and the Pope, rather a mix of practitioners who shared the same general belief of Rastalogy. There are several denominations that are referred to as Mansions of Rastafari. The biggest of these are the Nyabinghi, Bobo Ashanti, Ethiopian Zion Coptic Church and the Twelve Tribes of Israel.

Their belief includes a single God, Jah, making it a monotheism like Catholicism, who lives within all of us to some degree or another. The movement started among the poor and deprived Afro-Jamaican communities, with an Afrocentric ideology in reaction to the dominant British colonial culture. Two major influences on the religion were the Back-to-Africa movement by way of Marcus Garvey, and Ethiopianism.

Leonard Howell, known by many as The First Rasta, proclaimed that a Biblical prophecy had been fulfilled in 1930 by way of Haile Selassie being crowned Emperor of Ethiopia. Through the 1950s Rastafari counter-culture had seen frequent violent clashes with the authorities, but that all changed in the sixties and seventies thanks in no small part to the most famous Rasta to ever spark a spliff: Bob Marley.

On one visit to the Rasta's flat we had gone to see another dreadlocked friend of his to help plan how the Rasta was going to start smuggling his weed into Spain. Traditionally, marijuana has always been smuggled in the opposite direction – from the mainland to the island – but on this occasion there was apparently a demand for the Rasta's, or more appropriately the Yardies', weed in Europe because it wasn't passing their way on its journey to the UK. First, the Rasta only needed help smuggling a small amount over with him as a sample. We decided to hide a quarter ounce of the strong skunk in his dreadlocks. Apparently, my dreadlocked friends knew of other friends with dreadlocks who had been strip-searched at airports but never had their hair searched. The Rasta removed his wool hat and let his giant dreads fall loose. We set about placing the weed wrapped tight in a Ziploc bag in cling film onto the centre of his head, and then wrapped his dreadlocks back up and around the weed. It was perfect. Nobody would be any the wiser at a casual glance, or even a long stare. When I enquired about the possibility of Customs smelling the weed my two friends laughed loud and said that they always smelled of weed 24/7 anyway, even when they weren't carrying any.

The trip to Spain went without a hitch. The Rasta made contact and upon arriving back in the

UK started making plans with his Yardie suppliers. Due to the scale of the operation and new territories being explored, the Rasta was having frequent visits from his suppliers.

This caused a problem one overcast Sunday afternoon in West London when the Rasta got a phone call during our weekly smoke. The Rasta's black face turned pale when he ended the call and looked at me. "Dem man comin' roun'," he shook his head, "ya can' be 'ere when dem come."

"Why not?"

"Dem kill ya man!" he exclaimed as he got to his feet and looked out of the window. "Dey don' know ya man. So dem no trus' ya. Dey kill you an' me dey see ya 'ere wi' me."

"Shit."

"Maybe ya have time to leave." The Rasta moved quickly, gathering up my weed and smoking paraphernalia to pass to me. "Quick man, go—" his command was cut short by the sound of the buzzer from the intercom.

London

6

The London Yardie rise to power started in the 1950s in Kingston, Jamaica. The government had created social housing developments in many areas that included large public courtyards, as seen in the area known as Trenchtown. These big courtyards soon became the hub of all activity in the crowded housing developments. The overcrowding led to poverty, squatting and homelessness, which developed into drug abuse, violence and crime. At the same time, political corruption was rife and the two coincided by way of payment for patronage. Political parties such as the Jamaica Labour Party (JLP) and People's National Party (PNP) paid gangs and political supporters to intimidate the competition, which grew from threats into assaults and inevitably murders.

By the late seventies political violence and politically-affiliated organised crime was business-as-usual in poorer areas of Kingston. The gangs, from courtyards like those found in Trenchtown, became known as Yardies. They went by other names as well, such as posses and crews, but in the UK the name Yardie became notorious. The crews

were led by a Don, which was a reference to the
Sicilian Dons of the Mafia that began in Italy. The
status of a Don could only be reached by the most
violent, bloodthirsty and determined of Jamaican
gangsters. Yardies were involved in political
violence, intimidation and murder, but also made
their money from drug trafficking and other illegal
shit.

During the 1980s a cut in government budgets
led to a huge drop in the cash Yardies received from
their political backers. On top of this, the Jamaican
government were publicly cracking down on the
gangs and political criminality in general, the
violence being their main target to put a stop to due
to public outcry. However, don't get it twisted
fellow traveller – no sudden semblance of moral
decency ever existed in reality, that shit was all just
for show in order to keep the masses placated.

'Going foreign' seemed to be the way forward for
the Yardies to maintain their revenue, and their
foreign destinations of choice were the USA,
Canada and the UK. While the Yardies were
acquiring false passports and other documents
from their political backers to help them in their
smuggling and distribution operations, crack
cocaine was starting to put in an appearance in
both US and UK cities. Ronald and Nancy Reagan
advertised the shit out of those little white rocks
and a lot of old white fossils got stinking rich from
it. Just say no to this highly addictive, very cheap
and easily acquired drug that'll launch you into
space, kids. What a marketing campaign! National

TV at primetime with the fucking President who was once an actor, no less.

While the British police have never categorised the Yardies as an organised criminal entity, because of there being no clear structure like that of the military or Mafia, there are links and networks. The posses each have their own Don, not one to rule over them all, but there is cooperation between some of them. It is through these links and connections that word spread about the UK's encouragement during the eighties of immigrants to come to the UK for stable job opportunities within its shittier employment sectors. Just because slavery was abolished doesn't mean the good ol' Union Jack couldn't exploit our dark-skinned brethren for a few more decades.

The Yardies exploited the UK's open arms, the rise of crack, the corruption in Jamaica and the inability of indigenous gangs to stop the violent takeover of their turf. The UK news during the eighties was flooded with stories of Yardie gangs in shoot outs with machine guns, vicious fights with machetes, police killings and horror story after horror story of these drug-dealing, woman-raping, kid-stabbing savages from Kingston. Neither the British police, citizens or gangsters were ready for the extremes that the Yardies would go to. A British drug dealer might cut you for not paying him, but the Yardies would cut your hand off, torture you to death or spray your home with bullets from the favoured 9mm MAC-10 machine pistol while your family relaxed in front of the TV of an evening.

This was the Yardies at the height of their powers, this was the Yardies when Lester Lloyd Coke, aka Jim Brown, was still running Tivoli Yard in West Kingston, and before he was burned to death in a police cell for knowing too much dirt to be able to prosecute in a court of law. Just like Jim 'the dan danner' Brown can still be seen in Kingston by way of murals and graffiti, so to can the Yardie hallmark still be found in the UK by way of inner-city gangs and the violence involved in the illegal drugs trade. Neither the police or criminals in the UK had experienced violence like they did when the Yardies arrived, and to this day it is the Yardies that can be seen as a significant influence on the level and ferocity of the violence used by gangsters. Their legacy in the UK is one of brutal violence and death. British media have ceased giving gang crime the coverage it once did, but the violence still goes on in the shadows, behind closed doors and out of the eye of the general public.

London

7

The intercom buzzed again. The Rasta stared at the intercom and then at me, "Go upstairs!" he commanded. "Under da bed man!"

"What?!"

"No time talk," he said as he grabbed my arm and steered me to the bottom of the stairs leading up to the bedrooms. He gave my back a little shove before leaning into the intercom, "Yah man."

He waved me away. I ran up the stairs and went for the first bedroom I saw, all the while hearing the sounds of the Rasta letting the Yardies in.

I struggled to slide my fat arse silently under the frail wooden frame of the single bed, but couldn't get so much as a single cheek out of sight. The sweat began to pour from me as I eased my upper torso back out and then stood up and held down the panic bubbling in my stomach, which occasionally emitted some of my fear by way of rancid farts like a pressure cooker close to exploding. It might have been the fear leaking out of my gut or my short-term memory recall, I'll never know, but I suddenly remembered tiptoeing past the bathroom that I knew had a bath complete with shower and shower curtain. I knew my rotund posterior could adequately hide there.

After creeping from the bedroom to the bathroom like a cat burglar who'd indulged in too much vindaloo before setting off on the prowl, I stepped into the white tub and slowly, silently eased the curtain across. I let out a noiseless breath of relief at having made it to sanctuary. I listened intently at the sounds of business happening on the floor below me, each passing second easing my mind and sphincter a little. And then I heard the heavy footfall of someone ascending the stairs. Without thinking I stopped breathing. I suddenly found myself trying not to exist. I wanted to become a ghost, a non-entity that would be invisible to the human eye. There was a moment when someone entered the bathroom and I closed my eyes. For a brief time I pondered what difference it would make in that situation. Eyes open when discovered dead and mutilated, or eyes closed when found decapitated? Would it make any difference? I figured that at least with my eyes open I stood a chance of seeing where I was going when trying to make a run for the door, not that I liked my chances of making it as an overweight, stoned and heavy smoker in such a closed environment. Then there was a loud rush of water and the stranger walked out and back down the stairs. I felt a weird mix of emotions and bizarre thoughts. I'd survived undiscovered, which was an obvious relief, and the fella who pissed hadn't washed his hands, which was unhygienic. I have no idea why I was so aware of that at the time or why indeed I should care. At the time though I remember shaking my head in disgust, and then noticing the cascade of sweat drip down into the white bathtub that I cowered in.

I listened to the heavy thuds of steps down the stairs and the deep timbre of their voices, but was unable to make any of the conversation out. There was no laughter, only talk. The Rasta was a cheerful dude with a great sense of humour; we were always laughing together. Now there was no laughter, only the sound of my heart pounding in my ears and the deep boom of voices downstairs. After what seemed like an eternity the Yardies could be heard leaving and the Rasta finally called up the stairs, "Ya all good mun."

I returned to the kitchen and collapsed into a chair. The Rasta was filling his chillum/chalice thing, which he had made with his own hands back on his native isle. My hands shook like an epileptic rushing on speed at the climax of a rave. He explained to me that this was a traditional Rasta pipe. It looked similar to a bong, but there was no water necessary only a full quarter ounce of skunk. Any less than a quarter was not enough to properly pack the clay bowl, and once it was fired up you had to smoke the entire thing.

"Figure we nee' ta really relax man," the Rasta said to me as he sparked his lighter.

I'd spotted the old clay chillum in the past and asked him about it, but he always informed me that due to the large quantity of weed required to fill it he only used it on special occasions. It appeared that narrowly missing a brutal and possible bullet-riddled execution at the hands of London Yardies was cause to celebrate. Within seconds of the weed being lit the small boxroom kitchen was looking like a sauna, but with a lot more smoke and a lot less visibility.

When you're used to smoking less than a gram at a time, seeing seven plus smoked in one go is quite a sight. Well, until the smoke is exhaled and then you can see very little. The Rasta pulled on the pipe like he was playing a didgeridoo, taking violent and deep breaths in an out of time with jazz-like rhythm before passing it to me to play my own thick grey melodies. Within minutes we were both completely wasted and sat surrounded by the dense smoke in complete silence. After an unknown time the Rasta's woman returned home and stepped into the corridor to be met with a wall of smoke. She coughed and turned to see the two of us sitting and staring at nothing at all.

"What's on fire?" she asked us as she attempted to approach the kitchen, waving her hands before her to try to clear a path through the THC peasouper.

The two of us laughed long and loud.

Holland
2

Amsterdam

4

The unanimous decision had been made by myself, the Actor and the Writer to visit the Hash, Marihuana and Hemp Museum as well as the Cannabis College, both conveniently located on the Oudezijds Achterburgwal in De Wallen. Both were informative and run by friendly dudes who clearly enjoyed teaching people about all of the wonderful benefits this extremely versatile plant has to offer the world. At the end of the tour in the college the staff informed us that the three vaporisers they had on display were all fully functional and available to use provided we had our own weed. None of us had ever tried a vaporiser before but we were all intrigued.

The fundamental differences between vaping and toking are thus: the strength of the high and the speed at which it hits you. When you smoke a joint the paper and carcinogens cause your body's immune system to fight back, allowing the high to hit you faster as your internal defence mechanism is busy fighting the bad shit that some of the good shit just slides right on past unchecked and into your brain, but your immune system will prevent some of that good shit ever hitting you. A vaporiser doesn't have any harmful effects on the human body, and therefore there is nothing for your immune system to fight back against, so it keeps the THC at bay until satisfied that it is safe for the foreign body to pass into you and work its magic. Because there is no immune system fighting it, the whole impact of the THC can hit you – you just gotta give it some time. The Writer and I naively heeded the museum's advice and took it easy due to our need to get to the airport in a few hours to fly home. The Actor, however, decided that while in Amsterdam he would get a real buzz on and sucked the vapour out of it like it was oxygen and he was a man who had just been saved from drowning. The fact that there was no immediate hit warranted further blasts on the vaporiser as far as the Actor was concerned, much to the staffs' disapproval and warnings to the contrary. The Actor was having none of it and insisted they reload the plate and heat that bitch up again. This had been the theme of the whole trip – excess and overindulgence, which became a theme in this most wonderful of cities.

As soon as we exited Schiphol airport, trouble had begun on my second visit to the country...

Amsterdam

5

Something any savvy traveller knows is that when in a foreign land it is not always beneficial to show just how intelligent and clued up you really are. That can also be said for one's knowledge of the native tongue. There are many situations where it is better to play dumb and act like you have absolutely no idea what the natives are trying to communicate to you, and this is particularly true when you have clearly flouted the rules and broken some laws. The Writer had flown to Amsterdam before, unlike me who had only gone by coach on my first visit, and led us to the platform at Schiphol station under the airport. We caught a direct train to Centraal, which usually takes less than half an hour. Everything was going smoothly until a conductor turned up, clearly requiring to see our tickets that we had not purchased back at the station. The three of us played dumb and acted like we had no idea what the conductor was trying to say, despite the fact that damn near all of the natives in Amsterdam speak fluent English as well as several other languages.

"You need to purchase tickets. Back at the

station, before you boarded the train," a polite but weary woman informed us.

"Siarad Cymraeg?" I asked the puzzled uniform. This is another trick used by the cunning traveller – speak a language the other person obviously won't understand. I had asked her if she speaks Welsh, knowing full well she probably didn't. When you come from Wales you have the advantage of being able to claim that you are British as well as Welsh when the need arises. Or in this instance, speak Welsh instead of English. The Dutch conductor squinted her eyes and cocked her head at what appeared as nothing more than gibberish to her. In fact, most people think that of the Welsh language, even when they are fully aware of the fact that you are speaking a very real and very old dialect to them. The uniform in front of me had no idea what we were saying to her, and for that matter neither did we at times. The Actor was semi-fluent in Welsh, but the Writer and I couldn't even claim to be beginners in what should have been our native tongue. The majority of my Welsh lessons in school had been spent taking the piss out of the Actor and another friend for being diehard Bon Jovi fans. Over the years I'd picked up some stock phrases and vocabulary, but couldn't come close to holding down a conversation. In desperate circumstances the ability to imitate the Welsh language had been employed, as the other person couldn't speak Welsh anyway and would therefore have no clue what was being said. The three of us looked back and forth at one another and continued to jibber-jabber broken Welsh, held together by guttural sounds that could have easily passed for Welsh, while the conductor shook her head and tried her best to explain in fluent English and hand gestures that we needed tickets to ride the train.

When we finally arrived at the central station, we were accompanied by several conductors who also all spoke fluent English, and who followed us along the platform and down the stairs towards the exit while we muttered pidgin Welsh to one another, shrugged our broad shoulders and shook our heads. By the time we were halfway through the tunnel leading us to the exit and out to the centre of Amsterdam the uniforms all gave up and headed back to their duties. We briskly walked out of the station and into the skunk-perfumed air of Amsterdam. The no ticket and no understanding of simple instructions was further utilised on the trams in order to reach our hotel. The trams were an easier one to pull off as there is no conductor, just a driver who doesn't leave his seat and seldom gives a toss about idiots jumping onto the tram via the exit doors situated halfway down the long metal snake. The locals would tut, mutter and shake their heads at you, but fuck them – their city is far too expensive to be messing around with things like tram tickets.

The hotel was about 20 minutes away on the tram, but over an hour when walking stoned. It was a decent looking abode, but due to its proximity to a canal it had a problem with terrible smells coming up from the drains and toilet, as well as the occasional rodent home invasion.

At night, we would hear the little (or possibly big) critters rummaging through the bins looking for food. Of course there was no food to be had as we were all tokers and would therefor consume anything and everything edible before passing out. The munchies are a dangerous side effect in Amsterdam as it's damn near impossible to find anything even slightly nutritious to eat. Your choices are mainly waffles, pizza slices and kebabs, or crap out of vending machines. All perfectly delicious of course, but not exactly top of the list of recommended foods for a healthy diet. Granted, when stoned a healthy food option isn't usually what you crave, but it would be nice to have the option.

Our hotel was situated in an area that catered more for the straight-headed tourist. It was close to the Heineken (brewery) Experience in Stadhouderskade, which had practically no coffee shops. This meant that every day we had to travel into Amsterdam centre and back again. The journey in was fine via an unpaid-for tram. But at night when the cafes closed, there were no more trams to be had and the taxis are not something you can hop on and off without paying, so the walk had to be done. The journey was made even longer due to having spent all day sat in coffee shops getting wasted, which made the legs heavy and navigation sketchy. Every night we would take wrong turns, miss streets due to chatting and generally increase the length of time it took us to get back to the hotel. The plus side to this was that we got to see a lot more of the incredible streets that make up the beautiful city, with its insane architecture that includes buildings that look like they are leaning forwards and about to fall over and miniature flats that are piled on top of each other like early blueprints for the favelas in Rio, but with more of a fairy-tale aesthetic to them. Amsterdam has superb architecture that dates back centuries, some of it even having survived the fires of 1421 and 1452 allowing you to catch a glimpse of the city's medieval history. It's the Golden Age structures from the 17th century that most see around the canals in the form of gabled houses, and it was these that got us distracted during our long chilly walks back to the hotel.

Amsterdam

6

A huge problem I have always had is an inability to take mushrooms. It doesn't matter if they are of the magic kind or regular supermarket variety. Upon making contact with my tongue, the texture of fungus causes an immediate gagging reflex that inevitably leads to projectile vomit should I force said-texture to stay longer than a nanosecond in my mouth. I have tried on many occasions to force myself to swallow mushrooms and have always created the same hilarious outcome of watery eyes, choking, retching and body spasms. Obviously, none of this is funny for me, but to anyone watching – particularly drug abusers – it's fucking brilliant entertainment. The Writer recommended cutting the shrooms up into small pieces and wrapping them in rolling papers, which would stop my tongue making contact with the texture. This is not something I would recommend to anybody with the same affliction as me. The outcome, surprise-surprise, is exactly the same: gagging and retching and drooling. Others have suggested tea, but that had the same outcome too. I am doomed to never experience a magic mushroom trip. The Writer and

Actor did not have this problem.

We picked up a couple of packets containing the long brown fungi during a morning smoking session and then returned to the hotel for the two of them to consume the shrooms before we would go back in the centre to continue smoking. The Actor had never done magic mushrooms and the Writer couldn't remember what a safe dosage was – something none of us had bothered to check with the fella flogging the stuff. I swiftly recommended an appropriate dose – the whole pack. Each.

It wasn't long before the Actor was staring strangely at me and the room around us, his eyes big and bug-like, as his head flopped about and he occasionally muttered something incoherent. The Writer, on the other hand, was a different animal. Literally, a different animal. The Actor and I watched from our beds as he crawled around on all fours, stopping now and then to dip his hand down the side of his bed, which resulted in him recoiling with a look of panic. We would later learn that at this stage in the trip the Writer believed himself to be a tiger and that he was stranded on a rock surrounded by water. He explained that he had literally been testing the water, and had been unhappy with the results. After all, cats don't like to get wet. He further jabbered that not only was he a tiger trapped on a rock (actually his bed) surrounded by water, but that he had badly needed a piss. Thankfully he knew that in order to relieve his bladder he first had to make it to the bathroom, which he was unable to do due to the water around him. He had considered pouncing for the bathroom door, but was unsure of how far his newfound tiger form could actually travel through the air.

The tiger and my bug-eyed companion amused me for a while, but it wasn't long before I needed to head back into the thick of things and smoke more weed, having consumed the contents of the baggies we'd acquired earlier in the day. I announced that I would be leaving shortly, which got different reactions from each of my tripping companions. The Actor seconded the motion and managed to go to the bathroom for a quick wash before being ready to join me. The tiger, however, took a lot longer, along with a lot of coaxing or abuse depending on your point of view, before even being able to make it to the bathroom for that much-needed piss. Once in there were many strange noises and very little in the way of sounds of running water. The Actor terrorised the tiger by repetitively banging on the door and demanding that he get his arse out of there to join us on another journey back into Centraal. The Writer emerged at one point with a look of dread and fear, and said that he was unable to join us as he was having difficulty operating the shower, sink, toilet and everything else in the small room. The Actor and I told him to catch up with us when he was ready, figuring we'd get back later that night to find him sleeping soundly.

The tripping Actor and I did the usual journey back into the thick of things and toured some coffee shops, before making our way into our joint favourite: the Jolly Joker in Nieuwmarkt. We sat smoking and people watching for some time, enjoying our highs and the tunes being played. The sun was setting when we both saw a familiar face amongst the crowds of tourists, drug abusers and fiends. A tiger wandered amongst them with a somewhat pitiful look upon his face. The Actor said he would retrieve him while I stayed and kept our table occupied. I watched as the Actor, now recovered from his shroom experience, went outside and waved at the tiger, who pounced on his friend with an unabashed display of emotions. The Writer let out a couple of tears as he announced his fear of never finding us again. The Actor beckoned him into the Joker for a spliff to calm his nerves. We spent the rest of the night there, but not all of us were so jolly.

Amsterdam

7

The final day started much like the ones that preceded it, up and out into the coffee shops as soon as possible for excessive amounts of cannabis consumption in all its various forms – weed, hash, edibles, rosin, wax, kief crystals and shatter: whatever we could get our greedy little paws on. On this last day, we decided to do some touristy things just so that the Actor could lie to his girlfriend that he had actually been there as a culture junkie and not just as a committed stoner. He had sent her a photo earlier into our trip, which consisted of an extreme close up of his face with a woolly hat on his head and a scarf around his features. He had sent it with a message telling her how bitterly cold it was (it wasn't that bad, particularly for Welshmen), hence all the woolly garb. She was anti-drugs, so he had told her that we were there strictly as regular tourists, not fiends out to smoke the coffee shops out of product. The Writer and I had refused to be a part of his deception, hence the reason why the only photo he could send her was an extreme close-up selfie covered in wool. Our idea of touristy things to do consisted of the Ann Frank Museum, which the Actor went to alone as the Writer and I deemed it a waste of smoking time, followed by visits to the Hash, Marijuana and Hemp Museum as well as the Cannabis College.

After massive hits on a vape in one establishment, we ventured back out into the streets and along the canals to find another coffee shop so that we could continue our true purpose for being in Amsterdam and quit the tourist nonsense. We came out of the narrow alleys and onto a main road, which was still wet from the rain that had fallen earlier that morning. It was round about now that all three of us started feeling the effects of the vaporiser at about the same time we saw a fucking tank rolling down the road towards us. All three of us stopped in our tracks and involuntarily let our jaws hit the asphalt as we watched the Dutch army roll past us, all dressed in full greens as they convoyed in Jeeps, APCs, motorbikes and tanks. There were a lot of flags and a lot of noise. All of the soldiers looked like they were headed into battle, with grimaces on their faces and guns in their hands or slung over their shoulders. It took a while before I finally turned to my companions and confirmed that they were also seeing the rolling green army before us. We couldn't understand it. Why was the tooled-up Dutch army tearing through the streets of Amsterdam in the middle of the afternoon? I quickly racked my brains for any previous plans or chatter we may have had of taking over the country in some deranged three-man attempt to overthrow the government and turn Amsterdam into an annex of Wales. We would probably claim that Wales and Amsterdam both shared the colour green as reason enough for our sudden takeover of the city and Celtic coup d'état. I recalled nothing of a plan to take over Amsterdam with my two friends, and decided that the military riding past us probably had nothing to do with the three of us. It was probably just some Remembrance Day parade or their version of the territorials out for a play with their toys of terror.

After they had all rolled on past us and onto the next street we continued our walk to the comfort and safety of the Jolly Joker for one last session. We sat and smoked, sipping coffees and blazing nice fat biffs. It wasn't long before the Writer and I noticed that the Actor was looking a little whiter than usual. We asked him if the sight of the Dutch military in all their glory had given him the fear, assuring him that the Nazi's were not in fact making another go of it. He responded by declaring that he was in fact melting. We watched as he slid down and onto the table between us, face first, where he proceeded to dribble and drool onto the scuffed wood.

"Are you all right dude?" I asked.

"I'm melting," was the only reply.

The Writer and I laughed hard at our companion's level of highness right then, which prompted him to start laughing as well. The three of us laughed louder and harder as the Actor proceeded to melt all over the table and down the chair and onto the floor. A member of staff came to our table and enquired, "Is he okay?"

"I'm melting," came the reply from under the table.

It was clear to the three of us that those extra blasts on the vaporiser had done this, and that the spliffs in the cafe had tipped him over the edge. The waiter smiled, shrugged his shoulders and asked if we wanted more drinks. Upon checking the time we declined and made the decision to try to get to the airport for our flight. This caused the Actor's eyes to widen with panic.

"Move? Now?!" he asked.

The Writer and I smiled and nodded as we got to our feet and gathered our belongings. We strolled out of the cafe and back among the beasts, giggling every time we peered back over our shoulders at the Actor, who dragged his little case behind him like it was a 10 ton boulder. The Writer and I agreed that watching the Actor move like sludge for the entire journey was great entertainment; who needs enemies with cunts like us as friends?

England
4

London

8

My last year in London was spent managing a wine bar, which had a restaurant section and also doubled as a late night venue and after hours party spot for some of the big clubs. It was here that my previous three years of practice climaxed in a spectacular orgy of drink, drugs and madness. This is where I met the Kiwi, whose claim to fame was an ability to stay awake on X, coke and vodka for a whole week while still working a fulltime job and functioning like a semi-normal human being. This is also where I came to know Spike, the manager of the entire venue that I now managed the wine bar for. Spike was a young ex-footballer who loved drink, drugs and women. He had a full-time girlfriend that he lived with but he fucked a different girl every day of the week. Sometimes they were women he picked up at the bar, sometimes they were employed behind the bar and sometimes they were girls who just came in to enquire about work. He had that way about him – women just loved the skinny, spiky haired degenerate. Spike ran the venue but his father owned it. His father owned and ran over a dozen bars, clubs, pubs and restaurants all around London and was a 100%, true to the bone, genuine cockney villain.

He had made the money to buy his first pub by pulling off a daring feat of criminality back in his day. The Owner, along with two companions in hiding in London, but originally from Sicily, stuck a bank up on a London high street and then ran down the street to the next branch, which they also stuck up with their shotguns before legging it further down the street to a third bank and knocking that one over too. Three armed robbers, three banks, all on one high street. They got away clean and never looked back. The owner got into the pub game and it didn't take him long to expand further into the service industry, where he made a mint. The Sicilians became silent partners, as neither was in London legitimately and couldn't have their names on any form of paperwork or legal documentation.

Back in the Owner's day it was easier to forge documents as well as hide and move money around. In his time, putting your money into legitimate businesses was part and parcel of the criminal enterprise. He then learned another kind of racket – finance.

It was at the wine bar where I also learned about finance, as well as banks, and that most elusive of places called the City of London. The UK has had a longstanding tradition of maintaining what is referred to as 'the old boys' club'. This roughly translated as a network of highly privileged white men who give each other jobs and do each other favours to keep getting richer than they already are while avoiding jail time. These clubs can be seen all over the country in various shapes and sizes in damn near any sector of society, provided you know what you're looking for – as the saying goes 'It's not what you know, but who you know'. It was at the wine bar that some of the City of London's old boys network met for liquid lunches in order to discuss dirty deals. The Hogs liked to stuff their fat faces as well as their golden coffers.

London

9

To fully understand what was being said, I first had to get my head around how banks and money actually worked, or to be more precise how the financial system fucks people over. Money is the blood that pumps through the veins and arteries of every city and society, and yet most of us don't really understand anything about it, other than how to spend it of course. The financial system wears a shroud that is purposefully complex and smothered in lies in order to hide its true agenda of crippling, paralysing and raping each and every one of us. Most people find it far too difficult a thing to wrap their heads around, which is why approximately 1% of the population owns around 50% of the planet's wealth. This is why roughly 50% of people live on less than a pound a day. We are being financially fucked, and the rapist performs a little card trick before your very eyes while doing the dirty deed to distract you. Before you've had time to figure out where the king is there's a jack in your ace and you're now feeling like a queen.

In modern times, money comes into existence by way of the fractional reserve banking system. One afternoon, between mouthfuls of Cabernet Sauvignon and rare steak, several of the Hogs explained it to me.

"The way a fractional reserve banking system works can be summed up like this: a government decides it needs some money. That government contacts its central bank and requests the money. Let's say £10 billion for example."

"Peanuts," one of the Hogs interrupted, which caused an outbreak of snorts and chuckles from his fellow swine.

"The central bank says 'sure, we'll buy £10 billion worth of government bonds from you.' The government then paints some official looking pictures and letters on a piece of paper and calls them bonds. The central bank also paints some official looking pictures and letters on some paper and calls it money. The government and central bank then exchange their pieces of paper. The government then deposits the central bank's notes, known as money, into a commercial bank account. That money has now become legal tender, and that £10 billion has now been added to the country's money supply." The Hog sat back and took a swig of wine, confident he had explained the system accurately enough to me.

I nodded my understanding of the seemingly simple process.

Another Hog took up the mantel. "Of course, today there aren't really any pieces of paper as everything is done digitally, but it's essentially the same thing that's going on. The central bank is creating money out of thin air and exchanging it for an equal amount of bonds with the government, which it too created out of thin air. A bond is simply an 'I owe you'."

"But what do the government actually owe?" I asked.

The Federal Reserve Bank of America created a long, dry and tedious document titled 'Modern Money Mechanics, a Workbook on Bank Reserves and Deposit Expansion'. The book states on the opening page that its purpose is to describe the basic process of money creation in a fractional reserve banking system. Fortunately for me, I had drunk London Hogs tell me all about it between bottles of Bordello, Pouilly-Fumé and Champagne, so I didn't have to turn page after page to learn the inner workings of the system. The question was, did either the document or the Hogs really know – and want to divulge – the answer to my question or would there simply be some creative wordplay to further confuse the common citizen?

"So now that the government has placed its £10 billion into a commercial bank account, that money is now part of the bank's reserves," the first Hog continued while ignoring my question, "which is what happens to all deposits into a bank account – the money becomes part of the bank's reserves. Current regulations state that a bank must have 10% of its deposits in its reserves. This means that only £1 billion needs to be kept as required reserve, while the other £9 billion is classified as excessive reserve and can now be issued as loans."

Common sense, at that point, told me that every time the bank issues a loan, that money is being drawn out of the original £9 billion excessive reserve. However, this is where some of the financial fuckery in the system takes place and pisses in the face of logic. What really happens is that another 'imaginary' £9 billion is created from thin air by the commercial bank and this is what is issued as loans to businesses and the general public.

"...thus creating new money and expanding the money supply of a country," another Hog snorted boisterously.

So, from nothing a country now has £19 billion in circulation, although none of it actually exists for real (other than numbers on screens) or is backed up by anything like gold or other precious commodity. It's just made from nothing and in essence is worth nothing.

"A loan is made by the bank accepting a promissory note, also known as a loan contract, from a borrower – i.e. you. They then deposit credits, also known as money, into the borrower's transaction account. Whatever the original deposit is, another 90% of that amount can be created from nothing and issued as loans or new money." The Hogs all nodded and grunted confirmation that the words being spoken were both true and accurate.

"Banks are thought of as intermediaries, but they are actually the creators of the money supply," the first Hog continued, sounding smug and even a little condescending as he regarded me down the length of his fat greasy snout. "People think that banks take deposits and lend money, but the truth is that they don't do either of these things."

"In law, the word *deposit* is meaningless," another snout chipped in for my edification.

"If you give your money to a bank, it's not a deposit – you've actually loaned your money to that bank. Likewise, banks don't lend money to the public as they are in the business of purchasing securities. When you sign those bits of paper at the bank, what you're actually doing is signing a legal document that they then purchase from you. The paper says that if you don't give the agreed amount of money back to the bank by a certain date they will take whatever securities you have."

"Securities?" I asked, close to getting very lost.

"This is typically property and other physical things of actual value. When they make the deposit into your account, what they are actually doing is making a record of its debt to you – the public," another snout informed me.

"It's a fair estimate that around 97% of money consists of bank deposits, which is created from nothing. No actual money is printed or handed over, there are simply more numbers on the screen when you check your balance after signing the bits of paper. And this is the bank's record of its debt to you." Again, the lead Hog stopped to refuel with alcohol, and the lecture was continued by another set of wobbly jowls.

"New money takes its value from the original, existing money supply in society. If it is created regardless of what's happening with the demand and supply of goods and services in society then inflation occurs. As supply and demand level out, prices rise thereby weakening the power of the money."

"In other words, by increasing the amount of money in society, but not the goods and services, you will always create inflation," the first Hog continued. "Inflation is nothing more than a hidden tax for the people to pay."

Yet more financial fuckery for the masses I thought to myself.

"If a society has new goods and services, implementation of new technology – productive bank credit for example – then there will be no inflation. Loans can be serviced and repaid and you can have a stable economy without problems and with low inequality."

"Basically," a new Hog lent in, "money for production is good. Money for consumption is bad. Money for financial transactions is very bad. When you keep creating new money, but not new goods and services, you keep creating more inflation."

"Around 80% of the money being created today is for the purpose of giving someone purchasing power over existing assets, such as property, which in turn *drives up* the prices of these assets." The first Hog put a lot of emphasis on the phrase 'drives up' and threw a fist into the air as he said it like he was violating some young boy on his private yacht far out at sea and safe from prying eyes. "If the new money was being used to make new land and property, things would be fine. But it's not. The new money is being used to buy old assets, and this leads to..." more wine apparently.

Economic anal bleeding, I silently thought to myself.

"This process of creating new money can repeat, and keep repeating, until eventually the original £10 billion hits zero way down the line after a ginormous ton of new money has been made from thin air and sent inflation through the roof. During all of this there will be little goods and services created. The new money is being passed around for assets that already exist, thereby raising the price of the existing assets and weakening the strength of the money." Hog #1 needed more wine and clumsily filled his glass from what was left of the open bottle of delicious and appropriately named Dirty Laundry Vineyard Bordello on the table. I leaned in and uncorked a fresh one for them.

"In the UK, there are five main banks that make up 90% of deposits. The UK has the most concentrated banking system in the world. These five banks dominate the economy. Also, there is no accountability for these institutions. They are free to run things as they see fit."

To fully understand this lack of regulation I first had to learn a little history.

London

10

The British Empire was the largest empire the world has ever known. Forget about the Romans. The Mongols don't even count as they never sat still for long enough. For over 300 years Britain ruled. Its armies conquered all before it and its bankers established the awesome clout of its currency. But then the inevitable happened. More and more countries declared independence and started telling Britain to go fuck herself. As a result, Britain's wealthy and entitled made the decision to change from a colonial power to a financial dominance. The British Hogs set about proving that the pen was mightier than the sword or cannon if you set about writing out fictional numbers and legal documentation that most will never get their heads around.

The decline of empire meant that British commercial interests across the globe were under threat and losing money. In 1956 Egypt nationalised the Suez Canal. President Nasser seized the internationally owned canal, causing France and Britain to issue an ultimatum with only 12 hours for the president to accept or face a spanking. A few hours after the 12-hour deadline expired, Britain bombed five of Egypt's key cities, including Cairo. The USA, a country infamous for its love of war, opposed this British invasion of Egypt. The then President, Dwight David Eisenhower, who is famous within conspiracy circles for his 'In the councils of government, we must guard against the acquisition of unwanted influence, whether sought or unsought, by the *military-industrial complex*' speech, put pressure on Britain and France to withdraw their troops. Britain was humiliated by the lack of international support, and the political pressure weighed heavy on its shoulders. Essentially, the Suez Canal incident signalled the end of Britain's role as the world's predominate colonial power.

The demise of the empire caused the Hogs – mainly bankers, lawyers and accountants from the City of London – to set up an intricate web of offshore jurisdictions that captured wealth from across the globe and funnelled it to London. The City of London to be precise.

An unwritten agreement was made between the Bank of England and the other major institutions and financiers that a new London Euro-Dollar market would be created off the official books and on new unseen books. It would exist 'elsewhere', not in the City of London or even Britain, and therefore wouldn't be regulated by the Bank of England, like other British banks had to be. The US, as well as other nations, took advantage of this non-regulated banking and began moving their banks to the City of London.

The Cayman Islands were once famous for nothing more than mosquitos and its crystal-clear waters until the 1960s. This is when British lawyers and accountants flew in to draft the financial secrecy laws and regulations that make up the secrecy jurisdictions. The Hogs went all out with their illegal dealings on this one. All kinds of illegitimate money from drug money to terrorist funds was shipped in, and it all came in vast amounts that evaded any and all tax regulations. It was what would soon be dubbed 'a tax haven'.

The secrecy jurisdictions meant that the City of London was the place that banks could engage in business not allowed elsewhere in the world. The Hogs need not worry about jail or consequences as the lack of regulations and secrecy prevailed, and shrouded them like a blanket made from the skin of all the poor people they were fucking over on a daily basis. This new system meant that while your offices and Hogs were on UK soil, your dealings were 'technically' being done offshore and therefor out of sight and mind of the so-called regulatory body.

British banks no longer put their money into manufacturing. They put all of their cash into real estate speculation, financial speculation and foreign currency trade. The financialisation of the City of London deindustrialised the country because it enabled the pound sterling to be supported by this huge in-flow of hot and dirty money from criminality – illegal drugs, tax evasion and terrorism – from all over the world. The economy was no longer backed up by goods and services, it was built on illegal money and speculation.

Many of Britain's Hogs are politicians who sit on the boards of the very companies that they are supposed to be regulating. Instead of doing their jobs, they spend their time lobbying the EU to protect the interests of the City of London. They do this more than all of the other EU member states combined. Yes, the City of London has some very real power and a lot of voices crying out to protect her interests, because she is her own entity. The truth is, the UK doesn't have finance – the City of London does. The City of London is not actually part of the UK or the EU, and has no democratic elections in the typical sense of the word. In the City of London banks and businesses have had the vote since 1668, but she has existed for far longer.

Banks have an approximately 5000-year-old history. During that time they have perfected the art of misleading their customers and the public at large, which is exactly what we are told does not happen in the financial sector; after all numbers don't lie, right? Since the times of the Crusades, banks have been performing the fine art of financial fuckery with invisible arrangements between trustees and settlors, Anglo-Saxon secrecy forming the basis for complex offshore clandestine structures to hide the identities of the owners of assets that reach as high as $50 trillion in worth; from property to art to fucking race horses. The

Hogs have mastered the deception of ensuring the beneficiaries and trustees of a trust reside in different countries, that the shell companies and assets are kept in different countries and that the offshore lawyers that handle all of this black magic are never caught, prosecuted or bothered for doing what we, the public, are assured by our leaders never happens.

"And if anyone were to do something, who would it be?" I asked the Hogs during another of their liquid lunches. They snorted and guffawed before telling me that while all of these dirty deals were done in London, being registered offshore meant they were far from reach of any regulatory body, or "little shit that may want to actually do his fucking job properly," snort, snort, chuckle, chuckle.

Who indeed? In the UK, the regulatory body would be the central bank, which is the Bank of England. The central bank in all countries is the institution that issues and regulates the currency for that nation. They control the expansion and contraction of the money supply – inflation – as well as the interest rates.

Interest is the real financial fuckery that nobody seems to want to talk about. Interest is the real dick up the arse that'll make you scream and bleed out, almost literally. When the government swaps its bonds for that £10 billion, it is called the principal. But in such transactions there is always the principal to pay back, with interest, even for a government dealing with a central bank. Interest is not just something the public have to pay back to commercial banks, or foolish so-and-sos have to pay back to loan sharks for fear of a hammer to the kneecaps. No, even governments get charged interest. This, more than any other sign, should make it clear who is *really* in control.

I thought to myself, if all money is created and borrowed from a central bank and expanded by commercial banks through loans to the public, then surely only the principal is ever being created in the money supply? And so you scream as I did: where is the money to cover all of the interest?! Inflation occurs because new money is always needed to pay back the interest of the original debt, and the money required to pay back everything doesn't actually exist.

"In short," the first Hog concluded, "the amount of money owed to the banks will always exceed the amount of money in existence."

The lack of money in existence to pay back the interest is what causes the economical game of musical chairs you witness every single day. Defaults on bank loans and bankruptcies are actually built into the financial system. Yes, it was designed this way. It did not happen by accident. And the Federal Reserve even printed that book to help you understand it: 'Modern Money Mechanics, a Workbook on Bank Reserves and Deposit Expansion' if you were so inclined to read it one day. So why was it designed this way? To acquire what really has value, of course. Land, property... and *you.*

London

11

The Hogs laid it all out for me without a stutter or a pause – we are all vassals. The money supply is just modern slavery. Traditional slavery was the ability to do labour by way of owning actual people, but that meant caring for the labourers as well. Now they control the money, which controls the wages, which controls the labourers. Money is created in a bank, given to a company, that pays it to a worker, who puts it back into a bank. Economic slavery instead of physical slavery. Slavery enforced with numbers rather than chains. The modern helot competes in the job market in order to get enough money to buy what they need to survive. The more money there is, the more personal debt there is, the more national debt there is. Then we go global, my weary traveller.

In the nineties, the Hogs did a test run on what was labelled the South-East Tiger Economies. These included South Korea, Thailand and Indonesia. They did it in Japan too. They shifted the economy from manufacturing to financial services. This shifts an economy from high performance to recession and a crash relatively quickly. As the Hogs had already told me, money for production is good but money for finance is bad.

The establishment of international banking facilities in Asia allowed the Asian banking sectors to borrow money liberally from abroad, even though it could have been created domestically via a goods and services-based economy. But greed is a bitch, along with the pressure from outsiders like the International Monetary Fund (IMF), World Trade Organisation (WTO) and the US Treasury.

Asian central banks were taken over by foreign interests, who then made it more expensive to borrow domestic money. Commercial banks then had to lend to high-risk borrowers, eventually leading to a banking system burdened with bad debt that lead to bankruptcy. When the IMF set up its offices inside the central banks it started to dictate the terms of surrender for those countries one by one. The IMF demands new policies that typically include credit creation control, legal changes and rises in interest rates. It basically cripples a country and then forces its leaders to sell its assets off cheaply to foreign buyers. There is never any chance of saving the doomed economy or country, as the IMF know exactly what they are doing before they even set up shop in that country's central bank. That right there is a powerful statement. They set up office in the central bank, i.e. the economic centre of a country. They tell you from the jump, 'we go wherever we want', and then inevitably do whatever they please. And what pleases them most is taking everything. It is critical to notice that they do not set up their base of operations in any government buildings or royal palaces – no, they plant their flag in the central bank of a nation because banks are where the real power of a country lie, not its public leaders.

This trial run of how to destroy a country's economy and take it over was then played out in Europe on a large scale. The European Central Bank took control of all the other central banks, thereby centralising Europe. Then it implemented credit lending that would cripple the countries inside Europe, just as they had done in South-East Asia. The financial system was changed only after political concessions had been made. Unemployment hit 50% in some countries.

As usual, they got into power by promising to implement changes that would stop all of the problems that it later brought about. Say one thing, do another – think Orwell's Doublespeak. Give us power and we will bring prosperity and happiness, but by the time they are finished your country is bankrupt and on the verge of suicide.

The European Central Bank is an international organisation, unlike the Washington-run IMF or WTO, and it is above any of the nations that it operates in. It cannot be touched by any laws or rulers. The European Central Bank is independent, unaccountable, secret and has zero transparency.

My head spun with all of the information spat at me from the sagging jowls and chins lathered in saliva of the drunken Hogs. They had done their best to explain to me the parasitic nature of the financial system, and its institutions that have burrowed into society's skin to suck out the goodness to keep themselves alive unbeknownst to their hosts. I was perplexed while they were aroused.

The knowledge they had handed down to me was frightening and almost too much to believe. Did the world really run that way? Was this some giant conspiracy kept hidden in plain sight from the masses? I scratched my head while trying to take it all in and make sense of the beast. The Hogs touched themselves, rubbing their bloated bellies while spilling wine over their bespoke shirts while toasting the thought of all that money and power. It visibly excited them. I thanked my teachers and departed, making my excuses that there was work to be done behind the bar. I continued my shift in a daze, and for once it wasn't a sign of how many drugs I had consumed.

My lessons in the financial fuckery inflicted by banks had gone on for nearly a week. Each day the Hogs imparted a little more knowledge, opened my blind eyes to a bit more of the truth and had ultimately blown my fucking mind. It was both scary and sickening. Not only that this shit goes on, but also knowing that so many hide their heads in the sand from it. Whenever I would speak to people about my newfound-knowledge, they would shake their heads, either look confused or shocked, but ultimately go about their lives like I had said nothing important. It was completely understandable, for how do you stop such a behemoth as a global economic powerhouse?

London

12

I found myself jumping from bus to train to tube in order to wander the streets of that little understood place called the City of London. From what the Hogs had told me the days before, this is where it all happened. The City of London was where the masters of the universe did their dirty deeds and manipulated the entire planet. I'd never had cause to go there in the past, but after hearing so much about it I wanted to see it for myself. I wanted to see its original architecture dotted between the tall modern-day glass structures, all brimming with power and authoritarian grandeur. The hustle and bustle of dark suits and briefcases stalking from one crime scene to the next, disguised to the eye of the average prole.

The City of London is the financial capital of the world, and yet is only home to roughly 11,000 people. The City of London is a different place to the rest of the city where I lived and worked. My London had seven million residents, a government and a royal family. The City of London is a one square mile patch of land near the centre of the capital. It has its own mayor – The Right

Honourable Lord Mayor of London – and its own flag and crest. If the Queen (or King) of England wants to enter the City of London, they first need to get permission from the 'The Right Honourable' at a special ceremony. It is a most bizarre place indeed.

The City of London is more like a country than an actual city. The corporation that runs it is older than the United Kingdom as it is structured today by several hundred years. Nobody knows exactly when the City of London came into existence it's so old. The Romans established Londinium around ad 47 on the banks of the River Thames, but that wasn't the City of London as we know it, just the location where its buildings reside. This is partly how it gets the power that it has, because it is 'Time Immemorial', which means that it's so old that it *just is*. The oldest documents in the UK make reference to the City of London already being an established powerhouse long before they were written. Roughly 2000 years ago the Romans came to Britain and founded a trading post on the River Thames and named it Londinium. They then built a wall around it for defence, and it's this wall that makes the City of London possible today. After the Romans left Britain, the City remained within the walls and grew very rich trading with the outside world. In 1066, William the Conqueror came to Britain, but he couldn't conquer the City of London, partly due to the wall. In 1067 William made a deal with the City, agreeing to leave it alone in exchange for the City recognising him as King. After the agreement was made, the Conqueror – due to his inability to conquer the City – surrounded it with more walls, towers and buildings.

Westminster was built as the capital of a city named London as a power move in order to try to suck the wealth and authority out of the City of London. This was the real start of the second London, which grew much larger and merged with other towns whether they liked it or not to eventually surround the City of London.

As I walked around in the wet and greyness that reflected the giant structures of the modern time, it was difficult to spot the original wall that had made the City possible. Most of it has gone now. What does remain are the dragons. They guard the entrance to the City of London and are also on its crest.

The crest can be found in many places as a signifier that something is in fact owned and operated by the City of London, such as the Old Bailey, Epping Forest, Spitalfields Market, Paddington Station and Tower Bridge. The City of London is also home to the oldest Masonic Temple in the world. This combination of wealth, history and the freemasons makes for a conspiracy theorist's wet dream. There are many who believe that it is there, in that tiny one square mile plot of land, that the centre of the spider's web is. It's there that the true rulers of the world congregate, plot and plan on how next to steal your children to spill their virgin blood in some kind of dark and twisted offering to forces from other realms.

Despite what some believe the City of London isn't an independent nation, it's something different. It's a city inside a city (London) inside a country (England), which is inside a nation (the United Kingdom). If that wasn't complicated enough, then there's its elections.

The City of London has the most complicated elections in the world, which consists of Aldermen, Sheriffs, Committees, Common Councillors, Liverymen, Livery Companies known as Guilds – which are medieval guilds – modern corporations and Freemen. Three-quarters of the electorate are company employees working within the City of London, but not living there. The other 25% of votes is given to the residents. The reason for this seemingly unfair distribution of voting power is due to the fact that more people work in the City of London than live there, and so it must always be what the Hogs referred to as 'business friendly'.

Of course the City will always be business friendly, as it is a business in itself. The City of London is a corporation. A private company that performs the functions of a local council, with a private police force and private courts. The city called London gets its power from government, who get it from the Queen, who gets it from God. The City of London gets its power from corporations, who get all of their power from money. Serious money.

"Over and over again we have seen that there is another power than that which has its seat at Westminster. The City of London, a convenient name for a collection of financial interests, is able to assert itself against the government of the country. Those who control money can pursue a policy at home and abroad contrary to that which is being decided by the people." Strong words from Clement Attlee, who served as the UK's Prime Minister from 1945 to 1951.

Within Westminster the City of London has someone called The Remembrancer, whose main duty is to ensure that nothing the House of Commons does interferes with the City of London. This person is not elected and can never be removed. They ensure that no laws passed by the British government can touch the City of London. That's right, the British government can't fuck with the City of London and the Queen herself must first get permission from the Mayor before she can set foot inside it, yet alone try to do anything to it.

The City of London had been the beating heart of the British Empire, but that had long died by the end of the twentieth century. The City, however, lives on. It has adapted and survived in the modern world.

At the heart of the City of London stands the Bank of England. This is the central bank for the nation, and is also the financial regulatory body... or at least it is supposed to be. After the Empire died, the City used the Bank to attract other banks from all over the world with all of their money, and none of the regulations they had to abide by in their homelands. It adapted and survived. It preached one thing and did another, which is still how it operates today.

A clear example of how they operate can be seen by looking at the Bank of Credit and Commerce International (BCCI). It was in the early seventies when the Bank of England issued a license to the BCCI, who set up their head office in the City of London. Within 10 years, BCCI had grown into the seventh largest bank in the world. The miracle of zero regulations enforced upon you was clearly demonstrated to the world. Another 10 years later, the BCCI was bankrupt. The BCCI had done too much dirty dealing with the world's intelligence services, including the CIA, as well as terrorists. It had also engaged in far too much money laundering and financial fraud to keep going indefinitely. Greed is what eventually fucked them over. For years whistle-blowers had been coming forward to the Bank of England, the so-called regulatory body, informing them of the BCCI's shenanigans, but all the Bank of England did was try to cover things up. Eventually, gambling with dirty money that had no real backing brought it all crumbling down.

Money, banks, financiers, accountants, lawyers – they are all part of the same game. A game that we are all a part of, but most of us have already been dealt a losing hand before we even take our place at the table. As the Hogs had told me the day before, "If you didn't go to the right school or come from the right family, then you're never really going to be a part of it. If you're not part of it, then how can you be a winner?"

How indeed? As I wandered the rain-slicked City streets that reflected my puzzled face back at me, blazed and confused, I thought back to that time when I had truly realised that there is no God and that all religion is bullshit. The knowledge that the Hogs had dropped on me seemed to almost parallel that understanding about religion. And, likewise, it became a moment in my life when I saw the world differently and would forever be looking at it from a different perspective. They say that 'the truth will set you free', or at least the writers of the King James Bible, John 8:32, did. In this instance it seemed accurate to some extent. My mind was still traversing the details of what I had been told, but essentially I was already coming to the understanding that the game is rigged with insurmountable odds stacked in favour of a few, and therefore I was free to concern myself only with what I felt truly mattered in life. This is different for everyone. At the time, I didn't know what it was for me, but I knew it wasn't money or Heaven.

Not too long after my newfound knowledge of the financial system had sunk into my grey matter, I was made an offer by Spike and his father. They had decided that they would like to pay for me to get my landlord's license in order for me to take over one of the cockney villain's pubs. It was time for me to run my own gaff. It was a big deal, and a big compliment as to my abilities as a barman and manager. I was still in my early twenties and had only just graduated from university. They showered me with praise and promised me the world, so I thanked them and said, "No."

My recent awakening, along with past experiences and beliefs, had driven me to the conclusion that staying in London and running my own pub was not the best path for me to take in life. My future lay elsewhere. It had been a fun, drink- and drug-fuelled ride no doubt, but it was time to move on to pastures new.

Spike and I spent some time reminiscing of past exploits in a futile attempt to win me over and convince me to stay in London. We laughed about the previous New Year's Day, when we were still partying from the night before, and he had climbed onto a table in a packed pub, dropped his jeans and underwear around his ankles and screamed out loud, "Let's have an orgy!"

For the average citizen, this would be an abnormal and shocking sight, but for us it was just funny. Spike, with his cocaine shrivelled member being wiggled to a pub full of friends, co-workers and strangers while he swung his pint of beer and spilled it over the heads of all around him.

Cocaine was another reason why I felt I had pushed my time in London as far as I should risk it. I'd been partying and snorting for several years, but my time as manager of the wine bar had escalated into new territories of time with the white mistress, as well as ecstasy – the adult smarties.

London

13

There is a common misconception about what are labelled as 'hard drugs'. The media, politicians and probably your parents too have always pushed this agenda that stipulates all lives will be ruined by any drugs all the time. You are taught that there are no exceptions to this rule. Just say no, kids. However, like so much of the information that is pushed upon us this rule is in fact bullshit.

Like anything, too much can be a bad thing – that's what 'too much' means. Be it sex, shopping or sniffing cocaine. If done in a non-overindulgent way, there should be no consequences, only fun times. The lie that 'one hit will make you an addict' is nothing more than a scare tactic. Nothing in life becomes addictive after trying it once. Repetitive use on the other hand...

I had a lot of fun times with cocaine but had reached and surpassed that point of not overindulging. I was now clearly pushing my use, along with other drug abuses, way past acceptable limits.

By that time, a weekend started for the Kiwi and I on Friday morning around 10.00 am and went straight on through the weekend until around Tuesday. We would stay awake for anywhere from three to five days, snorting, smoking and rubbing cocaine into our gums. Added to the equation was plenty of hard booze, which would always be a mix of white Sambuca, vodka and JD. We would pop pills or crush them and snort the gravelly remains or possibly sprinkle them into joints. It was pure unadulterated fiendishness. The Kiwi and I pushed our bodies and minds as far as we could, and then a little bit further.

I took a lot of pills over those months, but can't say that any ever agreed with me, regardless of which way they were to send my mind and body. I hated the come up on Ecstasy. For me, coming up on E inevitably led to vomiting at some point as well as sweating profusely and feeling giddy. After that, you are euphoric and loved up.

On the other hand, cocaine agreed with me a little too much. The White Mistress and I were intimately acquainted for a very long time. I was never a poster boy for the media spun and politically motivated myths behind that white powder. Unlike what they tell you in popular media, I was a fully functioning abuser. Not only holding down a fulltime job but also being offered promotions too.

The reasons behind this perpetuated myth of cocaine and other drugs fucking up your life is due in no small part to the media and politicians, who choose to ignore all research to the contrary. It makes for much better movies and TV to have these demon substances turning women out on the streets to perform tricks and men into swivel-eyed rapists, thieves and murderers. It makes for easier voting acquisition to have all fear and no education about these substances, rather than speak the truth and educate people about the true nature of these substances and their effects on the human body and mind. A simple slogan by simple politicians for simple people: Just Say No. It's easier for politicians to blame drugs and say that they will wage war against them than deal with the actual problems that society faces. Unemployment, poor education, a lack of understanding of the universe and life itself – these are the big issues that require a lot of time, effort, energy and thinking to tackle. So the politicians said, "Fuck all that! Let's just tell them it's drugs and spend a shit-ton of their money on industries like prisons, police and treatment." These industries make a boatload of money from drugs being illegal. The pharmaceutical industry grew exponentially because of the illegal drugs market. Now, despite more and more people smelling the shit in the air, these industries are like living organisms, fighting to stay alive by perpetuating the myths about drugs. Slowly, each new generation realises the truth and changes are made. But this is slow – very, very slow.

In some countries drugs have already been decriminalised. This, in essence, makes them no different to traffic violations. If you're caught with more than a certain amount of drugs you can get a ticket or a fine, but you cannot be put behind bars.

This is the sign of a progressive society that cares a little about its people. It is surely a sign of a sick society when there are numerous repressive policies in place that are more damaging than the drugs they are trying to repress. You can live a normal life on drugs, but are well and truly fucked if you've ever been convicted on a drugs charge. Nobody wants to give you a job, money or a roof over your head if they know you've done time for anything related to narcotics in the UK.

Heroin withdrawal is no different from a severe 'flu. Alcohol withdrawal can kill you. And yet which is legal and indulged in frequently in the UK and so many other so-called free countries?

In the mid-eighties cocaine changed to crack cocaine as the No.1 public enemy in the mainstream media. They are both the same drug, despite what you may have been told by the media and others. Powder cocaine and crack cocaine give you the same high. The only small difference is in their chemical structure. Powder cocaine still has hydrochloride salt attached to it, crack doesn't. It is the lack of hydrochloride salt that makes cocaine smokable in a pipe.

The Kiwi and I preferred to just sprinkle cocaine into a joint or do the traditional bump up the nose. Some people also enjoyed mixing it with water and injecting it, which gives you a high in seconds like crack does, but of course has its obvious downsides. Seen those little black dots running in a line along someone's arm? Chances are they've been shooting up. Ever seen someone with little to no teeth and fucked-up gums? Chances are they've been rubbing their hit on those gnarly gums or smoking the pipe for far too long.

Originally, people would use ether to remove the hydrochloride salt impurities and then do what was known as 'freebasing', but then some clever so-and-so realised that the same could be achieved with baking soda and water without the risk of setting yourself on fire with the highly flammable substance that is ether. Base heads then changed to just plain old crackheads. The cooking of cocaine led to its sale as rocks in unit doses, so it appeared cheaper and allowed for mass distribution to those who couldn't afford to buy powdered cocaine, which was originally only sold in bulk to the rich and famous. This led to gangsters fighting and killing for turf to sling on, fuelling the bloodthirsty media and politicians and their hunger for propaganda.

Crack was blamed for a lot of things, but the truth is unemployment, a lack of responsible parents and crime all existed long before anyone stripped the salt from cocaine or the cocaine leaf was soaked in gasoline and pressed into that fine white paste in the makeshift labs deep in the South American jungles. It was just easier for society to blame those little white rocks and associate them with big scary black men. In America, the number of white cocaine users far outnumbers the number of black users, and yet if you say the words 'crackhead' or 'cocaine dealer' to most people they would more than likely picture a black man before a white man. And the prison system certainly reflects those racist sentiments.

In 1597, Sir Francis Bacon wrote that 'knowledge is power', but for me it was less about power and more about change. I had learned a lot living in the capital of the UK, but both times and people must change. I made the decision to turn down the offer to run my own pub, I handed in my notice at the wine bar, ended my contract with my landlord and said farewell to my new friends. I decided to go back to Wales to start a new chapter.

Wales
2

Llanelli

4

The soap crumbled terribly. When you heated it
with a lighter the rubber and plastic cocooned
within stretched out like melted cheese, and the
stench of petrol overwhelmed any possibility of
pretending it actually was hashish and not it's
atrocious, cheap and unhealthy knock-off that tried
to pass as hash in Wales.

Soap bar was smoked by everyone who puffed,
and eventually everyone came to learn the truth:
soap bar is not really hash. Soap bar used to be
hash... until Portugal. There, it is cut with a variety
of things that are extremely harmful when set on
fire and inhaled. Favourites include plastic and
rubber and diesel and shoe polish, because they
melt and are a decent weight when solid again,
which makes them ideal for mixing with hash in
order to make what appears to be *more* hash but is
actually just shit (another popular ingredient) soap
bar.

Once burned, crumbled, mixed with tobacco and
rolled in paper with a roll of card slid into one end
it is promptly lit and smoked. The blue tinge to the
grey smoke was rumoured to be an indication of a

high potency of hash and copious amounts of THC in the soap. It captured the attention of all present, but not all were believers in the myth of the blue smoke. Some knew that it was a clearer indication of the amount of chemicals you had just inhaled into your lungs, and let's not forget the further damage done by holding that smoke down to get more of a hit from those toxins. While not the same as a true high it did have the desired effect. Numbness.

First, the head got lighter. Not enough to make you fall if you were standing, but enough to make you hold onto something just in case. Next, the inability to communicate, which was usually accompanied by an inability to think. Staring blankly straight ahead at nothing. Then the heavy eyelids. Not heavy enough to close them altogether, just enough to make you look gormless as the bottom of the jaw got heavier in tandem with the eyelids to create a half-asleep, slack-jawed yokel look. Finally, after what seemed like an hour but was barely a minute, you get your senses back and are just left with the numbness. But the strength and duration of that numbness depends on the individual.

The White Horse was a perfect example of an individual who should stay clear of intoxicants of any and all kinds because it numbed one of his most important organs: his brain. He had earned the moniker after an unusually excessive night of alcohol in the form of cheap whiskey straight from the bottle, countless spliffs filled with high-quality green and a variety of pharmaceuticals that had either been swallowed whole with the aid of the whiskey or crushed, snorted and then washed down with the whiskey. The reason for this cocktail was to celebrate the joyous fact that there was real green buds available in town.

At some point during the night a question was put before the room. "Does anyone else see that white horse?"

In the front room of a semi-detached house in a small coastal town once famous for rugby, tin and steel, that was the question asked to a room where several drunk, stoned and generally intoxicated men sat listening to music. Laughter had drowned out the sound of music and the White Horse was born. Pale white, skinny to the bone, shivering slightly due to all that had been consumed, paper-cut-panda-eyes and a punch-drunk jaw. A fine specimen. There was no drool from the hanging jaw yet, which indicated partial freshness in the specimen. But the neck had already weakened and the pin that sat aloft was slightly circling. There was no real rhythm or timing to the small involuntary motions, despite the White Horse being a musical genius. There were no tunes being performed tonight though, just the occasional murmur about the mysterious white horse somewhere in the room.

"Shut-the-fuck-up! There is no fucking horse you tart!" bellowed the Bear before he burst into hysterical giggles.

The paper-cut-panda-eyes sprung open like a rusty electric garage door that needed maintenance and were accompanied by a sound similar to an American stroke victim being asked to explain a theory marrying quantum mechanics to classical physics in Cantonese.

More laughter filled the room. Some people can still function normally after consuming alcohol and narcotics. Some people turn into the White Horse.

The four of us, as well as several others, had regularly been hanging out at the Bear's home for many months. Almost nightly, we would descend on the building on the outskirts of town and spend time with each other, either wasting that time or using it to try to make art of one form or another. Some were writers, others musicians, actors or designers, we covered a wide array of mediums between us. Most of us dabbled in multiple forms of creativity, and we regularly tried to combine our efforts to make something new and interesting. The venue was a strange place, but it was the only one that offered us complete freedom and sanctuary from the outside world. Almost all of us were either unemployed or had part-time jobs, so we were still forced to live under our parents' roofs. For most this was problematic when it came to smoking weed and chilling out.

The Bear was a very sociable character, but deep down suffered from something that the Mohawk attributed to depression. I was never convinced of this, as the Bear had always been a jolly kind of a character and we spent most of our time laughing at one thing or another. The Mohawk insisted that the reason the Bear's home looked like a municipal waste site was a sign of some underlying mental melancholy, but I simply assumed he was too lazy to do any cleaning. It can't be denied that the Bear's cave was like nothing we had ever seen before it. He had been living alone for many months, having been through several housemates all of whom had departed for one reason or another, but mainly because of his lack of hygiene. Now the entire house was filled with rubbish. At some point he had decided to place black refuse sacks around the place for people to dispose their waste into, but at no point had he ever taken those bags outside. Over time the multiple black bags got filled, overflowed and then spilled out onto the carpet. It didn't take too many months before every room in the semi-detached was knee-high with rubbish. The Bear never cooked, he simply got take-outs and deliveries, the containers for which now littered the house. Almost a year's worth of rubbish and waste lay in piles in every room. The stink was just like the one you experience at your local rubbish dump. If you've ever watched documentaries or YouTube videos about poor Africans and other Third World people having to survive by living and foraging in rubbish dumps, literally setting up homes like that of Phnom Penh's Stung Meanchey landfill in Cambodia, then you will have a good idea of what the Bear lived like, except he was in Wales and in a semi-detached house.

As time went on the house slid further and further into disrepair, which damn near consumed the entire structure. And yet, some of us continued to go there in order to hang out, smoke and escape from the realities of the early 21st century.

Llanelli

5

The scenario was typical for a small Welsh town.
Young men with nothing better to do than spend
what little money they had on substances to help
them forget just how much spare time they had on
their hands.

A lack of industry creates job scarcity. No jobs
means no money and a lot of free time. In that
small town you either spent your time drunk and
fighting, or stoned and motionless on a couch in
front of a TV.

We were slightly different. We liked the arts and
driving. We preferred both when stoned, and when
you combined all three then you were in for a good
time. There's nothing quite like chucking a car
around narrow bends on muddy country lanes
while blazing a spliff, arguing artistic theories,
discussing new creative ventures and blasting your
favourite tunes into the night. Fun times in small
towns and villages.

Some people, mainly from previous generations,
have never understood this kind of entertainment.
The kind of fun that is derived from losing yourself
in drugs and calculated risks. When you are born

into a life of mundane slavery in a society that wants nothing more from you than to wake up, clock in, obey, consume and shut the fuck up there are one of three ways that you can go.

First, you can do as previous generations did. You can submit. Do as you're told, do whatever shit job they give you and work your fingers to the bone for nothing more than scraps that barely allow you to survive. Maybe if you're lucky you'll have a fortnight in Spain getting drunk in British bars with British tourists eating British all-day breakfasts.

Second, you go insane. There are many friends and colleagues that have taken this route. Previous generations blame the substances, always burying their heads in the sand to shield themselves from the bitter truth that the reason substances and alcohol were being abused in the first place is because the alternative was a mundane existence as a slave, constantly cowing down to a government that is owned by banks and who want nothing more from you than servitude. The question is often heard, 'Why would he do that to himself? Drink himself to death... swallow so many pills... die alone choking on his own vomit in his sleep on a cold bare floor...' but of course, the real question should be 'Why do we live in a society that tolerates such a common scenario?'

Third, you get high. Get high and find holes in the system. The more you learn about the system the less a slave to it you will be.

Know your enemy! The enemy is not some fellow homo sapien with a different skin tone living on a different patch of dirt. The enemy is the one who prevents any changes from occurring right there on your own doorstep. It's the one who hides the truth from you. It's the one who has you wasting the one life that you have. Were you really born to work a nine-to-five that you hate in order to receive fictional numbers that you exchange for essentials like food and water that are slowly poisoning you because big-business can get bigger bucks by turning natural healthy food and water into chemically tainted trash? We were once endless possibilities, now we are property of limited liability companies.

Few people are aware, and fewer still accepting, of a horrible truth. You are an owned commodity. When you were born you were issued a birth certificate – a certified copy of course, not the original – this is a record of your ownership, because someone – probably your parents – registered you by wilfully submitting to a higher authority. This is a document that proves you exist and who currently has charge of you. Your parents do not own you, for they are owned by the same entity that owns you. You are the property of a Limited Liability Company, an LLC. It is public record that every cabinet member, Prime Minister and even the Queen of England and the soil you live on are all registered companies. It is a little-known fact that when you register something – anything – you give up ownership of it and instead receive a Certificate of Title.

A Certificate of Title is absolutely worthless. It

means nothing and is evidence that you in fact own nothing. Not your car. Not even your children. Check your documents and you will see that you are the registered keeper of the vehicle and not the owner. Check with social services plc – if you don't raise the child the way the state wants you to raise the child, the state will take the child from you and you will be forever labelled as an unfit parent. The state insists upon mandatory vaccinations, mandatory schooling, holidays when they tell you to and not a moment sooner or later. The state tells you how to manage their property, and they will take it from you if you don't do it the way they tell you to.

Think of it like this. If you actually owned your car, could the government take it from you and crush it? If they didn't own your children, could they take them from you and do as they pleased with them? By registering something you hand over legal title – ownership – and you get documentation that states you are nothing more than the registered keeper.

How can your children be yours if the government can take them from you whenever they like? Wouldn't that be theft or kidnapping even? Would this in fact be breaking one of only two natural laws: no harm to others and no loss to others. But more than natural law applies to a person. Men and women obey the natural laws and common laws, a person obeys statute rules and policies.

When you were born and your parents

submitted your birth certificate application form, a legal identity was formed. This fictional person is known by a title, such as Mr, followed by your name.

A 'Person' was defined as fiction by the law society in Black's Law 3rd Edition, but by the 8th Edition, 'Person' was defined as natural person, firm, co-partnership, association, limited liability company, corporation or legal personality. Somewhere along the line, fiction has been defined as natural by lawyers. An abstract entity such as a corporation. Men created government, which in turn created persons, which are owned by the government. Your birth certificate means that you are not a man or a woman, you are a person and you are a legal fictional entity, and you are owned by the government that you are registered with. Inaction, as well as unknowing or knowing consent, to represent your person means that more than just natural and common laws apply to you. And outside of natural and common laws there is no justice.

When you go to court, which is a corporate place of business, you are immediately asked or referred to by your title and name. The reason being, this is your person and it has status, which is subject to all manner of legal trickery and judicial buggery. If you do not reply yes, or acknowledge your person, then the statutes and articles that apply to the fictional entity with legal personality do not apply to you. Of course, inaction isn't always going to save you.

Llanelli

6

"But…" the White Horse tried to explain himself but only produced air.

"Go to sleep!" the Bear instructed him, but there was no comprehension of the instruction, not even recognition of the presence of other life in the room except for that four-legged beast.

"How much have you had dude?" I asked the White Horse. His head lolled around and he groaned.

"He's gonna be sick," the Mohawk announced before firing the bong up.

"Don't be sick there you fuck!"

The Bear's words caused the White Horse to jolt awake momentarily. He managed to shuffle forwards on the cushioned chair to the point of almost sitting up straight. He forced his eyes open and looked at the three of us on the couch in a way that said, 'I'm back… kind of'. The White Horse's freshly opened eyes were suddenly filled with a humungous plume of thick grey smoke from the Mohawk's lungs, fresh from the bong. He choked on the smoke and coughed violently as he fell to his hands and knees, coughing and spluttering more and more until eventually passing out face down on the waste beneath him.

We laughed uproariously.

The Mohawk choked slightly on the smoke and laughter, which just caused harder laughter all round "Don't be sick you fuck!" the Bear reiterated his instruction.

The Bear's concerns were not ill-placed. The White Horse had a reputation not just for being sick while intoxicated, but for astonishing displays of projectile vomit that defied the laws of physics. The Mohawk had once found him lying face down on his bathroom floor with a patch of vomit on his back. No sick in the toilet, sink or bath. No vomit on the floor or his face. Just a disgusting patch of cold vomit on his back. How the fuck did he get it there?

One past temporary house of debauchery had a tiny bathroom under a staircase. The room had a stained toilet with a minuscule hand basin attached to the wall directly in front of your face when sat upon said toilet, with a shower on the other side of that. Again, it was the Mohawk who had the misfortune of finding the White Horse. He was found partially dressed sat on the toilet, fast asleep. The tiny bathroom was completely covered – walls, floor, ceiling and furnishings – in vomit. The Mohawk has always maintained that it should have been physically impossible for, firstly, the White Horse to be able to produce that much vomit and, secondly, for him to literally cover every single square inch of the small room with it. It was a masterpiece result of excessive alcohol and narcotic consumption by a beast not built for such adventures.

"He's done dudes," I said, stating the obvious.

Llanelli

7

We decided to call it a night. The Mohawk and I left the White Horse passed out on the Bear's rubbish-covered floor with the Bear curling up on his sofa that usually doubled as his bed.

Outside, the Mohawk and I went our separate ways in separate cars. As I drove home I smoked another spliff and continued to ponder some of those strange entities that make up our western society.

We believe that money is valuable, but it is in fact worthless – backed by neither gold standard or anything else. The work we do in order to earn money has value, but the money itself is nothing more than a promissory note. Money bears the term 'I promise to pay', but pay what if not your soul or physical being? There is no gold standard anymore and it was never replaced by anything. Some believe that a country's worth is determined by the number of residents it has registered in it via birth certificates and legal residency. They believe that the ultra-powers that secretly run the world are in fact playing out some god-like competition to own the most souls by having them on their patch of dirt. What they will do with those souls, who knows? Some think they're being harvested for inter-dimensional entities that feed on our fear, but I hadn't done anywhere near enough drugs to start believing in those kinds of theories. Yet. A promissory note is a promise you will receive something of value for the work you do, but in reality it is all just fictional numbers created from thin air by white guys with thinning white hair. Modern day slavery. Suddenly the car was illuminated by a blue light in the rear-view mirror.

I tossed the spliff out of the window and continued to drive. It's important in these situations to clear plenty of distance between you and the evidence. It's rare, but on occasion it has been known for the more enthusiastic piggy to go trotting back down the road to recover your abandoned goods, or even drive back in search of it if he believes it to be of substantial quantity. Once at a suitable distance I pulled to the side of the dark and deserted road, and then watched the pair of piggies park up and swagger over to the car.

During the confrontation I decided to use the Freemen-on-the-land philosophy against the members of the Law Society, represented that cold night by two large pork chops. I refused to give them my name, stating that I was not obliged to. I refused to stand under them. I refused and resisted non-violently as a man, not a person. I used silence and blank stares to show the pigs that I would not submit to their illusory authority over me and that I was in fact a free human being.

Llanelli

8

When I regained consciousness I found that the pigs at least had the decency to put me on the back seat of my car so as not to let me freeze to death while unconscious on the side of the road after midnight. The pair of piggies had given me a good old-fashioned stomping on the side of the road for my lack of submissiveness. My refusal to bow to their will had resulted in me buckling to their might. They beat me like a red-headed stepchild and then dumped me back inside my car to recover. I hadn't been out for long, maybe just a few minutes. Just long enough for the pigs to have a good chuckle and then depart, happy in the knowledge that they had shown me who was in charge.

Sat at the side of the road, still bleeding and sore, I rolled a joint and came to the realisation that knowledge is not always power. Sometimes a pair of big black boots and a baton is real power. Words, pseudo-legal mumbo-jumbo and far-flung theories won't do jack shit to save you. I turned over the engine and rolled out onto the asphalt, and as I did so I heard Eric Lynn Wright's voice in my head,

"While I'm drivin' off laughin' this is what I'll say,
Fuck the police..."

Llanelli

9

The walk to work was usually about 15 minutes, 30 after waking and baking. The shop opened at 9.00 and staff were expected to be there by quarter to. I usually left home around 9.30.

There were never customers anywhere on the retail park before about 11.00 and if we ever did see one in our shop it was usually after lunch. So, why did I need to be there at 8.45 in the am?

In the past I had been a money-hungry salesman, 'always be closing!', but now I just did the bare minimum to get my monthly pay. Most shifts started with a cuppa and a spliff with the others. There were four of us in total; a manager, an assistant manager and two salesmen. None of us gave a fuck. The shop sold ceramic tiles and bathroom suites, but we sold almost nothing. The most footfall the bathroom suites on display had were when we slept our hangovers off in the tubs. As the months rolled by we had to invent more and more creative ways to entertain ourselves.

We became notorious on the retail park. The shop where the staff spent their time drinking, smoking and playing. The store covered a large floor space and was split into aisles by A-frames that displayed ceramic tiles for the home. The length of those aisles had seen all manner of things travel down them, even motorbikes.

It started as a one-off laugh when a graphic artist I knew who had an office nearby rode a mini-motorbike into the shop and straight down the centre aisle. The shop was filled with the smell of petrol as we watched a plume of exhaust smoke travel down the middle of the store, away from us standing behind the counter at the front laughing in shock. The graphic artist popped a wheelie on the ridiculously small machine he was straddling as he rode back toward us. We followed him back out of the store, where he had come to a halt in order to try to control his laughter. This then escalated to people drag racing full-size motorbikes with engines as large as 1000cc-plus up and down the shop aisles. Needless to say that the once cheap grey wiry carpet that covered the floor soon developed bare patches down the centre and revealed the concrete beneath.

This did not please the area manager when he made his monthly visit. He wasn't like us. He didn't see the futility in spending our days re-cleaning the same gleaming displays that were never looked at by anyone, vacuuming the spotless carpet that was never walked on by customers, re-stacking the bags of grout and adhesive in more eye-catching ways and all of the other pointless and mundane duties that are devised for you when you work in a shop that never has anyone buying anything.

Summer days were spent lounging out the rear of the store, away from prying eyes and the general public. We would attach a bell to the main entrance that could be heard from out back, and there we would relax in the sun with cups of tea and big fat spliffs. The area behind the store was away from main roads and was used as a delivery bay for all of the stores in the retail park. The road stretched around behind all of the shops, which all had large empty areas. Almost nobody came here. We were free to puff away in peace for the most part.

That peace was shattered on one occasion when the bell failed to work and a police constable, in uniform but on a break, called in to check some prices for tiles to decorate his bathroom with. As he walked past the fire exit, which we used to get out the back, I popped into the store, fresh from stubbing out a spliff, the roach of which was still clamped between my fingers. I had planned to dispose of the evidence properly (flush it down the toilet), but was intercepted en route by the pig who had managed to creep into the shop undetected. The smell of skunk had overpowered the stench of bacon and he had trotted up on us silently. He must have smelled the weed in the air, seen the glazed look in my eyes and heard the stupor in my voice, and yet he said nothing other than his original purpose for being there. I dealt with the pig in a calm and cool manner, as I always do – giving off any sign of fear will only excite the piggy who's as twisted as his tail. My composure and professionalism threw the poor piggy off the scent and he left without trouble or incident. A close call but handled like a surgeon!

The Bear worked in the store next to mine and we often hung out and smoked weed on those long and boring days, but his co-workers and management were not so laid back. It was on this retail park that the Bear and I met the Welsh Terrier, a character like no other.

As the months passed, our boredom at the store grew and our antics worsened. From drag racing motorbikes and smoking weed we delved into acts of sexual exhibition, parties utilising the store's fantastic sound system, graffiti displays, violent destruction of various things in the name of scientific experimentation, fights, gambling, theft and fraud.

It wasn't long before the British economy took a nose-dive and the company we were employed by went into liquidation along with countless others all around the country. We were tasked with closing the store as part of our final duties. This involved packing up all stock and displays to be transported to some of the few remaining stores that the owners were desperately hanging on to in an attempt to stay afloat under a different trading name. As we emptied the store we filled our homes, our friends' and families' places and of course our pockets.

While picking the store's carcass clean like merciless vultures we also vented our anger born from the knowledge that once the shop was emptied we were unemployed with thousands of us in the county looking for work. The venting came by way of creative ways to make our time pass with the accompaniment of the sound of laughter. We played indoor golf, displayed our strength with throwing and kicking competitions, attempted stunts and created contemporary works of art with the aid of a sledgehammer. By the end, the store looked like a snapshot from a war zone. We had both emptied and destroyed the place.

When the area manager came to lock the doors for the final time his jaw hit the bare concrete floor where carpet once lay. He turned 360-degrees and took in the destruction around him. It was a glorious exhibition of golf ball-pocked walls blackened by fires and broken windows. The few remaining light fixtures hung from what was left of the false ceiling and flickered eerily. Bits of plaster would occasionally drift from the battered walls. Wires that hung and jutted out from random spaces sparked to warn there was still life in them yet. Giant dunes made from wood, ceramics, concrete and whatever else had once been part of the premises were scattered throughout the dusty, dark shell of a shop.

The four of us stood and watched the area manager without a drop of guilt, remorse or actually giving a shit between us. We all figured he'd be super pissed at the state of the building and would scream and shout at us like we were still employees who might give a flying fuck. But he didn't. Instead, he offered us extra work. The area manager offered us our normal rate, but our new job would be to travel to stores the company were closing and empty them. Our reputation for fun and vandalism spread throughout the dying company. Some of the former employees had not understood our attitude towards the job, some were even under the delusion that it was a poor work ethic like ours that had been the downfall of the business in the first place.

In times of stress and fear, many people stop thinking clearly and ignore the facts. The UK had entered into dire times and was about to plummet headfirst into a recession, many argued months later that it was in fact a depression that was wrongly labelled in order to prevent fear and panic from spreading throughout the kingdom. If you were clued up enough all that anyone could really be sure of was that the bankers had done it. They'd done it before in other countries, and now they were doing it right here on their own doorstep.

Llanelli

10

The line at the job centre got longer every week. The staff inside made less and less effort to hide their frustration at being overworked and underpaid, as well as completely under-appreciated for achieving a double IQ rating. I was one of the many job seekers who had zero appreciation for the employees in the job centre. They were a humourless and almost brainless bunch who had an air of arrogance about them. The saying that arrogance and ignorance go hand in hand fitted like a glove at the job centre.

For the most part, the job seekers were lazy and didn't care about whether they worked or not. The staff were completely indifferent to your wants or needs as a job seeker. I recognised this as I had exactly the same attitude before I lost my job. The whole purpose of the staff at the centre was to marry a suitable seeker to a suitable source of employment. Suitability depended on your experience, qualifications, skills and ability to travel to the job. Most of this didn't really matter to the staff at my local job centre though.

"I have both a BA and an MA," I informed the

middle-aged lady.

"So, you would say your highest qualification is...?" She peered over her spectacles, unsure what the answer to her own question was despite me already informing her.

"The MA, obviously." I stared unamused through my glasses, having to answer what should have been deemed a stupid or at best rhetorical question.

"Right," she stated before click-clacking on her keyboard for a few more minutes. "Well, we do have a commission-only position at a call centre for mobile phone insurance. Ooh, just around the corner from here on John Street. Can you travel there?"

"I make it here every week, don't I?"

She proceeded to stare at me in silence over her eyewear with one of those condescending looks that tells you the person is full of confidence that they have the upper hand and are not impressed with your backchat.

"Yes."

"Yes what?"

"Yes, I can travel there."

"And *how* will you travel there?"

"Does it matter?" I was genuinely confused by this latest stupid question. My records on the screen before her showed that I lived within walking distance of both the job centre and the employer, and as any native of the town would know there are no buses running between these locations due to their close proximity. My address was a grand total of 10 minutes away on foot, and that was at a leisurely stroll.

"I have to be sure that you are actually going to make an effort to attend the interview and can actually get there on time. We can't waste people's time with no-shows now can we?"

"You said the employer is one street away from here. You have my address on the screen in front of you. I've never missed an appointment here so—"

"There's no need for aggression."

"Aggression?" Again, I was confused.

"Do I need to call security?" She leaned back in her chair, her body language signalling her withdrawal from the conversation with no sign of distress. Her raised chin signalled the position of dominance she felt rather than any sense of fear from any alleged aggression.

"If you like?" I said unenthusiastically.

A staring contest began, which I gladly withdrew from. Her victory at out-staring me prompted the first smile I'd seen from the job centre employee in over two months of going there.

Several more stupid questions later, and a lot more posturing and attitude, then a paper was handed to me with the details of the job posting. Several signatures later and even more posturing, then I was free to leave the den of dumbness.

Past the slobs still wearing their slippers and bath robes, past the staff staring at seekers through empty eyes, and past the ageing security guards who had their heads buried in the sports section of the newspaper and out into the street. A street filled with fellow jobless and many fellow drug takers. Pot heads, like myself, were hard to spot, but the real junkies stood out clearly. Well, less stood and more leaned on strangers or lay down on the pavement. As you walked down the line you could see junkies at various stages of their highs. Some were nodding out where they stood, others shuffled about on edge, while calling their dealers to inform them that they were close to getting their cheque from the job centre to come and score. Mine got paid directly into my bank account, but not everyone in town was eligible for that.

A little further into town and a line of junkies could be seen outside the 'smack-converter' pawn shops. Months later the police would have to permanently station themselves on the street during the opening hours of these shops, as the more desperate junkies had taken to robbing people directly outside the stores and taking their phone and then walking straight in to trade their freshly ill-gotten wears. The shops didn't care, it was all profit to them. Capitalist vultures of the lowest kind. I once worked in one such store in London and was even offered a management position, but thankfully a better opportunity presented itself working as a painter and decorator; a more honest living.

I'd watched the town slowly rot from the inside out over many years, but now it had spiralled into a freefall descent headed for the deepest depths of Dante's Inferno. The crisis that had hit the British economy had left small towns like Llanelli in ruin.

What few businesses remained were laying off employees on a monthly basis, and there hadn't been any sign of an industry for decades now. Shops and businesses couldn't afford to employ anyone, so people had no money to go shopping or employ the services offered by the businesses. A steady downward spiral of despair for all concerned. Well, all except for the perpetrators of the giant game of musical chairs, but instead of music and chairs there were only bankruptcies and foreclosures and worry and misery.

The banks, aided by the governments, had well and truly fucked the citizens in the arse yet again. Another chair was removed, and another few thousand ordinary people were left on their bleeding rectums. No jobs, no money, no homes, no hope. The choices had been bubbling up from the subconscious for some time. Either think of a viable way to make decent money or turn to crime.

The only people making any money were the drug dealers, but even they were feeling the downturn. Some were stepping on their product so much now that they actually had to start trying to sell it to their customers with a creative sales pitches. There is something quite humorous and disturbing about seeing a heroin dealer have to try to pitch a sale to a junkie, "I got the best shit in town for you bruv for cheap!"

"I ain't trying to buy the stains in your knickers mate, I'm looking to get fucked."

A plan had once been pitched to go and rob some dealers. To turn to taxing and become a vulture.

Unfortunately, the dealers were damn near broke too. I considered moving back to London, if not for honest work then at least the chance to rob drug dealers who had some cash to take. This was an extremely dangerous idea. The dealers in my hometown would beat you, possibly cut you, for trying to steal from them. In London, they will kill you; sometimes with a pump action shotgun.

Job interview after pointless job interview rolled by, never bearing any fruit, only frustration. When you live in a small town that has little in the way of higher education, you find yourself in the unenviable and infuriating situation of being told that you are over-qualified for jobs. That's correct, not under-qualified – over-qualified. This seems like a paradox to many, including me, for how can you be over-qualified for anything? But in small towns, having a degree puts fear into the hearts of the management who have almost no qualifications and who got their jobs by working their way up the ranks, or having a relative already employed there sort them out because they turned their back on the education system. The thought of somebody new being able to step right into their shoes without clawing and brown-nosing their way up the ladder first is quite an intimidating thing. Many got a thrill out of telling you that they could see your potential to steal their job, do it better than them, improve on things within the organisation and therefore you were not getting hired. They wouldn't even risk giving you a cleaner's position for fear of you eventually outshining them and leapfrogging through the ranks to a position of authority.

One head of HR told me in a job interview that I couldn't get the position, or indeed any other position, because there was nothing mentally stimulating enough there at the company for somebody with my qualifications.

After months of nothing, two job offers came to me at the same time. Selling mortgages for a bank or assisting an administrator for a charity. It was a bit of a dilemma. Should I go and work for the masters of the universe or help those most in need? There was no real question to be answered. The thought of sitting at a desk and swindling people with mortgages was stomach-churning to say the least. Sure, the money would be a lot better. There would be far more benefits and job security. I could easily get on the property ladder myself, possibly at a relatively young age. But I would want to die every single day. If not by some form of arse cancer, then by my own hand.

I turned the bank down and started working for the charity. It was boring and mundane work as an administration assistant, but at least it was honest and you could go home knowing that your labour was contributing to society rather than crippling it.

Swansea

1

The Welsh Terrier barked. He always barked, but nobody had ever seen him bite. He yapped non-stop, even when he was stoned. His eyes would cloud up and his tongue loll from the side of that small but loud mouth and yet the barking would persist. He barked about his time in the military police and when he was at the peak of his boxing prowess, which was also when he got the moniker 'Welsh Terrier'. He told tall tales about all of the different giants he had vanquished in the ring, despite only being a fraction of their size; apparently weight classes didn't exist back then. Soldiers from various barracks all over the UK would travel to challenge the legendary Welsh Terrier – King of the Ring.

At some point in the Terrier's life he had left the military and somehow wound up working low-paid jobs as a security guard in Swansea and the surrounding area. He was very proud of being a security guard and claimed that he had always been an integral part of every company he had worked for, and yet he wasn't in a supervisor or management position and had never been.

He had become a legend on the site. Marching around the shopping park in his high-vis yellow sleeveless jacket over his grey jumper that covered a white shirt and red clip-on tie, much like a secondary school boy from a comprehensive school in the rough part of town. He goose-stepped around the park in his cheap black leather shoes, with laces that never needed tying or adjusting, and his pressed black trousers that never quite made it all the way down to his skinny ankles.

And he growled and he snapped. He barked at the general public, who were just there with friends and family trying to do some shopping. He barked at the shop staff, who were just trying to earn minimum wage and have a quiet and uneventful day. But best of all was when he barked at the management of the stores. Also known as the clients. These people represented the company that paid the Terrier's security firm, or at least the security firm that employed the Terrier. Because, despite his boasts to the contrary, he wasn't part of the ownership committee. He was just a minimum wage security guard with delusions of grandeur. When he barked at the store management they barked back, and this was something that drove the Terrier insane. In his mind, he was the ultimate authority and all should bow down before him. The title of site security guard meant a great deal to him, just not to anyone else. Especially not to the management of the stores who technically paid his wages.

This appeared to be a common theme among

security guards. Delusions of grandeur and putting on a front of being a tough guy, when in fact you didn't really care for violence or have an aptitude for it. Also, he was always telling past war stories while never actually engaging in any conflicts, unless they were verbal. While the Welsh Terrier often regaled people with stories of boxing in the army, backing up criminal friends with a razor-sharp katana and of course saving the day as the most courageous security guard in all the world, there was another security guard on the site who claimed to be the UK's number one underground bare-knuckles fighter. While the Fighter, at first glance, looked the part – good physique, shaved head and confident swagger – he never had any marks on his face or fists. He never so much as had a cut lip or a single bruise. He would often boast about travelling the length and breadth of the UK, fighting in barns and derelict buildings or at gypsy campsites. Occasionally he would offer people the chance to come and watch him, claiming that there was money to be won gambling on the fights, but of course whenever the offer was accepted there was always an excuse or a sudden bout of amnesia, then low-and-behold you've missed this chance but next time... *next time...*

The Welsh Terrier had been our supply for soap bar for a few months now. Things had dried up round our way, as was often the case, and so we were forced to drive to the Terrier's hood in Swansea and pay over the odds for soap that had been cut so much you could practically run a car off it with the amount of diesel poured into it. Every time you sparked the flint of a lighter in order to start burning the soap to crumble onto the tobacco you had visions of an explosion in your face from the flame and chemical compound reacting together in the most combustible of ways.

The Terrier had all sorts of tall tales about how his man was able to still deal, despite nobody else in the area having any soap or green. Some stories involved crooked cops, while others were straight out of an Essex Boys film script. The truth was that nobody really knew the truth and nobody really gave a shit. All that mattered was that there was some gear to be had, and despite the unbelievably poor quality of the hash it was better than no gear at all.

This is the junkie mindset. You know it's shit. You know it's doing horrendous damage to your mind and body. You know it's much more expensive than it should be. You know all this and more, but you also know that you don't want to be sober and straight headed – fuck that. Physical, mental and financial damage is far more acceptable to a junkie than having to deal with life in a hopeless, boring, parasite-infested hometown that you have lived in your entirely worthless life. The mundane reality of a straight existence is far more horrific than the fake nightmares broadcast by the media about the effects of drugs on the human mind and body. Especially once you've had first-hand experience of said effects.

Naturally, the law never entered into any of this.

The legality of cannabis was never really a question of right or wrong, more an occasional pondering of what fucking business is it of anyone else's if I want to get high? Police only entered the picture when they turned up in your rear-view and there was that feeling of '*oh shit, is today the day I get busted?*' But it never came. Even when the police did stop and search they never found the gear stashed in a... well, wherever one stashes these things...

Soap was easy to conceal. No smell. Green on the other hand left you fucked-on-all-four-fronts before the search began. Green stinks. It's incredibly pungent in a way that makes both users and pigs drool in anticipation.

Swansea

2

The stop and search mentality of any pig is the same: be a cunt! The notion that the police were there to *protect and serve* was a long-forgotten idea, which may have never been put into effect in the first place; simply a marketing ploy to get the public on board with such an institution. There is an unwritten mindset of the typical pig – 'bully the public with any and every means at your disposal'. The average Welsh male pig is fat, but has some muscle under it somewhere and so he'll always be sticking his pecs out like he's a champion bodybuilder, but were you to stick your finger into it then there would be nothing solid – just a warm feeling as your finger sunk into blubber. If you looked carefully in the rear-view mirror while hiding your stash, you'd see the same approach.

First, they heave out of their car via the handgrip on the roof (leg and core strength not being sufficient to pry their weight out of their seat) and then they'd straighten up and breathe as they sucked in their giant potbellies, transferring the fat to their pectorals for that fake pumped chest look.

Next, some alpha-male posturing and glances

around as if they were in need of surveying the surrounding area for threats from terrorists, gangs or alien invasion.

Then the swagger! All pigs have the swagger. Some believed it must be taught in police academy, but the truth is they must already have it in order to get a job as a pig in the first place. In order to qualify as a candidate to become a piglet-in-training you have to have a particular 'attitude', which is always accompanied by the swagger. You can't strut that way unless you have a certain kind of mentality to begin with. It's a mentality that most can't and won't ever relate to, unless you were the school bully or the kind of kid that murdered small animals and masturbated into your sister's underwear drawer with an angry frown on your face. In most Western countries police forces require candidates to perform a psychological test before an application process is completed. If you don't score the same as an antisocial-psychopath then you don't pass!

After swaggering over to your vehicle there will be the condescending look, the one that tells you you're scum just because you are not of the same breed. You are not even the same species. You are human, they are swine. Because of this there is nothing but contempt for you in the pig's beady eyes. The Suidae family cannot relate to other species, after all you are merely chow to them, nothing more than feed for a greedy piggy.

The next part of the obligatory stop-'n'-search is the question, "Do you know why I've stopped you?", which is of course rhetorical as most times they have no real reason other than a quota to fill and of course hatred in their black heart for all who are not their swine brethren.

There is much the average citizen does not understand about pigs and that which they mockingly represent, i.e. the law. Few understand that when a pig asks for your name and you supply it you then make yourself a victim of many statutes, rules, regulations and articles that, in fact, aren't laws at all but can put you in prison and bankrupt you anyway. Never tell a pig your name! Remember that you are a man or a woman but never a legal person or pig! And never tell a member of that sordid collection of soulless entities known as the law society that you understand, for those tricksters may use English words but they speak their own language: *legalese*. To them the word 'understand' does not equate to 'comprehend'. To the police, lawyers and judges of the world the word has two components, 'under' and 'stand'. When these two words are inverted it is what you do when you say 'yes' to them. Do you understand? In legalese, it's the same as asking if you stand under me? As in, do you agree to be beneath me and submit to my authority, which is in fact a social construct that only has the power you give it. The use of legalese, as well as a tapestry of other lies and cons, make it almost impossible to fight the giant money-making machine that is the legal systems of the west. And never be fooled – it is a money-making machine. It was designed and built to be exactly that. It is another registered company, and as most know a company's only goal is to turn a profit.

Of course in reality none of this matters. The pigs have complete authority to do as they wish, and no amount of pseudo-law, or real law for that matter, will ever make a difference to your rights as a free individual. If they want to throw you in a cell, roll you in a thin mattress and then beat the living shit out of you with their nightsticks, guess what? If you decide to press charges and fight the police, good luck with finding a lawyer who'll take the case on. If you go on the run, they'll punish your loved ones. Make no mistake about it that in Wales, like so many other countries, the pigs are a species all to themselves and will violate any and all of the laws of man, nature, corporations and whatever else is necessary to get their own way.

I once knew a political activist who was wanted for questioning in relation to the petrol bombing of some military barracks. When he went underground to evade capture the pigs kidnapped his wife and waited for him to call her. They then got her to inform the activist that if he didn't return and hand himself in immediately she would be gang raped by the swine and then beaten to within an inch of her life. This would continue until he was sitting in a cell at the wrong end of a collapsible baton. It's stories like this that made me realise the pigs were nothing more than mercenaries used by the bankers in order for them to keep making money. Arm the swine and let them loose on the public, ensuring the Hogs are undisturbed when lining their pockets.

Swansea

3

The Welsh Terrier wasn't interested in profit as he
believed that family came before everything. A very
good way of thinking and living, if not a little
Disneyesque. He was married with two children, or
so he claimed. In all the years that I knew him, we
never saw any of his family. Any time that we paid
him a visit, whether it just being social or to pick up
some soap, his family were always out. We had
always 'just missed them'. We were always arriving
at just the right time for the Terrier to see us in
peace, without fear of interruption by his alleged
other half. No worries of his kids bothering him for
attention or a hand-out, we were free to sit and
share a cone.

He lived in a semi-detached in the rough end of
Swansea city suburbs, but kept the place looking
homely. There were the usual family photos on the
walls, including some of him and a blonde that he
claimed to be Mrs Terrier. The Mohawk and I
assumed that either he was telling the truth and we
were simply well-timed with every single visit or he
was actually divorced. It's not too big a leap to
make to assume that the man lived alone but still

didn't want to admit to himself or anyone else that he was separated and that his family had left home and were now living elsewhere. It made sense to us that someone so argumentative would now be single and living alone after an attempt at family life had failed due to his hot temper and uncontrollable mouth. It also made sense to us that a sad and abandoned divorcee would be working a minimum wage job that often required him to do night shifts, and then spending all his free time smoking and dealing soap.

It was the Bear who had another theory. He had always liked diving headfirst into wild and fantastical theories about the universe and mathematics, but now his mind had turned to far-out thoughts about the Terrier and his strangely absent family. The Bear surmised that there was no family, but for reasons other than divorce. On one late and profoundly stoned night the Bear suggested to us that the Welsh Terrier was something akin to Norman Bates from the Psycho movies.

"It's too big a coincidence. How many times have we been there in the last month and he's been alone?"

We laughed long and hard, but the Bear persisted, "Not once have we seen or heard anyone else in the house day or night, or indeed any evidence of other people – toys, kiddie books, clothes, washing up that needs doing, you name it. It's fucking impossible odds, I'm telling you!"

We wiped the tears from our eyes while he

continued trying to convince us.

"Prove me wrong! Let's start dropping in completely unannounced. No phone calls or texts to say we're coming. We just turn up at the door from now on."

"That'll prove nothing," I interjected, "it'll just be more of the same."

"Bullshit! We're gonna fucking catch him in a dress and wig carrying a big fuck-off blade, I'm serious! If we go up there tonight he won't be expecting us because we picked up yesterday. I'm sure we're going to see something!"

"See what?" asked the Mohawk, giggling in anticipation of the possible answer to come.

"Something! He'll be fucking dancing around in his dead wife's underwear or using his kid's flayed faces as fucking masks or something. It'll be like the fucking Swansea Chainsaw Massacre with a secret room filled with furniture crafted from bones and dried flesh! He's probably got a fucking coffin to sleep in or those giant fucking hook things to suspend himself from via his back skin or scrotum or whatever!"

We laughed some more.

"He's a psychopath, I'm sure of it!"

"And what about the pictures?" I prompted the Bear to go deeper with his theory.

"That's what I'm saying. There *was* a family. He *was* married. He *did* have kids, but now they're all dead. He fucking killed them, but he can't admit it to himself. You know how much of a bullshitter he is! He's probably been deceiving himself for years.

Telling himself that he's still a family man, as well as head of the security company and not just a minimum wage toy cop working the night shift. That's it! He's probably the Terrier by night but thinks he's his wife or kids during the day!"

We laughed harder.

"You watch! If we go up late at night or in the early hours of the morning and peer through the windows when he thinks he's all alone, we're gonna see something weird. If we took shovels and dug up the garden we'd probably find their decomposing bodies."

"Sounds fun and everything, but actually fuck that! If he is as crazy as *you* say, or as dangerous as *he* says, then we'll be at the sharp end of a fucking machete before he even knows it's us," the Mohawk cautioned us of the madman we spoke of.

"Don't be such a whiney bitch! A stabbing never hurt no one."

And so the theory went. The Welsh Terrier had been decent to us but now there was a point to prove. The Bear insisted that we set out to discover if the madman was as crazy as he thought or as he appeared to be. It had to be seen with our own eyes. The Terrier doing more than sitting alone and sucking on a bong was needed to prove that what the Bear thought was a reality was not some stoned and creative madness of his own fractured mind.

Of course we didn't go through with it immediately. Being stoners, weeks went by where things ticked along as normal. We would arrange to pick up puff and then we would laugh long and loud as the Bear speculated wildly about the missing family of the Welsh Terrier during the drive back to Llan. We continued to hang around his house as much as possible and smoke with him while always looking around for clues that might corroborate the Bear's 'Bates theory'.

The theory morphed and twisted over the weeks. Sometimes it was speculated that he had murdered his family for trying to leave him. Other times there had never really been a family. The people in the photographs were old friends, nieces and nephews, but never a wife or children of his own. On rare occasions it was thought that maybe, just maybe, even the photos weren't real and that the Terrier had manufactured them himself with painstaking effort and a keen eye for detail. Our random unannounced visits continued and so did the wild and crazy guesses about the truth behind the Terrier.

Swansea

4

It was a Saturday afternoon when things started to unravel for the Bear. We were all chilling in the Terrier's living room, stoned, relaxed and watching Alan Parker's 1978 film Midnight Express. The Bear had gone to the upstairs bathroom. When he returned he looked pale and there was an urgency to his voice, "We gotta go," he said to the Mohawk and I.

"What?" the Mohawk enquired in a slow and stoned Welsh drawl laced with petroleum fumes.

"I'm really high. We need to go. Cheers man," were the Bear's last words to the Terrier before he walked out. We blinked at each other as we sat slumped on the couch, then we heard the front door open and close. Reluctantly the Mohawk and I thanked the Welsh Terrier and followed our companion out to my car.

We knew something was wrong. The Bear was never unable to handle any amount of gear. He was never too stoned to continue, none of us ever got like that; we were professionals. As the Mohawk and I followed the Bear to the car we both looked at each other in that way that said, 'we know something's up, but we don't know what.'

In the car, I drove us away from the Terrier's house and we were on the next street before the Bear finally said, "I was fucking right!"

"What?"

"I went to the toilet. Then I went snooping," the Bear informed us as he took his mobile phone from his pocket. He proceeded to display a photograph that he had taken, "In the bedroom," he informed us. On the screen was a picture of a full-sized samurai sword mounted on a wall above a double bed.

"I fucking told you he was mental!" the Bear yelled with a triumphant grin.

We put forth the argument that the mounted steel meant nothing more than the Terrier having delusions of being a hardcase or possibly living out some shōgun fantasy in his own mind, but more than likely it was just a decorative piece probably made of aluminium hanging there instead of a picture or mirror above his bed. The Bear was convinced that he was right. As far as he was concerned, the Welsh Terrier had butchered his entire family years earlier with the sword above his bed. He was sure that we'd find bones or remains or scraps buried in the back garden, like something from a horror movie. If we had the means, he was convinced that DNA traces of a missing person – probably a female with blonde hair – would be found on the blade. Wild speculations were posited, one even being that the blonde in the picture hanging in the kitchen was a woman who's hand he'd asked for in marriage and then cut off – along with other appendages and organs – when she turned his proposal down. The Bear was sure that somewhere in the archives we'd find news articles featuring her picture along with headings and text along the lines of 'missing person', 'family worried sick' and 'local girl still not found'.

With stoned determination, the Bear had now made it his life's mission to prove his theory true regardless of the consequences. He and the Welsh Terrier worked in the same retail park – the same one I had previously been employed on. The days that the Terrier worked the Bear would casually interrogate him about his family. He would make passing remarks about their absence when we visited, ask directly when their birthdays were and how old they were now. The Bear made it clear he was unrelenting in his pursuit of evidence, but always mindful not to give away that he suspected foul play. The Mohawk and I nodded. We were merely stoned observers, very likely to forget about the whole thing within half an hour. For us, the idea that a real-life Leather Face may be living in the rough end of Swansea, smoking soap and working security, was idle amusement and nothing more.

Swansea

5

It was a Friday night when the laughter dried up and the horror began. As usual, we drove up to the Terrier's place to score a nine bar of soap. He was now working days so we had to travel to see him late at night at the time when the pigs were out in full force and looking for easy pickings.

Once you were away from the town centre there was a window of safety where police presence was very low, at least until you got to the bridge leading out of both the town and the county of Carmarthenshire. They often sat in a lay-by there, waiting to catch drunk drivers returning from Swansea after a night on the town. It was the same bridge that years earlier I had smashed my car into when racing at night with the Actor. Tonight we smoked what soap remained and listened to tunes as we casually cruised the dozen or so miles to our destination.

As usual, the Bear had insisted that we don't let the Terrier know exactly when we were coming. We'd told him how much we wanted days earlier and paid the full amount up front. He had told us to come and pick it up the day before, but the Bear wanted to prove his theory true and needed the element of surprise on his side in order to do so. We said nothing of it on the drive there, and neither the Mohawk or I even thought about it.

The Terrier's house was the last on a short road with poor street lighting. The houses all had scabby litter-strewn front gardens as well as a lot of boarded-up windows. Some even had boarded-up doors. There were cars up on bricks as well as a couple of burned-out shells. Even in the sunlight the place looked sketchy. At night, you kept your wits about you regardless of how high you were.

As the Bear drove his little silver Pug over the last speed bump he turned the lights and engine off and freewheeled the remaining distance to the front of the Terrier's yard in silent darkness. We knew what he was playing at and found it amusing. Once we were at a stop, the three of us got out and closed the car doors quietly, as per the Bear's instructions. He opened the rusty gate like a ninja before we watched his giant round frame creep down the driveway towards the house. There was a light on in the living room, which was at least a sign to us that the Terrier was still up and about. We followed in his wake, stepping lightly so as not to disappoint the amateur sleuth leading the way.

Instead of knocking on the door the Bear silently moved from window to window, attempting to see inside while listening intently. Of course there was nothing to see or hear. There was light coming from the living room, but all the curtains were drawn and the place was silent – no TV or music playing.

The Bear crept around to the back of the house while we waited at the front in the shadows. Time passed slowly and we considered lighting a joint, but unfortunately that first required rolling one. The Mohawk and I agreed that we may as well wait until we were sitting comfortably inside. Then we realised how long we had been waiting for the Bear.

We decided to go searching for our missing comrade at the rear of the domicile and were both intrigued and surprised to not find him; instead we found an open door. Surely the Bear or Terrier would have called for us if they had met and gone inside? We peered through the door and into an unlit room that we knew to be the kitchen, although we couldn't see it at that time. The Mohawk and I looked at each other for a plan of action, but neither of us had any idea what to do in the circumstances. It seemed obvious that the Bear had opened the unlocked door and sneaked inside uninvited and unannounced, so calling out to him would only alert the owner of the house to both our presence and possibly the Bear's. We weren't about to give up our foolish third man that way. Staying by the open door and doing nothing seemed foolish on our part, as we did look somewhat suspicious just standing there in the dark by an open door to someone else's house.

We both listened as hard as we could for any sounds, and kept our eyes focused on the blackness inside for any signs of life. I have no idea how long we stayed like that for. Eventually we saw the shape of the Bear in the gloom, his hand beckoning us to

come inside. We shrugged our shoulders – I had
rolled and sparked a clumsy spliff in the moonlight
and we figured, 'fuck it, why not?' The Mohawk and
I tentatively stepped into the kitchen and crept
toward the shape of the Bear, who was now
receding deeper into the house in the direction of
what we knew to be the living room. There was
light coming from a crack in the open door, which
gave the Bear's bearded face a kind of horror movie
countenance. To make it more fitting he was also
giving us a very wide-eyed maniacal look that
screamed we were about to be shocked by
something.

The Bear quietly opened the door to the living
room, his large frame slowly becoming more visible
from what was obviously the light from a TV that
was still on but muted. He led us inside to witness a
sight that was both creepy and comical. Laying on
the couch in what can only be described as a coffin-
like pose was the Welsh Terrier. He was on his
back, completely straight and flat, with his hands
folded on his chest, just like a corpse about to be
cremated. Not an unusual way for a man to snooze
on his worn-in mid-nineties style beige couch you
might think, but what was unusual was that this
man was sleeping while wearing a dress and blonde
wig. He lay with his eyes closed and mouth slightly
open, his face completely covered in cartoonish
makeup. His skill at applying it was evidently
terrible, even in the poor lighting, which added to
the horror/humour of his appearance. The dress
was a flowing flowery number. The wig was long

wavy yellow strands, obviously cheap, and it had slipped halfway across his forehead because he was lying down.

The three of us stared in silent shock at the sight before us. The Welsh Terrier, in a dress and wig, just as the Bear had predicted. He looked at us, ear to ear smile, as he nodded his head and gave us two triumphant thumbs up. The Mohawk and I were not so happy at the sight. It was creepy in the way that the idea of old priests and young altar boys is creepy. It made your stomach turn and made you unsure of whether or not there really was any good left in the world. A man dressing as a woman is fine – if that's what you're into then have at it. But the unexpected sight – the amateurish makeup and garish women's clothing – and the fact that the Bear had called it right and that it was only a smaller part of a much darker and sinister theory, that's what gave it all such an air of evil. And it was made all the more unnerving by the room being lit by the muted flickering television. I forget what was playing on the screen but was thankful that it wasn't animal porn even though that would have somehow been fitting for the freakish scene. For a moment I wondered if this was some kind of bizarre acid flashback that I couldn't fully recollect from my London days. Something I had shut out of my consciousness and into some locked and lead-lined box deep down in my psyche to hopefully never be seen again. The moment passed and the reality of the Avon monstrosity passed out in a dead man's pose and looking like Nosferatu's dead sister sent shivers down my spine and a shrinking sensation in my scrotum.

For me, the next course of action was clear – leave and never ever never mention what we saw to this strange and twisted creature that we call the Terrier. However, the Bear had other plans. He took his phone out of his pocket and pointed it at the sleeping freak snoozing before us. The Mohawk and I both shook our heads in disbelief, not only of the Bear's calm reaction but the scene in general. The Mohawk tried to silently get the Bear's attention and communicate that he wasn't feeling the idea of getting a snapshot of this special moment. The Bear ignored him, continued smiling, and then pressed the button.

click

On the screen, the Bear saw the transvestite-Terrier's eyes snap open as if he'd been jabbed with a shot of pure adrenaline. The whites of his eyes bulged and were given a ghoulish effect by the hue of the television set. As soon as his eyes clapped onto us he let out a loud banshee-like scream. In turn, this caused us to scream in shock as well. Standing in the TV's half-light, staring down at the skinny man in a bad woman's dress and cheap wig, the three of us screamed in shock as he lay there looking up at us and screamed back. This lasted for who knows how long before the Terrier launched his bony frame up and onto the Bear like a jack-in-the-box on meth. The impact sent the pair backwards and then down onto the low coffee table in the centre of the room. They landed with an almighty smash of glass and cheap metal frame onto the threadbare carpet that covered the floor. The Terrier came back up onto his knees and was on top of the Bear MMA style, and just like a cage fighter the transvestite began pummelling the Bear's face with hammer fists, all the while still howling like a demented dog on crack.

It took me a moment to return to my senses. I watched the madness unfold like I was merely a spectator at a street performance. It was up close, but I wasn't a part of it. Then my mind snapped into action. The Mohawk must have been going through the same thoughts and emotions as I was, as he was simply standing and staring at the madness as slacked jawed as I was. Who wouldn't in that scenario?

Once we were back in the moment we dived forwards. The Mohawk grabbed the Terrier's shoulders to pull him off the Bear, while I had decided to use my foot to achieve the same outcome. Between my kick and the Mohawk's hands, we removed the insane tranny from our fallen brother and got him on the floor. I ripped a picture from the wall and slammed it down on his head but the Terrier was unimpressed. He rolled over and began to kick wildly at us, all the while still trying to smash his clenched fist into the Bear's stomach. The Mohawk followed my lead and the pair of us began kicking feverishly at the tranny-Terrier who screamed insanely at us. The Bear was by now bloody and beaten. He lost control of his faculties and grabbed a shard of broken glass from the carpet and heaved himself up and brought the jagged splinter down into the Terrier's flowery getup. The glass pierced the dress and went deep into his chest. At first my fellow stomper and I didn't notice what had happened. We were both so caught up in the moment with our adrenaline rushing at insane levels that our flurry of feet never stopped or even hesitated for a single second.

It wasn't until the Terrier stopped screaming and moving that we stopped kicking and stomping. The Mohawk and I looked down at the poleaxed tranny and then over to the Bear. He was breathing hard and was wet with sweat and blood. He stared at the corpse and then up at us.

"What the fuck just happened?!" the Mohawk said, eventually interrupting the sounds of heavy breathing.

"He's fucking dead," the Bear stated as he got to his feet. As battered and beaten as he was, the adrenaline was still coursing through his system and keeping the pain at bay. "We fucking killed him!"

"Don't say that!" the Mohawk retorted.

I knelt down and felt for a pulse. Under my index and middle fingers of my right hand I could feel those final pumps of life gently fade away to nothing. The cold and vacant eyes, framed by smudged black mascara, of a man we'd known for years and shared many a spliff with looked up at me. What a horrible way to go and an awful way to be remembered. An ill-tempered tranny, beaten and lacerated on the floor of his own living room on a Friday night while stoned on shit soap bar. The look on my face was all my companions needed as confirmation that, yes we had just killed a man.

The three of us sat down and rolled joints. We each smoked our own spliffs and considered our destinies. A normal human being in this situation would simply call the police and an ambulance. Get the emergency services to come and clean up the mess, while law enforcement took your details and began the process of stripping you of your freedom and basic human rights. But we were not normal people and this was far from a normal situation. The Terrier had clearly been living a lie. It now seemed very realistic that the far-flung theories of the Bear were indeed all true. With that in mind, I had to ask myself whether or not the dead transvestite lying on the carpet before me would really be missed. Sure, his employer would wonder why he hadn't shown up for work and the alarm would soon be raised after that. But there were no real family. Clearly the Terrier was a bachelor and considering his actions on this strange and unusual night he may well have killed and skinned his family just as the Bear had theorised. Clearly I had never had much time for the law. I'd spent most of my life consuming, transporting and/or selling illegal narcotics. Sure, this was different. Now a man had lost his life at our hands, and whether you justified it as self-defence was highly debatable. We had entered his home uninvited, unannounced and clearly unexpected and now he was dead. We were still alive, while he lay on the floor with a shard of glass protruding from his chest. As far as I was concerned, shit happens and as we had come out on top there was no point in voluntarily going under now, so that was a no to getting the police involved. I quickly presumed that my two companions would be just as inclined to avoid dragging the authorities into this mess as I was and it dawned on me that the only real question was whether or not we buried him in his garden or the woods. No need for some long drawn-out and deep Dostoevsky-like deliberation over our wrongdoings. I decided to wait until I had finished smoking my joint before discussing the options with the Bear and Mohawk.

When the cherry reached the roach I stubbed it, got to my feet and then looked solemnly at my two friends. "The woods," they said in unison. None of us spoke again for hours. We set to cleaning the house and wiping any traces of us ever having been there. Then we cut a section of the blood-soaked carpet, rolled up the body in it and transferred the lot to the car.

There were no cameras in the rough neighbourhood where the Terrier's house was located and he lived at the end of an almost derelict street, which meant there was little risk of prying eyes observing us moving the corpse to the Bear's car or the police showing up while out on some random patrol.

Stuffing the carpet corpse into the tiny Peugeot was hard work, but we managed it. The drive to the woods was slow and silent. We stuck to the speed limit, drove sensibly and only stopped to pick up the required tools from the Mohawk's pad that we placed next to the thick roll of carpet stuffed in the boot. If we had been stopped there would have been no chance of getting away with it – the fucking thing stood out a mile in the rear of the hatchback.

Once in the woods we took shifts digging until there was no danger of our crime being discovered. I thought back to my teenage years and the things that had happened in these woods that I now used as an unmarked burial site. We were far from the first to do this here. In fact, our biggest danger was being discovered by fellow criminals rather than campers, farmers or pigs.

In my youth the woods had been notorious as the place where bad people took dishonest cunts for punishment and a severe scaring. The general method was to take you blindfolded deep into the trees where nobody would hear you regardless of how loud you screamed. Then you would be tied to a tree and left there for a few days. Sometimes, your captors would go that bit further and douse you in petrol as an extra threat of burning you alive while tied to said tree or wipe something like jam or honey on you to attract the wildlife. Slumped on the damp forest floor, blind and restrained, many a man has cracked and given up what was desired of them. Sometimes your kidnappers would stick around. Stay silent for several hours and then start fucking with you by making noises and brushing things against you. A lot of people never made it back from their trip into the trees. There were tales of some people taking their victims into the woods and forgetting where they had left them. A warning gone very wrong.

There was no warning tonight. It had already gone horribly wrong. All we could do was try our best to clean up the mess and then cover our tracks. It was clear from the silence that we were all thinking the same thing. Common sense said that sticking around South Wales, or indeed the UK, was not a smart move. Sure, running could be evidence of involvement in something bad, but only if there was reason to suspect foul play between you and the missing person. Almost nobody knew of our relationship to the Terrier, after all we were scoring puff from him – not something you advertise to the masses. We could also reassure ourselves by believing that as there was no body, there was no crime. Who's to say that the Terrier didn't suddenly just up and leave for a new life in a new city or another country? Stranger things have happened.

The burial went as smooth as it was silent, as did the drive home. We parted ways that night still unclear of what lay ahead for us. We hadn't discussed a plan of action yet alone agreed on one. We were exhausted and still in shock from the night's bizarre turn of events. Transvestite Terriers, manslaughter and burials in the woods during the dead of night were not commonplace for three stoners from an ex-tinplate town like us. We weren't gangsters or hardcore criminals. We were writers, musicians and dope fiends. Our illegal activities centered around drugs, not death and violence.

Swansea

6

The next time I spoke to the Bear and Mohawk I told them about my idea. Years earlier I had been in a relationship with a girl who spoke fluent Welsh and English. She had told me about how in Chubut Province, Argentina, there is a community of Welsh expats dating from the 1860s who were desperate to employ Welsh natives to teach the next generation the language and culture, so they may keep their roots and heritage even in a foreign land. I deduced that there must be opportunities for fluent English speakers on other continents and in other countries, as I had no hope of teaching Welsh. There must be teaching jobs available for people in countries where English wasn't the first language. This thought quickly blossomed into a new career in what is known as either the TEFL or TESOL industry: Teaching English as a Foreign Language or Teaching English as a Second or Other Language if you go by the second acronym.

The Mohawk loved the idea. You get to be a teacher and travel, both of which were things he wanted to do. The Bear on the other hand was not sold on the plan. He had no desire to leave Llanelli and also argued that running would eventually lead to someone pointing the finger at us for the crime we had committed. I put up the counter argument of no body equals no crime, and also no criminals in the country equals no convictions for crimes. The Bear disagreed.

Days had passed by the time of our teaching English abroad conversation, and so far there had been no news or rumours concerning the dead Terrier. No alarms had been sounded, no news in the press and no pigs sniffing around with awkward questions. The Mohawk got straight onto the case and began researching how you get into the business of teaching English in foreign lands.

Several months later the Mohawk and I had the necessary qualifications and even officially stamped certificates to prove that we were fully qualified English language teachers. We were as surprised as anyone and set about applying for jobs in countries that took our fancy, always with the same recruitment agencies as each other.

Then the offers came via emails – jobs with a private language school in Tokyo, Japan. It was all set. The Mohawk and I would leave for the Orient to start our new lives. The Bear would stay in Wales and continue with his existence like nothing had ever happened.

Little comeback came our way about what transpired that strange night in the woods. The security company that employed the Terrier only went as far as trying to contact their missing employee by phone and letter. Apparently the manager had once gone to the Terrier's home and knocked on the door, but that's as far as he got involved. It seemed that the Terrier really had been living a lie. His talk of a family was nothing more than a figment of a deranged imagination, and whatever friends he had really didn't care that much about him to sound any alarms with the authorities. Presumably there was a dealer of soap bar who was missing his custom, but evidently not enough to risk going to the authorities and demanding anything like an investigation or search. He seemed to simply vanish from existence, leaving us free to flee the country and begin new lives in exotic lands.

After drug-fuelled emotional farewells with the Bear, the White Horse and a handful of other fiends, the Mohawk and I left Wales. Our third man stayed and continued living his life. The authorities never came asking any questions and nobody snapped from the pressures of guilt, one day feeling obligated to make a long and teary-eyed confession to a paedophile in a frock while on their knees in a dark booth in an expensive monument to a fake deity that constantly needs more money.

In other words, life went on.

Japan
1

Tokyo

1

The plane was packed, so the Mohawk and I had to stick to our assigned seats, which had been bought separately and were therefore situated at different locations and not next to each other as we had hoped for. I found myself sat between a middle-aged Japanese lady and a mid-thirties Nigerian man. In typical Japanese style, the woman kept to herself. The Nigerian, however, was keen to make conversation. He informed me that he was on his way back to his home in Japan where his wife and children were waiting for him. The topic he really wanted to get down to though was the business dealings that had taken him to London – the oil business to be precise.

Tokyo

2

Oil was discovered in the Niger Delta by Shell in the late 1950s and was being exported by the seventies. Oil – aka black gold – was supposed to have saved the poor country of Nigeria, but instead brought gangs, violence, weapons, militia, uprisings against the government and even a global increase in the price of the black stuff. The Niger Delta has roughly 3% of the world's oil and was supposed to be America's backup reserves so it didn't have to depend on the Middle East. While it did make the politicians and foreign oil companies wealthy, it predictably didn't help the natives. And so what was hoped to be a more stable supply of oil rather than relying on Bedouins became a battle with militias and pirates. The Nigerian natives were given nothing for the oil beneath their feet except pain, misery and pollution. Most lived on less than a pound a day in shanty towns that have no electricity or clean water.

Originally, many of the natives had been employed by the oil companies, such as the new friend I made on the flight to Narita, but once the companies could drop them and bring in their own people they did. The oil companies brought in foreign workers to replace the locals. This left the Nigerians jobless, oilless and penniless. The youth organised themselves into gangs and set about extorting and robbing the oil companies and their foreign employees. Oil pirates navigated the narrow rivers of the Niger Delta looking for victims. As the youth had once worked for the oil companies they knew their inner workings and found it easy to attack their shipments and even their flow stations. The sabotaging of the stations had dire consequences for the environment and surrounding villages and towns. Add to this accidents and an ever ageing infrastructure and you have all the ingredients you need for the death of the surrounding habitat and all that live there.

The combination of polluted lands, corrupt politicians reaping the financial benefits and the locals getting fucked over led to the formation of yet more gangs, pirates and militia. There were some who believed that peaceful resistance was the way forward, and their leader Kenule Beeson 'Ken' Saro-Wiwa, along with nine others, were hanged on trumped up charges by the country's then reigning dictator General Sani Abacha for his efforts and beliefs. His work and message continues by way of the Movement for the Survival of Ogoni People organisation, but most natives saw his murder as a sign that it was better to tool up and throw down before they found themselves at the tight end of a length of rope too.

The gangs and militia were slowly gaining

numbers, power and momentum to take the fight to the corrupt government and foreign companies. A single gangster was trying to show that guns and violence was the way to take back the Nigerian oil for the benefit of the people.

My new friend didn't think that this gangster would live long enough to see his dream become a reality. The Nigerian figured that even if the gangster took back the oil, no other nations in the world would want to buy it and risk dealing with a known gangster and criminal. They preferred their villains to keep their shit hidden from the public eye and wear suits, not balaclavas.

Tokyo

3

The Nigerian was trying to make money legitimately selling what he considered to be the purist oil on the planet, which came from his homeland. He wasn't the first Nigerian I had ever met, but he was the first and last one who didn't immediately tell me that he was a hustler.

Nigerians are world famous hustlers, always out there grinding for cash, always into something. This Nigerian was only interested in oil money though, and despite me telling him that this was my first ever trip to Japan and that I had absolutely nothing to do with the oil business he still insisted on trying to perk my interest in getting involved with him and trying to sell Nigerian oil on his behalf. We spoke at length about Japan, living in foreign countries, our different cultures and of course Nigerian oil. All of this was fine, but then he steered the conversation to his other passion: Christianity.

It was here that he lost me. Any person of faith who insists on telling me all about their beliefs quickly lost my interest, and in no small way my respect. If you want to believe, then go ahead and believe, but leave me and the real world out of it. I was soon invited to attend his church and get involved with their nonsense, to which I politely informed him that I was tired and would try to sleep for some of the flight. This was both the politest and most convenient way I could think of to get out of the conversation. I felt that telling him to fuck off was not the right move on a plane high in the sky with many hours left to go until we reached our destination. The fact that he was missing his little and ring fingers on one hand also made me weary of insulting him – after all, we were flying to Japan, the land of the Yakuza who are known for chopping off fingers as punishment. Was he connected with organised crime? Not a completely unbelievable scenario for a Nigerian trying to start an oil business in Japan.

Despite him giving me his phone number and offering to be of assistance to a first timer in Japan I never learned the answer to that question, as I lost his number soon after arriving in the land of the rising sun. I figured that my first contact in a foreign land shouldn't be a Nigerian oil salesman with possible Yakuza connections who wanted me to join his Christian congregation. His possible connections to organised crime and the oil pirates were fine, but religion is a dangerous business full of crazy people.

Tokyo

4

When I say that my family is deep in the church, I
mean balls-deep. My father's uncle literally built
the chapel with his bare hands in the Welsh village
where he lived. Obviously he had help, but that's
the kind of commitment to religion that side of my
family has. After aiding in the physical construction
of the chapel he went on to pastor there for the rest
of his long life. His son, my father's first cousin, not
only followed in his father's footsteps to preach at
the local parish, but then went on to become the
head honcho for all of Europe. Their belief system
was part of the Community of Christ if I remember
rightly, formerly known as the Reorganised Church
of Jesus Christ of Latter-day Saints until around
the turn of the millennium. I don't recall exactly as
I turned my back on both religion and that side of
the family at the tender age of seven. I think they
have some sort of connection to the Mormons, but I
could be wrong. It's all the same to me – Catholic,
Christian, Buddhist, Muslim, whatever.

I see religion as no different to sport. If you're
into it and have a favourite team, good for you –
just don't bother me with it. Religion has a long and

sordid history, whether the believers wish to admit it or not. Numerous wars and crusades, the inquisitions – there's a long list of atrocious and ungodly acts all carried out in the name of something that cannot be proved real. A complete waste of time and life. There are many who will argue that it is not religion that is to blame for many of the evils done to mankind, but there is no denying that in many of those cases, be they ethnic or economical, religion was an easy way to get the public on board with it. A useful technique to stir the dumb masses into a cry of war, vengeance, hatred or extremism. Considering most religions claim that their holy texts and deities promote peace and love, its leaders and practitioners seem easily swayed to pick up arms and kill in the name of their faith.

There appears to be something much deeper in the holy texts, there is no denying that. The Canadian clinical psychologist Jordan Peterson delves into them and does his best to extract their true purpose and meanings in a series of fascinating lectures, but the institutions that govern these theologies appear to be nothing more than out to control the populace.

Just look at the Family, or Fellowship or whatever name they go by these days. An American group of Christians who are almost all working in or with the government. Their leader, who denied that there even was a leader, ensured that every president of the USA since Eisenhower joined in a weekly breakfast prayer attended by the who's who of ruling elite from countries all over the world. America was supposed to be one of those nations that separated church and state – they even had it written down in their constitution just to be sure – and yet every one of their presidents for the last several decades has attended these breakfasts and bowed their heads in prayer. All claim that they are just there for Jesus, and yet it's well known that CEOs, rulers of nations and heads of banking cartels attend these breakfasts and then attend less public gatherings behind closed doors.

Religious institutions appear to be nothing more than a means of enslaving mankind and making them obey. Get on your knees, bow your head and don't ask any fucking questions! Because we don't know the answers and can only give you riddles and bullshit in place of facts and honesty. This was what led me to turn my back on the whole institution, along with most of my family; I asked too many questions and never received any real answers. You find it's that way with most theologies – ask too many questions and you either get bullshit answers, kicked out or killed. I walked away and studied the bullshit from afar, so as not to vomit from the stench or get any in my eyes, which may cause blindness like it has done to so many of the faithful.

Tokyo

5

The Mohawk and I stood outside Narita International Airport, smoking cigarettes and gulping energy drinks. We were both hyped to have landed in our new home: Tokyo. Two white Welsh males. Large in frame, low in morals and filled with excitement at what adventures lay ahead.

Two policemen strolled past and we paid little attention until they both stopped, turned and then approached us. At first, the encounter was polite and procedural. They requested to see our passports and enquired why we were in Japan. After explaining that we were about to start new jobs as English language teachers and that this was our first time in the country we were given warm and friendly welcomes, and then we asked the two nice policemen to please recommend some good bars where we could go and get pissed. To our surprise the conversation spiralled into a broken English, complete with amusing mimes, questioning of whether or not we were looking for some girls to fuck. We laughed hysterically as the two uniformed police officers, complete with pistols and shiny badges, gyrated manically in front of us while making hand gestures of drinking.

"You wan' girl? Beautiful girl? Good girl, pretty girl? Japanese girl bes' girl!"

We laughed to the point of tears. This was our second encounter with the Japanese authorities, the first being the emotionless customs officials at immigration and now these armed police officers who rambunctiously encouraged us to find some native girls to fornicate with. Not what a British native expects of representatives of the law. We loved it!

Tokyo

6

A couple of hours later we were in our hotel in Hanzomon near the classy Ginza district, which is where the Emperor's palace is located. We were, of course, like most young and dumb first-timers in Japan blown away by the toilets. Such a simple and uninteresting thing in any other country immediately captivated the attention of us two stoners. A multitude of buttons, lights and dials ran the length of an arm at the right of the bowl, most of which made no sense to us. Some of the pictures on the buttons gave you a clue as to what would happen when pushed, but most just bore kanji logographics.

We showered and then headed out into Tokyo. It wasn't long before we found a shop filled with rolling papers, pipes, bongs and a strange substance sold in small bags that kind of looked like weed but wasn't. Less than a day in Japan and we had discovered spice. It would be another year or two before this substance really started to make headlines around the world and get the terrible reputation it has now, but at that time it was a new substance for us to buy, try and get high on.

Unfortunately, both of our systems were still flooded with tetrahydrocannabinol from years of smoking weed in Wales, so the spice had little effect on us.

We spent the evening wandering around the world-famous Shibuya district, jaws agape at the sheer scale of the place. To go from a small Welsh town to one of the world's biggest megacities is quite a change in environment. Giant towers, narrow labyrinths, all manner of neon lights and huge numbers of people swarming everywhere. The only comparison I can make to the masses that filled those Tokyo streets is the Y2K New Year celebration that was held along the banks of the Thames in London. The streets were flooded with bodies, which often forced you to go wherever they were going, regardless of whether you wanted to head in that direction or not. We dined, drank and continued to wander the streets of Shibuya. We got confused in one area that had giant billboards bearing the smooth and shiny faces of young Japanese men with spiky hair and stylish suits, all looking like they could be male prostitutes. We assumed we were in a queer neighbourhood but would later learn that they were advertising host bars to Tokyo's busy female go-getters who had no time to find a boyfriend or get married.

Tokyo

7

By 2010, host bars were becoming somewhat of a boom industry, catering to wealthy females who were career-driven but still wanted male companionship. Some women would ultimately get addicted to the attentions shown to them by particular male hosts and would fall prey to the Yakuza bosses who ran those establishments, who would turn them out to work the street in order to pay back their hefty debts to the host club. It wasn't always businesswomen who got addicted to hosts, some regular housewives starved of attention also fell into the honey pot and wound up turned out to pay back their debts.

In the eighties and nineties housewives had gotten addicted to crank – aka methamphetamine – but in the 21st century they were getting addicted to compliments. Essentially that's all hosts do. They whisper sweet nothings into a stranger's ear and make them feel wanted, sexy, special – like they are the only person in the room. It doesn't matter if it's a female host pressing herself up against an ageing salaryman on a Friday night or a male host pouring drinks for a middle-aged housewife, it's all the same outrageously expensive hustle. There are, of course, some host bars and clubs where for the right price things can go a lot further than just flirting, drinking and singing karaoke, but the real money is made in making the customer feel wanted. The real hustle is in making an emotional connection.

In a megacity of more than 9 million people, the thing most missing from peoples' lives is human contact. Not just the physical kind, mainly just the ability to sit and talk to someone. To connect with someone. Japanese people are very reserved and many live by the proverb '出る杭は打たれ', which translates roughly as 'the nail that sticks out gets hammered down', and so most people just toe the line. To stand out and be special is dangerous, so to be made to feel unique and wanted can be an addictive thing in a dark room, one-to-one, away from the public eye. In the workplace many Japanese people will not share their feelings with one another, and even with their family and friends they often don't want to reveal their true selves. Their feelings, thoughts, wants, desires and pains are constantly suppressed. But when you're alone with someone hanging on your every word and filling your ear with nothing but positivity, the reassurance that nobody else can hear either of you over the loud tunes from the speakers can fill you with something very moreish indeed.

As an outsider in Japan, in a position of what many Japanese consider to be a place of authority and wisdom, you are sometimes privileged to learn aspects of the culture you would have never thought possible. When I taught group classes there were very few voices to be heard, mostly just my own. Most Japanese students didn't like to speak in front of their peers for fear of standing out – maybe because of poor English or indeed the opposite. Having superior language skills to your classmates would often embarrass a student into not speaking again. In one-to-one classes some students, particularly females of all ages, would share some of their most intimate thoughts and feelings with you, which can sometimes put you in a very precarious position for different reasons. I've had students ask my advice on an array of topics, from accepting job offers, to getting divorced, to committing suicide. Nobody taught me how to deal with that in my one-month teacher training course.

Tokyo

8

The Mohawk and I stayed in the hotel for two nights, and then we met up with a company employee who would take us to our new home. She was late and had no idea how to get to where we were supposed to go. We would have probably found our way quicker without her, but us being new to the country and her being a native we naively put our faith in the twitchy woman.

Hours later we finally arrived at the shack we would be calling home for the next year or so. It was a white, wooden building way past its due date to be renovated or demolished. The irony of its name being the White House was not lost on the two crackers fresh in the land of the rising sun. The building had eight apartments, all meant for company employees, and of those which were occupied only white faces lived there. Some of the flats were empty and waiting for new teachers to arrive.

When the company had found out that the Mohawk and I knew each other they asked if we would like to live in two single quarters or share a flat to reduce the cost of rent and utilities. We opted for the cheaper option, figuring that as we spent most of our time together anyway we may as well save some money.

It was highly unusual for two male teachers to start working for the company and live together at the same time, and so it wasn't long before rumours spread that the Mohawk and I were a homosexual couple. After all, the flat we were in was meant for a couple to share, and there were already two heterosexual couples living in the White House. By the time we started our first day as English language teachers everyone working for the company thought we were a white Welsh gay couple. The Mohawk and I being the sick-minded deviants that we are decided not to tell anyone differently and used their assumptions about our sexuality to have some fun. Even though neither of us are of the pink, we decided to walk a little differently when around the other men in the company. We started to talk with a slightly sassy tone to our voices. We would regularly compliment each other on how we looked or how we were dressed. The most fun was squeezing our large frames into the already full lifts when occupied with male teachers and lean into them, all the while blowing kisses at each other and licking our lips while wiggling our eyebrows suggestively.

These actions did of course disturb some of the less secure heterosexual teachers who we worked with. We found it interesting to note that none of the women were in the least bit bothered by having two gay men work with them and openly flirt with each other in their company. However, many of the men were less than amused. Most went out of their way to avoid us and refused to make eye contact. We found it all hilarious, as did one of the teacher trainers who guided us through our first week at the company. She was also a Welsh native and understood our demented humour all too well. She found it most amusing that we spent our time winding the other guys up and exposing them as the insecure and possibly in denial little boys that they were. Not all were that way, of course – some of the guys, like the girls, couldn't care less about our sexual leanings and accepted us for the happy little homo couple that they thought we were. They too found it sidesplittingly funny when we came clean that we were actually just straight friends trying to save money and fuck with people's heads. Our reputations within the company quickly spread. Be careful with the two Welsh guys, they will fuck with you – one way or another.

We settled into our new lives and country with ease. Both the work and the place suited us. Past indiscretions and crimes were brushed under the carpet and new lives were started. It wasn't difficult for two fiends lacking much in the way of morals to forget what they had done to inspire moving to the other side of the world. We were new people in a new land with new jobs and new lives as far as we were concerned. Let the past stay in the past and let the dead rest in peace in deep unmarked graves somewhere in the woods.

Tokyo

9

I turned a new leaf in Chiba, which is where I was living. Chiba is the prefecture that sits on the eastern border of Tokyo, which is where I taught most of my classes. I wasn't smoking weed everyday but I had gone back to drinking alcohol, something that I had stopped for a time after leaving London. I drank in moderation at first and even began exercising regularly. Due to my ink, the gyms and swimming pools were off limits to me, what with Japan still having a strict 'no tattoo' rule to keep organised criminals away from the general public.

I set up a mini-gym at the White House, went running around the neighbourhood we were living in and even started practicing martial arts on my days off. I was a new man and learning much about human biomechanics, nutrition and weapons, as well as Japan and Japanese people.

It is perhaps the only country that I have never heard a bad word against. Everyone I've ever met who has lived there or simply just visited has had nothing but positive things to say about both the place and its people. The Japanese are among the friendliest and most welcoming people in the world. Their culture instils a sense of honour and pride in being Japanese, which in turn makes them try very hard not to tarnish their homeland and fellow nationals. For tourists, Tokyo has to be one of the safest and easiest cities to travel around. Not only is their public transport second-to-none and their crime levels almost non-existent, but it's also the people there. They will literally go out of their way to ensure that sightseers get to where they want to be, even going so far as to travel on trains and buses with them to be sure they get there safely. They ask nothing in return and will simply wish you a pleasant trip before smiling and departing to get on with their day.

We lived in South Kashiwa, or Minami-Kashiwa as it was known to the locals, which was a tiny place with nothing more than a handful of shops and restaurants, along with a couple of supermarkets. Not too far away was the city of Kashiwa, which has bustling streets during the day and a thriving nightlife. The White House was surrounded by Japanese houses in a labyrinth of narrow roads. It had signposts regularly dotted around to ensure you wouldn't get lost in the maze of small structures that looked nothing like the architecture back in the UK. Due to the large number of earthquakes experienced in Japan, buildings are very different to anything seen in the West. I quickly learned my way around the urban maze that surrounded my flat by regularly going jogging, something that was also necessary to try to cease the creeping waistline that was slowly increasing from my new diet.

British food is bland and boring, but Japanese cuisine is delicious and addictive. I quickly discovered that not only could I use chopsticks very easily, but that I also loved to use them to shovel as much food as possible into my mouth. I fell in love with sushi, ramen, karaage, gyoza, yakiniku, shabu-shabu... the list goes on and on. I also fell in love with sake, both hot and cold, but especially hot during the winter months. I never liked shochu as it gave me some of the worst hangovers I have ever experienced, but sake was divine and didn't hurt me any worse than Asahi Super Dry the following day.

My new-found love of eating, along with my return to drinking alcohol, motivated me to do a lot of exercise in my free time in an attempt to stop my stomach from ballooning to ridiculous proportions. I was in a land overflowing with gorgeous women and had no intention of being too fat to flirt or fuck.

My days off were spent practicing Muay Thai and Bujinkan taijutsu. Both brought on a healthy sweat and were teaching me new things about the human body, my own in particular. I eventually became a healthy specimen, over time even cutting carbohydrates and sugars from my diet. I did a lot of cooking at home so I could find the time for healthy relationships with women instead of the usual one-night stands.

The relationship aspect was something I said I would never get into for fear of it tying me down to one country. I also had a moral awakening in the form of a cute little lady on a weekday morning.

As was quite common, the Mohawk and I had met up after teaching for something to eat and then decided to go for a few drinks. The night had been slow and uneventful until we wandered into our favourite scene of debauchery around our way – The Mars Bar. It was a place mostly frequented by Japanese salarymen who wanted to keep drinking until the small hours and hostesses who wanted a drink to unwind after chatting up salarymen all evening at the clubs they worked in. It was a small and dark place, the kind of atmosphere one expects in an all-male establishment built for barflies. At The Mars Bar we would often drink colourful cocktails or shots of Rémy Martin between draft beers, which inspired the Mohawk to paint the bathroom walls in colourful ways that the staff hated to clean up. The owner – Mars – was unlike most Japanese people in that he could handle alcohol like a champion, almost seemingly to never get drunk – or at least as drunk as he should be considering how much he put away with us. His bar became our local on the nights that we really felt like drinking hard.

Because of my newfound clean-living regime it was rare that we really tied one on of an evening, especially during the week, so when we did things got very messy very quickly. I didn't remember much else about that night. I woke up naked with a bastard behind the eyes and was just in time to see a petite, dark haired vixen smile and blow me a kiss by the apartment's front door. I smiled and waved at her, having no recollection of who she was or why she was there. I thought I'd try my luck and beckoned her toward the futon, but she said, "I can't, I'm late for class," and then it suddenly dawned on me as she walked out of the door that she was wearing a short navy skirt, which was the norm for Japanese schoolgirls. I convinced myself that she must have been a college girl, a lot of whom still wore schoolgirl-like uniforms. The Mohawk suddenly peered around the door and shook his head in disgust.

"Are you sure that was even legal?" he asked condescendingly before heading to the bathroom with another disapproving shake of the head. I lay back and tried to remember more details, but it just made my headache worse. I took painkillers and returned to sleep, trying to forget what may or may not have been a bad thing I'd done the night before. A subconscious decision was made to start making my sexual appetite as healthy as my diet.

Tokyo

10

It was when the Bear, or Kuma-san as he came to be known to us, and D. Lynch came to visit us that things took a turn for the debauched and never recovered. By this time I was living alone and the Mohawk was shacked up with his girlfriend. We were both living in the same city, but at different ends.

The Bear got his name from his physical appearance. D. Lynch got his name from one of our many trips to Amsterdam. It was there he showed us that just like David Lynch's movies, he was a dark and disturbed creature. It was in the midst of the Red Light District that the full-length black-coated figure, with his pale milky skin and pervert-predator eyes, made his true self known to us. We discovered that his odd walk, with his hands stuffed deep into the pockets of his coat and shifting eyes quickly trying to take in as much of the flesh on display as possible, was a key sign of how dark his mind really was. In other parts of the city, and indeed the world, he walked like a normal man, but down those narrow alleys his gait changed and his mind went to other places. He unintentionally made it known to us that he was the submissive type when he accidentally announced outside one window, "My God, she looks so dominant! She wasn't even smiling!" and then he shivered with a pervert's delight. Hours later he met us in a cafe, weaker, exhausted and a lot lighter of wallet but with a giant perverted grin smeared across his face. D. Lynch had made himself public and would never go into hiding again.

When they came to Tokyo the drinking started hard and fast and didn't relent. One cold night in Akihabara, aka Electric Town, while the Bear and D. Lynch wandered around inside a shop, the Mohawk and I smoked cigarettes in the street and discussed where we'd go for more drinks. Then a young lady approached us smiled and handed us a flier before walking off down the crowded street. The flier bore the pictures of yellow smiley faces puffing on joints and said something along the lines of 'happy smiley time'. On the back was a map to a shop and prices of bags in increments of grams. We couldn't believe it. Had someone just spotted the stoners on the street and given them a flier of somewhere to purchase weed? Surely not! Once the Bear and Lynch joined us we went to the spot. It was a spice shop, and so began our new love affair. A paranoid and often desperate relationship that never should have been.

Vietnam

Hanoi

1

We were in Narita International Airport when the trouble started. The Mohawk and I had planned the mission well, or so we thought. We'd learned about where to go and what to avoid. What to do and what not to do. We'd read a lot of information online about our target destination. We'd also spent a lot of time drinking alcohol, smoking spices and consuming various pharmaceuticals in lots of different ways. This was possibly the reason why during all of our late nights researching the mission neither one of us came across one small fact.

"You cannot board plane without visa," the polite but firm man said with a slight bow and momentary closing of the eyes.

"Sou-desu," came the obligatory support from the fellow customs officer.

"We're only going for three days, what do we need visas for?"

The answer to that question was simple. It doesn't matter if you're going for a three-day adventure, a three-year job posting or a three-fucking-minute piss in the toilet – you need a visa to enter Vietnam.

The Mohawk and I did not have visas. Our plane would leave in two hours. Narita Airport is more than an hour away from the centre of Tokyo where the Vietnamese embassy just happens to be. The Vietnamese embassy issue visas, but the process can take anywhere from hours to months to complete.

"Fuck," the Mohawk contributed to the conversation between the two customs officials and me, which had now increased to more of an unwinnable debate.

The customs officials suggested contacting the embassy to try to find a solution to the problem. How do you get a visa stamped into your passport when you are several hours of travel and administration work away, and you have a plane to catch in less than two hours? We contacted the embassy. A game of cat and mouse unfolded before us as we were told to send emails immediately, but first had to find some accessible wifi. Further instructions came to transfer payment via Western Union, which was a hard and crowded 15-minute sprint through the airport across various levels of the multi-floored building, before reaching a locked door bearing a closed sign.

"Fuck!" came another contribution from the Mohawk, who was as sweaty from the run as I. People who consume as much liquor and narcotics while chain-smoking as us should not break into a sprint but needs must! More calls were made and a compromise was reached. We would be allowed to board the plane at Narita International and fly to

Vietnam provided that we paid the visa fee immediately upon landing at Hanoi.

Deal!

The Japanese customs officials took some persuading to believe our arrangement was for real, but eventually relented in order to allow us to partake in one more mad dash to catch the plane before it departed.

We crashed through random passengers, knocked over luggage of every colour, shape and size and spilled peoples' food and drinks. But we made it to the plane. Sweating profusely and screaming curses between cries to hold the plane we barrelled along the boarding tunnel until finally crashing onto the plane to a sea of Asian faces staring at us in alarm and disgust. We smiled and nodded as we moved down the aisle to our seats where we promptly collapsed and breathed heavily through tar-stained lungs.

"I know where the snake village called Le Mat is just north of Hanoi city where we're gonna get all caveman and carnivore-like. I know that all of the suit shops are on Hang Gai Street, also known as Silk Street. I kind of know how to ask if a women takes it in the arse in Vietnamese. How in the name of fuck did I not know you needed a visa to enter Vietnam with a British passport?"

"Fuck."

The night-time journey passed quickly due to sleep brought on from the day's substance abuse, stress and physical exertion.

Hanoi

2

When I opened my eyes it was Vietnamese rain that I saw hitting the window. It was Vietnamese writing that I saw on the airport and its vehicles. And it was Vietnamese soldiers carrying guns that I saw inspecting everything. We moved amongst the mostly Asian passengers along the aisle and then out into the night. The heat and humidity were not much more to contend with than what we had just left in Japan, but now there was warm rain to go with it. Sandwiched amid the dozens of smaller passengers we moved our bulky Caucasian frames toward the steps. A voice barked for my attention from the bottom of them. I looked around, dazed and confused, trying to locate the source of the voice. I also searched my brain as to who in the hell would know my name in Viet-fucking-nam not two seconds after I stepped off the plane. Who would be calling my name this early in the trip? Had I done something in my sleep during the flight over here? My eyes landed on a uniformed figure at the bottom of the steps. He held out an outstretched finger that pointed right at us. His hand motioned for us to join him. We looked behind us to the entrance back into the plane, which was empty now. Thoughts of hijacking and taking the cabin crew as hostages flooded my mind before looking back down at the soldier.

"We have been waiting for you."

"Fuck," groaned the Mohawk as we descended the metal steps into Vietnam and straight into the hands of its military.

We were led past security and customs to a small office rammed full of military uniforms that all screamed and yelled at each other on phones and at other passengers waiting behind a window through a thick haze of cigarette smoke.

"Wait," said our escort before disappearing into the smoke.

We waited and took in some of the madness that is Hanoi Airport. Bodies moved everywhere, all in a hurry, all aggressive, all trying to get somewhere else. And we just got here. Another military uniform joined us and demanded our passports. We complied. He disappeared into the smoke. The airport looked like something from the 1970s, harsh strip lights, everything coated in yellow and furnishings that had seen far better days. The first uniform returned and lazily held out his hand in front of us, palm facing the nicotine yellow ceiling. I placed the equivalent of £50 sterling in Vietnamese dong onto the open hand. The uniform took a drag on the half-smoked cigarette that was glued to his lips. The Mohawk leant over and added his currency to the pile.

The hand stayed open.

"They said that would be enough... at the embassy..." I informed a plume of smoke that was directed my way "...in Tokyo." I closed my eyes from the harsh dryness caused by the insult thrown my way by the uniform. His hand stayed open until the Mohawk and I had sufficiently stacked enough dong on the pile, and then he disappeared into the smoke again.

"Are you guys having visa problems too?" an American female voice enquired from behind us. "Fuckers have really screwed us!" she continued as the Mohawk and I turned to see two white faces. The female was short and fat, which stood out all the more because her boyfriend was so tall and gangly. "Are you guys from around here? Can you help us at all?"

"That's actually why we're here. Well, you and some other cases of possible crimes against the People's Republic." I immediately brought them up to speed. "There has been a lot of trouble with visas these last two days. False documents, red flags, illegals crossing the border. There was even talk of old war tunnels in the jungles being utilised. Apparently two team spy cells, dressed like flaky-pot-smoking-hippie-faggots, are being deployed by unknown enemies of the Peoples' Republic." They stared at me in bewildered silence. "Now, tell us your side of the events, comrades."

"Well—" the woman launched straight in.

"Who are you guys?" the boyfriend looked very confused and slightly suspicious of us. "You don't look like you work for the embassy."

"It's two-in-the-damn-morning man! You think we sleep in grey suits with gold cufflinks polished ready to come and help you with your life!? This is Viet-fucking-nam son, your Western ideals don't apply here," the Mohawk barked at the boyfriend.

"Shut up!" the female put the boyfriend back in his place. "As I was saying," she gave her lover the look of an angry parent, "we've been here about two weeks and arranged all the correct visas and documents from the embassies to cross over into Cambodia. We only went for a week. Now we've come back to Vietnam and they're telling us that we didn't have the correct visas. They're threatening to arrest us as spies and all sorts—"

"Spies?!" I burst out.

"We're just backpackers, man. That's it," the boyfriend chimed in again and was once more on the receiving end of a reprimanding look from his boss.

"Our papers, passports and visas are all present and correct. We paid the money. Got the stamps, got the papers, we got they're fucking permission to go AND come back! All our stuff is at the hotel!" the woman began to get teary eyed.

"Take my advice." I got in close and hushed my voice. "Listen carefully." I glanced around the immediate area. "White meat is a rare delicacy in this part of the world." I paused for signs of recognition of her understanding my meaning.

"They do eat a lot of dog here," the boyfriend said curiously.

"Corruption is the bedrock of this society," I

whispered. "You've already witnessed that." I rolled my eyes to the smokebox that was serving as the customs office. "If you've got the cash," I smiled, "but if not..." I shrugged my shoulders and pulled a jib, "...there's always white meat." I gestured like I didn't know anything and raised my eyebrows. The Mohawk nodded in agreement and smiled suggestively as he eyed the boyfriend up and down. The girl shook her head in denial of the horrific and sordid suggestion I was making.

"You think I should... that I would—"

"Who said anything about you?" I cut her off. "They prefer," I looked at her boyfriend, "lean meat." I nodded as I eyed the lanky backpacker up and down.

"Hey, fuck you man!" The panicked boyfriend took a step back. "What kind of embassy officials are you?"

"Here you visas." The first uniform was suddenly between the Mohawk and I. He held out our passports and smiled satisfied in the knowledge that he had just robbed another two tourists. We took our passports and promptly checked them.

"So, are you going to help us?" the slow female asked.

"Green dong or white meat. That's all that's gonna help you." The Mohawk and I smiled at the pair as we turned and walked away.

Hanoi

3

The journey to the hotel was sketchy to say the least. After being robbed by customs we were out into the thick of things in Hanoi Airport. Picture a Wall Street stock exchange rammed full of white men in suits screaming and waving pieces of paper as they curse at the top of their lungs, all trying to hustle as much money as they can as fast as they can. Now, change the Caucasians to Asians. Pretty much the same thing. Lots of people who want your money, all crammed into one place and all hustling any and every way they can to try to get cash from you. We negotiated a private driver from inside the airport, already having been advised on the internet to avoid the street cabs.

The drive was a blur of headlights that we weaved between at high speed along with the blare of horns that joined the continuous rhythm of the windscreen wipers. Screeching between oncoming traffic while sliding from one side of the road to the next at 100-plus miles an hour and mounting pavements along with small islands of dirt that acted as dividers was a great way to take in the sights Hanoi has to offer at three o'clock in the morning during a tropical storm. Our driver made little attempt at conversation and we made even less. We'd learned how to say 'hello' and 'thank you' from the cute hustler who had convinced us that her private taxi firm was the best in Hanoi, but had already forgotten it. We sat back and enjoyed the ride.

The hotel was small and jammed between two other buildings on a downtown street. The SUV dropped us off and we entered to be met by a young and slight guy dressed in black trousers and a white shirt. It is common practice in many hotels to ask for guests' passports, which are to be returned upon checking out. This was unacceptable to the Mohawk and I. After intimidating the receptionist and then verbally abusing him for representing a hotel with no bar we were shown to our room, passports in our pockets.

Heading back out into the night and the waning storm, we noticed that the young boy secured the hotel door behind us with a bicycle lock – very safe and inventive we agreed. The rain motivated us to walk quicker through the deserted and dark urban landscape. Thoughts of dumb tourists getting lost and into trouble because they neglected to inform anyone where they were or where they were going flashed between thoughts of alcohol and curiosity that wanted to be satisfied. What was Hanoi all about?

We weren't sure if we'd find anywhere open to quench our thirst, but figured from all the stories we'd heard in the past from people who had lived here that it was worth a shot. It didn't take us long to find a seedy looking bar in almost complete darkness, with loud music blasting from within and a large number of fellow white faces coming and going. The Mohawk and I wanted to get out of the rain and into some liquor. Coming from Wales, rain is never a welcome type of weather. In Wales it rains more days than it doesn't. But for many of the patrons of this bar, the rain was something to stand in and enjoy with your drinks. We barged past the wet idiots and into the blackness, then immediately headed for the bar and ordered bottles of beer from the big, hairy white guy that bobbed his head behind it. After clinking bottles, we drank. Then we drank more and more and more. We continued this trend until the bar eventually closed. At no point had we bothered to speak to anyone except for the barman to order more drinks and each other. After the travelling and visa fuck-up, we just wanted to pound booze and then pass out back at the hotel.

Hanoi

4

We knew that there would be at least one crazy and fucked-up meal eaten on the trip. We were sure of that. However, once we saw what madness Hanoi menus had to offer, we knew that more than one unusual and bizarre dish had to be sampled. After a little deliberation we opted for tortoise.

By far the craziest thing offered to us was dog flesh. There were many eateries offering to serve us up some canine, but the Mohawk and I are pet lovers and have both been dog owners at different points in our lives, so we were sickened by the idea rather than tempted.

Multiple kinds of sea creatures, unavailable in other parts of the world, were on the menus as well as pigeon, which is actually a common treat in places like Egypt. We opted for tortoise. Neither of us could explain why, but the four-legged, hard shelled herbivore seemed like an acceptable choice to make. There are many who would consider the decision to be just as fucked up as eating a dog, but for us it was completely different. We both loved dogs but didn't give a fuck about tortoises. It turned out to be a pretty poor choice, as tortoise don't have much meat on them and don't make for particularly tasty eating. Neither of us would go so far as to say it tasted bad, but then neither of us would ever bother to eat it again.

After indulging in exotic cuisine and cold alcoholic beverages, we set about completing phase one of the mission at hand – find a suitable place to get our bespoke suits made. We walked from shop to shop, bargaining, negotiating, harassing and in some instances outright abusing different retailers and tailors. Eventually we settled on a small establishment, the walls of which were lined with framed pictures of the owner and head seamstress standing with various dignitaries and celebrities from all over the world right there in their little shop. The woman spoke great English and had an amazing sense of humour, which we stretched to its limits and possibly beyond. The Mohawk and I insisted that she made a three-piece suit for each of us from scratch, along with shirts to match and silk ties to complete the ensemble. Everything was to be made from new cloth, not some old garment refitted and rejigged to fit us. No, everything was to be brand new, done in two days and sold for a fraction of what they were worth.

"Please! You ask too much!" the poor woman yelled at us.

We loomed over her tiny frame, almost a full two feet taller than her and at least double her weight. Our demonic grins and crazy eyes informing her that there was no further negotiation to be had. We knew what we wanted and how much we were willing to pay, and that was that. Eventually, she reluctantly accepted the measly offering of dong presented to her provided we pay most of it upfront. This also took some haggling to accomplish, as neither the Mohawk or I are particularly trusting people at the best of times. After handing over the down payment we were measured and then we left the store in search of more booze to celebrate a successful job well done.

Outside, the streets of Hanoi can only be described as utter madness. Crossing the road is not for the faint of heart. It is impossible to see the tarmac when in the centre of the city due to the insane number of scooters that jam the roads up like an entire city fleeing from another American occupation.

The roads are all covered by one giant metal and rubber snake, slithering forwards in a continuous motion that kicks up smog and smoke that mixes with the insane jungle heat and humidity to create an atmosphere very different to that of Japan, the only other Asian country we had been to. We had been advised that when trying to cross the roads in Hanoi you just step into it and keep walking until you reach the other side. This seems like lunacy when you actually see the traffic with your own eyes. When you are there, stood on the pavement with countless cars, trucks, scooters and tuk-tuks screeching past you at full pelt, it is hard to believe that the advice you've been given is accurate and not just some bad joke being played on you in an attempt to end your life. Some strange social test, like the Milgram experiment, to assess your logic and ability to come to your own sensible conclusions based on first-hand evidence.

We played the part of the fools, we stood at the side of the road and then stepped out into the oncoming traffic. Just as we had been told, the traffic parted for us like the fabled story of Moses and the Red Sea. Every single vehicle swerved to avoid us, but none slowed down. Every fibre of your being insists that you are about to be hit by a speeding scooter ridden by several natives, but the collision never happens. You are never so much as scratched, yet alone smashed into and ridden over.

Searching for traffic lights or a crossing is pointless. They don't exist, or at least we never saw any. No, in Hanoi when you want to cross the road, you just do it. Don't think about it, don't plan it and don't hesitate, just step out into the road and keep walking until you are back on the other pavement. Don't even look at the oncoming traffic – observation is their job. Yours is to merely walk and not to stop until out of harm's way. Even walking around the city made you thirsty for a beer with that kind of daily madness to contend with.

Hanoi, like many cities, has another dangerous thing to deal with: thieves. Vietnam is not a wealthy country, at least not for the citizens. Occupations and a very long war, combined with communism, resulted in a country bereft of benefits and bucks. It is not usual for small and malnourished criminals to try their luck against two big and far from weak white guys, but something any Caucasian traveller has to remember is that in foreign countries where the locals are of a darker complexion than you, the thinking is that you are nothing more than a walking cash machine. If they can't hustle that money out of you, there are those who will simply try to steal it.

The Mohawk and I encountered one such foolish fella in the midst of sweltering heat and noisy roads. Not being naive to the ways of this world, we had spotted the runt of a man following us and being less than discrete about the fact that he was doing it. Studying us. Waiting for an opportune moment to steal our shit. We decided to not take the chance of him giving up due to us being in broad daylight and on busy, crowd-filled streets where there were any number of witnesses. We brought the opportunity to him. We welcomed him to our pockets. We went out of our way to find a quiet and witness-free narrow back alley, seemingly naively getting lost and wandering off the beaten path and into a dark and deserted area where our wallets were ripe for the plucking. Like any poor and desperate thief he took the bait. Once we were sure nobody could see us we stopped walking long enough for him to catch up and make his move.

Blood is not difficult to wash off when it has been freshly applied to skin. Only after it has dried does it become a little more difficult to scrub off.

Hanoi

5

Speeding along the almost empty motorway the
night air was damp and a little cool against the
skin. This was a welcome break from the heat of the
daytime. The towering and occasionally leaning
motorway lights kept us from relying on the tiny
scooter headlight. Images of war movies flashed
through my mind, in particular Kubrick's Full
Metal Jacket. A superb film, which stood out all the
more for depicting bombed out cities in Vietnam
(even though it was shot in the UK) rather than the
jungle like the majority of Vietnamese war movies.
The crumbling walls separated the motorway from
the towering blocks of flats and mazes of tiny
streets that contained all manner of shops,
restaurants and whatever else you wanted.

The area we cruised through off the motorway
had 15-story buildings with huge sections of the
outer walls missing, which gave you a clear view of
the flats on multiple floors and the people still
living in them. The area looked like something from
a post-apocalyptic nightmare, the remains of
Kubrick's vision of Vietnam with a few decades of
human survival and stubbornness grown all over it.

This part of town was not as well-lit as the motorway, which forced the tiny woman steering the scooter to rely on the small and dying headlight as she manoeuvred around rubble, rubbish, potholes and animals. This would've been a tricky ride in daylight as a solo rider, but at night with my weight riding pillion it was a miracle we hadn't crashed yet.

As I wasn't wearing a helmet it was decided the best form of safety was to drink more of the stale beer that was getting warmer in the oversized bottle in my hand. When I'd bought the bottle earlier in the night it had been ice-cold and had a great taste to it, but now it was a giant blue glass bottle of piss. I drank more and thought back to the bar I'd bought it from earlier in the night.

Hanoi

6

I'd wound up alone in the two-story bar, which was long and narrow on both floors. The Mohawk had returned to the hotel earlier in the night leaving me alone in Hanoi. Wandering the streets, light rain cooling me slightly, I bounced between shopfronts and the vehicles parked opposite them like a giant pinball. We'd consumed a lot of liquor over the course of the day. It was our final night in that strange and crazy city so the drinking had started early and got hard fast. I got my focus back to find myself perched on a bar stool looking into the young, shiny-smooth face of a barman who didn't look old enough to get into Disneyland. He was smiling widely and nodding at me.

"Beer," I blurted.

"Which beer?" he chirped merrily.

"Uhh…" I tried to remember the name of a good beer and struggled to focus on anything behind the bar. The multi-coloured bottles twinkled magically and looked fantastic, but my vision couldn't handle reading. "Whatever's good dude." He brought me a tall, sweating glass of cold beer. "And one for yourself," I generously said. He skipped away and poured himself a draft beer immediately. This was a good sign. In the UK it is illegal for bar staff to drink alcohol while working, but here this rule didn't seem to apply and this kid took full of advantage of that, which I liked. He came back sipping his beer.

"Thanks mister," he said between slurps.

We continued to drink more beers while trying to out-do each other with various shots done in over-elaborate ways. My favourite was white Sambuca. That sickly clear aniseed liquid looks cool when set alight and consumed to the casual observer in various nightspots around the globe. After multiple shots and beers the ambitious suggestion was made to go to the second floor.

Hanoi

7

The entire floor was one room and the whole space had a Middle Eastern vibe. There were no chairs, there were just rugs and cushions. The low tables were covered in drinks, ashtrays and smouldering hookahs. You couldn't see much through the grey clouds that was the smoke and the small number of tiny lamps didn't help when drunkenly trying to find your way through the room for the first time looking for a place to slump. The kid guided me to an area in a corner that would have allowed me to look down the length of the room were it not for the smoke-filled darkness that made taking in my surroundings almost impossible. The room was packed with bodies, and many of those bodies were wrapped in tiny tight designer dresses. They dripped with gold and designer labels. There were girls everywhere and they were all stunning.

The kid came and sat next to me. I'd lost track of time and had no idea how long I'd been staring around the room for.

"I order good flavour. Nice flavour. You like I sure." He passed me another beer and smiled as he bobbed his head to the thumping pop music.

As we smoked the giant, bubbling hookah the topic of women came up. The kid had laughed at the idea of me meeting a woman here. He explained that all of them had the same checklist with the same two requirements on it. First, you had to already be living here in Hanoi. These women were only interested in long-term relationships, therefore one-night stands were out of the question. Second, you had to be rich. After several attempts to prove the kid's theory wrong I gave up and admitted that he was in fact right.

He smiled more, "I tell you. I from Hanoi. I know Hanoi girl. You last night in Hanoi. Hanoi girl not like you."

I decided to change the subject by questioning him about the soldiers that had entered the bar earlier in the night. I came to learn that licenses for owning bars were not enough here. As well as having all of the proper and correct legal documents all in order, you also had to pay off the military police for that part of the city. As far as the military are concerned, the license got you open, but if you wanted to stay open into the early morning you had to pay extra. In cash. Every night. The bars had the choice when the soldiers arrived to either pay and stay open or if there were not many customers spending lots of money in your establishment, don't pay and close up for the night. Simple, no fuss, no stress, no violence or backchat. There were no repercussions if the bar decided not to pay, they simply had to close the doors until the next working day began. According to the kid, this bar was one of the most popular in the city, and so every night the soldiers got a fat wad of cash. I had only been in Hanoi for three days but had seen cash-in-hand payoffs right from the start. There was nothing you couldn't get in this place if you had the cash to pay. With that thought in mind I passed the hose of the hookah to the kid and asked, "Can you get anything else to smoke here?"

"You smoke Marlboro Gold, yeah?" he innocently asked.

"That's not what I'm talking about dude." I smiled mischievously.

Hanoi

8

The third floor was actually the roof. Most of it was open to the night sky, but there was a small area for sitting that was sheltered. As the kid offered me the small bag of weed he naively enquired, "You sure you want smoke this now? You very fucked up."

It was weak bud but packed enough punch to do the trick due to the huge quantity of alcohol that had already been consumed. After finishing the baggy of weed and bottle of beer, we went back down to the ground floor. I resumed my place on a bar stool and he resumed his position behind the long bar. But now we were both very fucked up and using the bar to hold us semi-upright. On the stool next to me sat a surly white male. He drank alone and looked like he was in no mood for company or small talk.

"You live here?" I enquired.

He spoke with a gravelly thick Australian accent without really making eye contact. "No."

"He businessman," the kid informed me, with a look that screamed *leave him the fuck alone, he's trouble!* "He sell meteor."

"What kind of business?" I drunkenly pursued.

"Rocks."

"Lot of rocks here in the jungle. Must be good business," I said sarcastically.

"Do I fucking look poor?"

I eyed the Australian up and down on his stool. He was dressed casually, just jeans and a T-shirt, but there was also a black leather sheath on his belt that looked like it should have a giant hunting knife tucked into it. He was built like a military man, lean and muscular with perfect posture despite sitting on a bar stool in the early hours of the morning with a bottle of beer in his hand. I, on the other hand, had almost no posture as I almost sprawled across the bar to take a closer look at him. "Is that a digital watch?"

"What are you after mate?" He turned and looked at me with more disgust than hostility. I sat upright and spread my hands as I smiled drunkenly.

"What any red-blooded drunk heterosexual man wants at this time of the night. A woman!"

"You won't find that around here mate. Not unless you wanna pay for it with one of them lot outside." He referred to the numerous prostitutes that cruised the narrow streets on scooters trying to pick up johns. This option had crossed my inebriated mind but was a last resort and the night was not over yet. The Australian read my face and saw what I was thinking. "You can come with me after this beer if you're up for it."

"Sure. Where?"

"No, no mister," the kid spoke up with fear, "you

go clubbing down dock, yeah?"

"That's right." The Australian shot him a look of hostility.

"Bad people there. Gangster and bad man. Dangerous place," the kid informed us.

"Do I look fucking scared to you?" The Australian was clearly very offended by this notion. The kid stared at the ground for a few moments before leaning into my ear.

"You no go there. Bad place. Bad people," he whispered.

Hanoi

9

I woke up still sat almost upright on the stool, with my upper torso spread across the bar. I had no idea how long I'd blacked out for, but nobody around me seemed to care. The kid was restocking a fridge at the other end of the bar and a single Vietnamese customer was propped up against another section of the bar. The Australian was nowhere to be seen. I figured this was for the best as he had seemed a particularly angry individual who was clearly in the mood for violence. I noticed the large bottle of beer to my side was full and looked like it was still cold. The icy bubbles gave me a slight shiver that woke me enough to make the decision to leave. Bottle in hand, bouncing from side to side, I staggered out of the bar yelling something about seeing the kid again later in the day.

The rain was warm and slick, and it impaired my vision. When the tiny toot from the scooter's horn eventually caught my attention I could barely make out the rider's gender. It was her squeaky voice that confirmed her as female, which also confirmed the suspicion in my head that she was in fact touting for business on this empty wet street at ridiculous-o'clock in the morning with a very obviously drunk stranger. She ordered me onto the back of the two-wheeled death-trap.

I swigged beer and held onto the back of the seat as we whined along the spot-lit street. Less lights were followed by less buildings and then eventually the black flatness of what passed as a motorway in North Vietnam. Moments of clear thinking occasionally penetrated the fog in my mind and spelled out the potential trouble I was putting myself in with a clarity that could only be washed away with more beer.

Once we were off the motorway and through the labyrinth of small streets and alleys, we eventually pulled into a garage built into the ground floor of a tower. We entered the decrepit structure and I was led up numerous floors, past many identical brown doors until finally coming around on my back – too much booze often gave me blackouts like this. Sprawled out on a double bed I saw the scooter rider undressing in the en suite bathroom. My giant bottle of beer stood on a dresser under a large window opposite the bed. My companion was yelling something in her native tongue, which may or may not have been directed at me. I started to undress. While stumbling around the dimly lit room I managed to partly strip and drink more beer. The small woman approached, all the while still mouthing off in Vietnamese, and she helped remove the rest of my clothes.

The sweaty, out of breath, beer and cigarette smoke-smelling sex was made all the more weird when the prostitute made a call on her mobile during a brief burst of high energy doggy style. The heavy breathing, grunting, fake sex noises and the headboard slamming against the wall went on for an unknown length of time before being interrupted by a pounding on the door. Suddenly aware that I was naked, in an unknown location, my last known whereabouts a mystery to anyone, very drunk and quite possibly about to get robbed, raped, beaten, murdered or a combination of all the above made me dive from the bed, now semi-sober, and arm myself with the giant glass bottle of beer. I took a swig before gripping the neck ready to do battle with only a condom and bottle to protect me. In the meantime the little Vietnamese hooker had semi-dressed and gone to open the door, all the while still muttering in Vietnamese. I swayed slightly as I closed one eye and tried to focus on the door into the room as it opened. Behind it stood two more Vietnamese women, both obviously workmates of my current companion, and both blatantly filthy.

The miniature gangbang went on for a while and ended just as sordidly, stickily, aggressively and loudly as everything that had preceded it. It appears that Asian women don't like cum in the eye as much as Caucasian women.

After a brief rest and quick wash, the four of us staggered out into the hallway. One of the women waved and spoke to her friends in their native tongue as she walked away down the brown coloured hallway. The three of us headed back down to the scooter. The sun was yet to start its ascent, the air was hot but it felt good on my face as the tiny engine struggled to transport the three of us back toward where I'd originally been picked up. The small rider in front of me gripped the handlebars hard and still muttered as she steered us along a lit part of the motorway. The dyed blonde hair sitting behind me wrapped her hands around my body as she held tightly in hope of remaining on the scooter. I sipped more beer and chuckled at the position I found myself in.

The two women giggled and waved as they sped away on the half-dead scooter, leaving me standing on a street I'd apparently been on before. I finished the last of the beer in the oversized bottle and started to stagger. Occasionally a landmark seemed familiar and eventually I made it back to the hotel.

I rudely woke the terrified boy on night duty and laughed something at him between slurs as I barged past to go to my room.

I burst through the door like some deranged wildebeest on roller-skates, laughing and howling, turning lights on and off while trying to remove my shoes and bounce off walls and cupboards. After I had finally face-planted onto the mattress and quieted down some, the Mohawk eventually asked, "Have fun then?"

I giggled mischievously for a time before stating mysteriously, "There were three of them."

And then I laughed long and loud while the Mohawk sat upright, intrigued by my words and the condition I was in.

Hanoi

10

For our final day in Hanoi we collected our new suits and arranged our trip to Le Mat, aka snake village. At the tailors we paid what was owed and then thanked the very tired-looking seamstress before having some pictures taken with her.

Neither the Mohawk or I are famous, and yet we still felt the need to have our picture taken with the lady and informing her that she could frame it next to all the other pictures of her with high profile customers on the walls of her shop. We told her it would probably sit well between the pictures of an African president and a world-famous football player. By this point the woman had all but lost her patience with us. The high demands and low profit margin, coupled with the insane time schedule, robbed her of her otherwise jovial character and left us looking at a thin and wiry woman in need of peace and quiet; not two fiends jesting about having their pictures taken to adorn her walls and forever remind her of this most tiresome of encounters.

After collecting the suits we went back to the hotel to drop them off and jump into the taxi we had booked via the receptionist. The drive was calm and uneventful. It took us over the Red River and into Long Bien District and Le Mat, where things are a little different.

To say that the snake village looks primitive, third world and sketchy as fuck would be a massive understatement. For the most part the place looks like an abandoned industrial site. There are short grey very large buildings everywhere and a lot of young men, seemingly unemployed, waiting around outside these buildings like they are just biding their time for a victim, or victims, to drag inside to abuse, rob, rape and murder, not necessarily in that order.

Small rivers and what is left of the jungle intrude upon the grey buildings. In the beginning it was probably the other way around – grey intruding on green. But now it looks like the remains of the jungle are a virus spreading across the broken concrete.

As our taxi cruised through the narrow labyrinth that makes up the heart of Le Mat, we sat mouths agape and stared out at the village around us. The locals stared back at us with for the most part noticeable disdain. At one point one of the young men ran alongside the taxi attempting to open the door and banging on the window. Neither the taxi driver or us were fazed by the young man's actions, we were more perplexed as to what he thought he could accomplish. He banged and shouted as he sprinted to stay alongside us, and we just looked at him with puzzled faces. He eventually gave up and we continued to cruise around until the taxi finally stopped and the driver pointed up at a large wooden sign on one of the grey warehouses and said something to us in a tongue that we didn't understand. It was only the picture of the cobra on the sign that allowed us to understand that we had more than likely arrived at our destination.

We had already paid the fare back at the hotel when he picked us up, so we arranged for the same driver to collect us in a couple of hours. We thanked him and then got out of the safety of the car and into the dodgy streets of the snake village.

From the outside the restaurant just looked like a warehouse. A typical kind of grey square building you would expect to find on an industrial estate anywhere in the world with nothing but storage space and pallets inside. When we entered our tiny minds were blown away.

The bare grey concrete walls had water running down them from the torrential rain North Vietnam had experienced over the last few days. There were large chains hanging, some for the giant shutters that acted as doors, some just for decoration or who knows what. Then we saw the cage. A large wired enclosure that ran almost the entire length of one of the walls, home to peacocks and some other exotic birds. At the centre of the entrance area were wide stairs that led up and split in two, both flights then leading to the same balcony area. The entire staircase, like the walls, was bare and grey.

A young woman dressed in a black skirt and white shirt approached and asked if we wanted a table for two. We replied yes and we were then led up the stairs and into a different world.

The upper area was all decked out in plush red velvet drapes and curtains, which hung around heavy teak chairs and tables. The internet had informed us that this was the best restaurant in the entire village, and while we were at first dubious to these claims, it now seemed apparent that we were in the right spot. Gold and red were the main colours, a stark contrast to the bare grey on the ground floor. The heavy wooden doors and the dividers between areas and booths were all ornately carved. Large porcelain pieces decorated the heavy traditional furniture and made for a spectacular area to sit and eat snake meat. We figured at this point that the driver had probably dropped us at the staff entrance by mistake, as he had clearly had trouble finding the restaurant in the first place.

The waitress led us to a clean and well stocked table on an outer balcony that overlooked the jungle surrounding the village.

There are no longer any snakes in the immediate countryside for the villagers to catch; snake wrangling being the primary trade in the village for generations. Instead, the locals now farmed the reptiles in enclosures to supply the numerous restaurants that catered for the ever-growing tourist industry and wealthier natives.

The menu had a variety of snakes to choose from, but by far the most expensive and our number one choice was the king cobra. We wanted to order two, as an important part of this experience is not only to eat the snake meat, but to drink its blood, drink its bile and to swallow its still beating heart. The waitress informed us that they cook and use every single part of the snake and absolutely nothing goes to waste. This meant that if we each wanted to swallow a heart, two whole snakes had to be consumed, and this the waitress informed us would be too much food for even two large travellers like us.

We ordered the one king cobra, and the Mohawk said that he was more than happy to pass on the experience of eating a fresh heart. The waitress returned with several young men, one of whom carried a wriggling sack. He tipped the sack upside down and let its contents fall to the concrete floor. There, only a couple of feet from our feet, hissed a more than annoyed king cobra. The man then proceeded to bang, poke and prod the snake to make it even angrier than it already was. It writhed around and flared its hood at us. The Mohawk and I laughed with fear at the killer on the floor next to our table hissing its fury at us. Once the snake wrangler was sufficiently happy that the king cobra had been shown off enough and was angry enough, he promptly smacked it on the back of the head to stun it, and then with lighting hands snatched it up off the floor. He held it with one hand and used the knife in his right hand to slice it lengthways down its scaly belly.

At a small table off to one side the wrangler and his helpers quickly drained some of the snake's blood into two shot glasses, along with two shot glasses of luminous green bile. This was then mixed with rice vodka that had already been poured into the two glasses. Next, the still beating heart of the king cobra was placed onto a small white dish and then all five items were brought and served to us.

The waitress and young men all stood back and waited to see if I would swallow the heart, and that both the Mohawk and I would drink the reptile's still-warm blood. We looked and chuckled at the red lump of organ still pulsating on the small white porcelain dish placed in front of me. I tried to figure out how to eat it. Was I supposed to cut it with a knife and fork like a civilised chap? Was I supposed to let it slide into my open mouth from the dish? Was I supposed to pick it up with my fingers and bite into it like a savage before standing and beating my chest like King Kong? I had no idea. I attempted the third option, but before I could take a bite the waitress stepped forwards with a giggle and poured the beating heart into my shot glass of blood and said, "Swallow in one."

I did. I threw the shot glass back and emptied it of both the heart and all the blood in one giant swig and swallow.

It tasted fucking delicious.

The Mohawk stared wide-eyed at me and then let out a raucous laugh.

"You fiend!" he yelled as he giggled.

I smiled and nodded, 'yes' for both confirmation that I had done the deed and that I was indeed a fiend of the highest calibre.

The young men all smiled and nodded approval

before disappearing with the dead snake. In Vietnam they believe that the snake's heart, especially that of the king cobra, brings strength and virility to men. The waitress approached with a smile and pointed at the shot glasses filled with what looked like liquid kryptonite, "You drink slow with food. Very strong."

She then took the empty shot glass and dish, still stained with blood, and walked over to the kitchen area.

The Mohawk and I each took a sip of the cobra's bile. It was indeed strong and tasted like piss mixed with bleach. This, for anyone who has ever drunk real Mexican tequila knows, is a sign of just how fucking strong it really is. Strong alcoholic beverages are never smooth and tasty. They are always harsh and taste vile.

When they said that they cook the whole snake, they weren't kidding. Every single part of that reptile had been grilled, fried, baked and fuck-knows-what. Even the skin had been deep fried into what resembled prawn crackers, but with the colour pattern of the cobra's scales still visible on them. It was amazing. Some of the dishes were a little bland, but most were scrumptious and served with tasty dressings.

During the meal I felt what is usually described as 'a little funny'. My friend watched and chuckled as I momentarily slipped in and out of the conversation, meal and my surroundings. It came in waves. First, long intense fuckers, but then as time went on the spaces of normality between them grew longer and the highs became less intense and for shorter periods of time. I had no idea what was happening to me.

"I feel a little light-headed," I said to my companion. "I think I must still be really fucking drunk from last night dude."

The Mohawk laughed and sat back in his chair to watch the show.

"It's the fucking heart you just swallowed you idiot." He laughed more.

"What?"

"It's full of adrenaline. Didn't you know that?" More laughter.

I didn't know that. I had read a little about the snake village and the different restaurants located there, but not much else. The Mohawk had read about it and proceeded to inform me about the fact that the heart is full of adrenaline that acts very similar to a stimulant, such as amphetamine for instance. And so there I sat, riding wave after intense wave of king cobra adrenaline, sipping its bile between swigs of beer and bites of its flesh. We even ate its bones. What a meal!

Once the snake had been eaten and the bill paid, we waddled away from our table and back down the bare concrete steps. We took a different turn and came out in a different part of the ground floor, which was almost identical to the way we had entered save for a stand at the foot of the steps holding a glass case. Inside was a stuffed king cobra in a typical half-coiled, half-erect pose with its hood flared and fangs on display. Standing close to it was a man with a gimpy hand. It was distorted and bent in an unnatural way, like it was about to curl in on itself and burrow into his wrist. The man greeted us with a warm smile and then set about explaining to us that the snake on display had been the fucker who bit him and caused his misshapen hand. The man was the owner of the restaurant and had killed and stuffed the cobra on display in the main entrance of his restaurant as payback for what it had done to him. He chuckled and nodded as he rested his good hand atop the display, all the while staring into the reptile's dead eyes with a 'fuck you, buddy' glare. We complimented his restaurant and then stepped outside in search of our taxi, who was there waiting and had apparently never left. A clear sign of just how much over the odds we had paid.

Hanoi

11

We were both full and exhausted after the madness of Hanoi. The two of us fell asleep in the taxi to the airport, despite the drive being as crazy as the one that took us from the airport. We boarded the plane without any trouble and then slept all the way back to Japan.

Before the short trip we had only seen Vietnam in American war movies, which never really showed you much other than green jungles. Kubrick's movie depicted bombed-out urban areas and was a far more accurate portrayal of what we saw first-hand decades later, despite Kubrick never setting foot on Vietnamese soil. It was a country that had recovered in part from decades of war, as well as both French and Chinese occupations. It was only in the 1990s that Vietnam was opened up to the outside world and things started to really progress. But, of course, these things take time.

Japan
2

Tokyo

11

Spice – synthetic cannabinoids – changed
everything. I turned away from practicing martial
arts, weight-lifting, jogging and studying. I cared
less and less about the job and my students. Living
conditions and responsibilities mattered not. There
was only the ever-increasing desire to smoke more
spice.

The addiction to the stuff creeps up on you
slowly and subtly. Easing its way into your brain
like a slow-moving parasite that doesn't want to
cause pain or discomfort in order to avoid detection
and ultimately its own death.

We started on a five-gram bag a week between
two of us. By the end, we were doing at least a bag a
day – each. Spice was marketed as synthetic weed,
but in truth it is absolutely nothing like cannabis.
The Japanese authorities continually tried to
outlaw the product, but all they could do was make
one particular element of the overall concoction
illegal. So the manufacturers would just use a
different chemical to replace the one which was
now illegal. This cat and mouse game of the
authorities classifying one substance illegal and the

spice makers replacing it with another went on for years. The effect on the product was a substance that was being punted to the public without anyone really knowing what affect it would have on you. It would have been wiser, safer and more humane to just legalise weed, but that was never going to happen as far as the Japanese authorities was concerned.

And so the spice continued to flow. And flow it did, from our regular hook-up in Akihabara to our lips and lungs in joint after joint of chemical concoctions that even the chemists were clueless about. It went from a weekend treat to a junkie necessity in the space of a few months. From a social smoke with the boys in the comfy confines of a flat to a paranoid shaky hand sucking down rapid drags in the dusty concrete stairwell that was used as a fire escape at a teaching centre for young students.

There is no exact way to describe a spice high, as each baggy contained a slightly different mix with a sometimes drastically different outcome. You might feel mellow and numb, other times you were a water droplet falling from the clouds and taking its journey down the gutter alongside the paving slabs until you descended into the almost pitch-black sewer systems beneath the busy neon streets of Tokyo and winding your way out into the polluted rivers that ran through the expansive metropolis and eventually splashing into Tokyo bay to merge with the ebb and flow of the waters out to sea. What a trip – the Mohawk was never quite the same after that one. I had watched, bug eyed, as he lay on his back in the middle of my single room, kicking and scratching at the air with his eyes closed and a steady trickle of drool descending from the corner of his mouth. When he came to, he told me about his water drop journey and we smoked some more spice to calm his nerves.

Many an evening was spent alone, confined in the tiny Japanese bathroom made for single quarters so as not to stink the non-smoking apartment out with spice smoke. This only added to the claustrophobic and paranoid mindset that would often come from the high, which should almost always be described more as a low. Countless nights had been spent rolling around on the futon, howling and wailing into the blackness for no apparent reason other than my brain was soaked in spice.

Like true fiends, the Mohawk and I found any number of places to smoke spice privately while in the midst of the world's largest and most densely populated metropolis. We would find ourselves wandering the narrow alleys and dark side streets in search of a quiet place to roll and blaze before returning to the teeming crowds; two pale white faces with slack jaws and droopy eyelids. Sometimes the chemical concoctions would induce momentary lapses in consciousness while you were walking across a crowded crosswalk in the centre of the city. You would find yourself walking across a road, surrounded by people, and then suddenly realise that you had taken the last several steps while sleeping.

There were some spice companions who didn't manage to stay on their feet. One such spicer told me of how he had been standing on a busy train, staring at nothing, and then woken up with his head in the lap of a stranger informing him not to panic and that medical assistance was on its way. The news of the imminent arrival of paramedics did indeed induce panic in the poor addict, and he promptly made his escape from the train at the next stop and hurriedly barged his way through the busy station and out into the street to disappear into the crowd. Just another spice junkie lost in Japan.

Over the months of overindulging in the stuff there were more and more news reports of Japanese citizens losing their minds on the semi-legal toxin. Taller and taller tales of people freaking out and getting violent erupted in the mainstream media to scare the population.

On we smoked.

Tokyo

12

While spice was being smoked by stoners unable or incapable of finding weed there was another drug on the market – bath salts. The first-hand descriptions of bath salts from fellow travellers confirmed my lack of interest in trying the powder. Everyone spoke of rushing in an unpleasant way, few even mentioned tendencies towards violence. There were global mainstream media stories of vicious acts perpetrated by users of the drug, including the eating of faces. We stuck to spice, and it stuck to us like a thirsty vampire to its first victim on a cold and moonless night.

On rare and special occasions in the past we had gone through the tedious trials of scoring real weed in Roppongi, Shibuya or Shinjuku, but spice had put an end to that. Scoring real weed was far more of a trial and went as follows:

Take a train and tube journey to the chosen part of Tokyo. For us this took about an hour and a half. Wait all of the half a nanosecond it took for a Nigerian hustler to approach you and ask if you wanted a sexy girl. Tell him no, but you wanted to score some weed instead. Follow the hustler to a lift, which takes you up to a Yakuza-owned strip joint, where a variety of women of varying nationalities will accompany you at an overpriced table while you are cajoled into purchasing extortionately priced and watered-down drinks. Sit and wait. Keep waiting. If you are so inclined and have the cash to burn, chat to the girls and buy them drinks. Eventually, another Nigerian will approach and ask you to follow him to the toilets. Here, you will pay crazy amounts of money for tiny one-gram bags of stale and weak Thai stick. If you're lucky, the bag will be a gram of weed and not a mix of weed, sticks and seeds. The bag, or baggies, should then be placed down your pants or in your footwear for the walk back out into the busy streets where the gaijin and trendy Tokyoites go to play and party. Keep it concealed until you return to your home, and then make sure you are able to smoke it behind closed doors with no smoke detectors ready to sound the alarm or nosy neighbours ready to do likewise.

Occasionally, we'd get lucky and just do a deal in a quiet alley behind the bars, eateries or strip joints. A quick heavy handshake and then all was well and we were on our way. You could be out of there in 15 seconds. Of course, all of this fucking around could be avoided once you meet the right people and make the right connections, but if you're a tourist or don't have the right hook-up that's how it's done, fellow curious travellers.

All of that was redundant for quite some time because spice was just a simple stop in a shop to purchase with no worries of the law tapping you on the shoulder and deporting your arse. Bags of spice were legal to purchase and have on your person so long as the makers had stuck to the rules and printed the words 'not for human consumption' on the packet. When we asked the young Yakuza member working in the shop what it was used for if not for human consumption, he just shrugged his shoulders and explained that all he knew was that he was to tell customers it wasn't to be ingested, even though that's what everyone was blatantly buying it for.

Tokyo

13

The Mohawk and I would regularly purchase our synthetic weed from a store located at the top of some steep steps on the seedy side of Akihabara. This is a famous part of Tokyo. For the mainstream traveller it's famous for electronic goods. For the traveller who wanders down the darker end of the streets, it has a very different side. It doesn't take much of an open mind or open eyes to see the less savoury side of this part of town. There are sex shops and suggestive billboards everywhere. Most Japanese natives never go to Akihabara, as it's known for being an urban sprawl full of techno-geeks and porno-freaks. It's not for regular people.

There are also maid cafes. For those not in the know, a maid cafe is a really shit cafe where the staff are all young females dressed in old-school maid outfits who are ready and willing to serve their master (or mistress), a bit like cosplay only a lot stranger. They're almost all in their teens and have hem lines just below their tiny arses. Maid cafes are in fact innocent places, not just knocking shops disguised as coffee shops like we had first suspected. Groups of Japanese friends, couples and families of tourists can be seen eating and drinking at them. They are just a novelty, much like the cat or owl cafes. And much like these two other novelty venues, the maid cafe has a dark underbelly hidden from the surface and general public. All three styles of cafe are exploiting their workforce, whether it be bird or pussy alike. The owners dress the young girls up in a way that makes you think about more than just coffee and cake. They are encouraged to be happy, subservient and welcoming. They sing, dance and exude an air of innocence that is perversely lusted after by many men in the neon-lit urban sprawl.

There are some places where for the right price you can have the maids serve you privately at a more discreet location, such as a regular hotel or a love hotel. These are where you can pay for four-hour or eight-hour stays. They are mainly used by teenagers who can't fuck at their parents' pad, or by parents who are having affairs.

In order to attract customers, the cafes have the girls stand around the streets and back alleys of Akihabara, handing out fliers and encouraging people to go to their place of business for a beverage or snack. They stand there regardless of the weather, dressed in tiny maid costumes baring their flesh to thousands of ogling strangers, trying their best to attract as many customers as they can to whichever cafe they work for. Most are just regular chicks trying to make some honest money, but others are after more than just minimum wage.

Tokyo

14

The darker side of Akihabara and Tokyo in general is apparent if you dip your toe into Japanese manga or anime. It won't be long before you're seeing a plethora of images involving schoolgirls or maids being violated in any and every way imaginable. Walk down the right street at the right time, and these animated fantasies can be made into reality. Walk down the wrong alley at the wrong time and you will instead be conned into an entirely different experience altogether.

Take the Hitcher for example. He was a guy the Mohawk and I had first met back in Swansea. He had studied at the same time as us for his teaching qualification, and he had a wild side that was attracted to our blatant use of weed and flouting the law. He joined us a couple of times for a smoking session, but his low tolerance meant that he never really remembered much and he never really gelled with us. We'd been in Japan over a year when word got back that the Hitcher had come to work for the same company that employed us. He had gained quite the reputation in a short amount of time... as had we.

The Hitcher was a true free spirit and proper traveller. He had gone to Canada after finishing college and hitched all the way from the east to the west coast. He did the entire distance using only his thumb. No public transport, no rentals, nothing but his thumb and a big set of balls.

In Tokyo, he became infamous after showing those balls to not only a bunch of his co-workers, but also a whole lot of Japanese staff and strangers at a karaoke bar, and then the surrounding neighbourhood. The karaoke bars are very popular in Japan. For foreigners they can also be fun places, either just to sing or more commonly because they are open 24 hours and can be used as a spot to keep drinking on the cheap until the trains start running again the next morning. Japan doesn't have night buses or 24-hour public transport like other cities in the world, so if you miss that last train home a karaoke bar is usually your cheapest option to while away the hours.

One Saturday night the Hitcher had joined some fellow teachers and Japanese staff from the school for a night out. As is the norm, they wound up in a karaoke bar after the trains stopped running. He proceeded to get horribly drunk and then strip naked before deciding he wanted to walk home. The Hitcher had woken up in a public park the following morning, still butt naked and freezing cold with a stinking hangover. To get home he had to steal something from the clothesline in some poor git's garden not far from where he had woken up, and then sneak onto the trains by walking crotch to arse behind strangers going through the gates at stations. His legend quickly spread throughout the company.

It was also the Hitcher that brought awareness to another darker side of Tokyo. Down the right streets during the party hours, there can be seen many men in shirts or suits touting for business. Usually they just want to take you to a bar or strip club or some other seedy joint. Some want to take you to get laid. One late night, the Hitcher had said yes to one of these men and had followed him to a small nondescript doorway where he was charged a fairly large sum of cash. He had been instructed to go through the door and all the way to the top of the stairs where he would meet a beautiful young lady. The Hitcher did as instructed after handing over the yen. But at the top of the steps and through a red-lit door, he was met by something altogether different to what the Japanese fella's sales pitch had led him to expect. Inside there was an almost completely bare room. Its only contents were a used and soiled mattress on the floor, a single red naked bulb dangling from the ceiling and a lot of grime. The Hitcher said that the entire room, floor to ceiling, was covered in crap. The place had obviously seen a lot of action but had never been cleaned. And the same was true for the mattress. Plenty of action, zero cleaning. Then he saw the woman and he said you could describe her in the same way as the room and mattress. Very old, very used and very dirty. He spoke of how he had recoiled in horror when she smiled at him to reveal only gums and a couple of shards that still remained from the teeth she once had. He was almost sick when he saw all of the scabs and bruises on her bare flesh. His nostrils nearly bled when she spoke to him and her breath removed what little paint still remained on the walls.

He said that it was the worst fuck he had ever had.

This was a common thing in Tokyo, and indeed the world over: conning horny male foreigners into thinking they are going to have sex with a hot piece of arse, and then sending them into a room to be met by Tutankhamun's uglier grandmother. It is rare that Johns kick up any kind of a fuss in those scenarios, especially in Tokyo. For in Japan, it is the mindset of the police that the foreigner is always the one who is in the wrong. If a fight breaks out, which it almost never does, and there are white faces anywhere near the fracas, then the police arrest them on sight. You could just be a casual observer to the incident, simply walking past as it all kicked off. It doesn't matter. As far as the Japanese police are concerned, you're part of the problem until you can prove otherwise.

The Mohawk and I had no time for such things. We had spice to smoke. Like many narcotics, as your desire for consuming it grows your interest in other things diminishes. My libido was damn near zero some days. There were nights I would do my usual run into Akihabara after work to purchase another baggy, and somewhere along the way a hot little lady would smile at me and make an offer that would tempt the average swinging dick. But I wasn't interested. I had spice to smoke. I would keep on walking, maybe flash them a smile so as not to be rude or offensive, but that's about as far as it went.

Most street walkers are not pushy in Tokyo. The females will usually just stand in one spot and casually say, "Massage?" as you walk past them. It's the hustlers who are persistent. And by hustlers I mean Nigerians. These guys will walk with you for blocks and blocks, talking nonstop about how they can take you to the best spot with the best girls for the best prices for whatever your heart desires. Most have a pretty funny approach to their hustle and can be very entertaining.

Regardless of who tempts you on the tarmac, there's never any certainty of who'll be getting undressed with you indoors. One visitor to Tokyo said yes to a gorgeous Brazilian hottie in Roppongi one night and was sent into a room with a massage table and a Chinese horse. He was drunk enough and unseasoned enough to actually kick up a fuss, but fortunately it worked out in his favour. The management sent in two of their finest-looking girls to shut him up and make him happy. It was rare nights ended that well in such circumstances. Many a gaijin have been held and the police called to haul their drunken and horny arses away. Japanese cells, like most jails and prisons, are not where you want to end up after a night on the town.

Tokyo

15

Like many jails and prisons all around the world, in
Japan they are unofficially run on the inside by the
gangsters. In the case of Japan, it's the Yakuza.

Like most criminals, whether they be in criminal
organisations like the Mafia or not, Japanese
gangsters like to gamble. And in Japan, the Yakuza
had its origins in gambling. During the Edo period
(1603–1868), there were social outcasts called the
bakuto, which means gamblers, and they were
considered the lowest of the low in decent society.
Over time, they formed into the Yakuza along with
the tekiya, who were the guys who bought and sold
stolen goods. Even the name 'Yakuza' derives from
gambling. In the game of Oicho-Kabu, a card game,
the worst possible three card hand to draw is 8-9-3.
In Japanese these three numbers in the game of
Oicho-Kabu are pronounced ya-ku-sa. So more
than any other criminal fraternity in the world, be
it Bloods and Crips rolling dice on the streets or the
Mafiosa dealing out poker hands, the Yakuza have a
long and intimate history with gambling.

Today, members of the Yakuza either associate
with the tekiya or bakuto, and the entire criminal

organisation shares a strange relationship with society at large. Like the Mafia, the Yakuza have had a long-standing rule that its members never fuck around with what are deemed civilians. Criminals are to only engage in criminal activities with other criminals or members of the law – no outsiders allowed. There exists a strange balancing act between criminals and society as a whole. The presence of the Yakuza in a neighbourhood actually diminishes crime to almost zero. Their presence deters other criminals from setting foot in those areas, yet alone committing crimes there. Society, however, always looks down at these organisations because they are after all earning money from crime.

It was well documented in the mainstream media that after the 2011 Tohoku earthquake and tsunami the Yakuza provided faster aid than the Japanese government, just as they had done after the Kobe earthquake in 1995. Japanese people seldom talk about the Yakuza – it is something that exists but somehow doesn't. Something that acts against the norms and rules of society, and yet rushes to its aid when it needs it the most.

When you prowl the streets at night illuminated by the neon, there can be no doubt in any seasoned traveller's mind that the cat calls he's hearing are mainly coming from whores owned by the Yakuza. One of their trades is supplying women for various carnal pleasures and another is trafficking them for this role. Don't let the knowledge of their good deeds after earthquakes fool you, they are a ruthless criminal organisation through-and-through. The Yakuza have been linked to all manner of shady activities, from porn to extortion to bad hairdos; just check out the punch perm online. Like Japan in general, they have put their own unique twist on the crimes they commit. For example, they don't just extort or offer protection to small businesses, they also buy shares in large companies and then turn up to stockholder meetings. At the latter they have been known to use all manner of intimidation tactics to get the results – and money – that they want. They have been known to threaten CEOs with exposing them as having an affair or other shameful things, whether true or not, in order to coerce them into giving up the goods. As well as petty theft and corporate theft, the Yakuza also have links to some of the biggest thieves in the world. Politicians.

The Yakuza have long had strong links to the uyoku dantai, who are extreme right-wing political groups in Japan. If you visit Tokyo, you will see small black vans cruising around with the old Japanese 'rising sun' flags flapping from them and annoying voices screaming from loudspeakers. These guys want to bring back the good old days of Japanese imperialism, when they invaded China and tried to take over the world. It seems that two atomic bombs just aren't enough of a deterrent for some people.

Hiroshima

1

The Mohawk had had a morbid fascination with
nuclear war for as long as I could remember, so it
was not entirely surprising that he wanted to visit
Hiroshima. He often had strange nightmares that
involved experiencing the fear and drama of a
nuclear blast or surviving one and trying to live in
the post-apocalyptic world. Often these dark
dreams would weave their way into his lyrics when
writing songs and influence his style of music when
recording.

I'd never really liked the thought of it. In school
we had been made to read novels and even watch a
movie that dealt with the subject of nuclear war and
how the world would be afterwards named Threads
made in 1984 – an awful movie for schoolchildren
to watch, or pretty much anyone else for that
matter. For most, the idea of nuclear Armageddon
is terrifying, but for others like me it's simply
abstract and dark in ways that I feel waste my time
thinking about – time that could be better spent
thinking about other things. I have never had a
problem with the darker things in life, but unlike
the Mohawk I've just never been interested in the

subject of atomic annihilation.

I agreed to go with him, not to visit the Hiroshima Peace Memorial Museum like he wanted to, but because we both felt the journey should be made by road. We loved long drives, and from the west of Chiba down to Hiroshima was a hell of a trek.

We made arrangements to rent a car, score some real weed and stock up on spice for the journey. From where we were staying in Kashiwa it was approximately 850 km that should take roughly 11 hours to drive if we didn't make any stops. We had one long weekend – four days – to drive there, see what we wanted to see and then get back in time for work. In the UK, it would be roughly the equivalent of driving to Germany and back.

Accompanying us on our road trip was the Rabbit. He was a weed smoker like us but had only sampled spice on a few rare occasions. He figured that we would be doing a leisurely drive to do some touristy things and wanted to join us, as in all his years in Japan it was one of the cities that he had never had the opportunity to visit. We welcomed him along for the ride and he was grateful. He got into the car, all calm and relaxed, but things would soon go sideways for this little bunny.

Hiroshima

2

We left Kashiwa city in the late afternoon, not being the kind of travellers who set out in the early morn' or anything of that nature – we had to sleep off the effects of the night before to be safe and responsible drivers. The Mohawk and I already knew that we would be splitting the long drive between us for two reasons. One, we enjoyed long drives and wanted to split it fairly. Two, the Rabbit couldn't drive. We picked our new traveller up from his home and we welcomed him into the rented vehicle with smiles and civilised pleasantries. He was happy and looking forward to our trip.

Only hours later, the Rabbit found himself trapped in a car with us two dope fiends. Hurtling down the dark road at 100-plus in a rental car while being hot-boxed with weed and spice fumes, the once ordinary man turned into the Rabbit. A wide-eyed specimen who would be momentarily illuminated by vehicles travelling in the opposite direction of the lonely and mostly deserted highways as we sped to our destination. He was indeed a rabbit trapped in headlights shaking and reacting badly to the sounds of our demonic laughter.

When you do long drives at night in Japan there are seldom fellow travellers on the motorways. Mostly large lorries doing long-haul to make deliveries or pickups. And then there was us in a little silver rental, unfortunately an automatic with a tiny engine, speeding along the outside lane. We couldn't understand the Japanese sat-nav built into the dash but we could use the map to zoom in and out and that was enough to let us know we were headed in the right direction. We would use the road signs, which bore the names of the cities in romaji – Romanised Japanese writing – to know we were on the right track.

When not driving at night, the Mohawk would almost always pass out in the passenger seat to recharge his mental battery before his next turn at the wheel. His navigation skills were always far superior to mine, which often led to me hitting him awake and screaming, "Which fucking way?!" And on the first night of this trip his only response was, "South! Just keep heading south!"

I would nod, wild eyed and very high, before focusing my attention back on the blackness ahead of us. Occasionally I would turn and look into the backseat, where there was almost always the same pair of bulging white terrified eyes of the Rabbit looking back at me. Sometimes he would be under his jacket shielding his face and mind from the terrible reality that he was in a speeding vehicle operated by a very stoned and possibly lost fiend headed to fuck-knows-where.

The fact that the Rabbit was very high didn't help him at all. It made matters even worse for him that we had been spiking him with spice for the entirety of the journey. A cannabis high and a spice high are very different animals. That animal can be terrified when it doesn't understand why it's feeling the way it does despite having smoked weed for many decades. Our backseat cohort was very inexperienced with spice, and now he was doing it unknowingly and in conditions that would be described as less than ideal for such high volumes of any drug consumption. Not only did the Mohawk and I know we were smoking copious amounts of the stuff mixed with weed, but we were used to it and our tolerance was sky high. The Rabbit was not, and it showed in those eyes peering back at us from the blackness in the rear of the car. There were multiple times when he passed on the joint being shared, already knowing that he was past his limit and anymore could be fatal to his sanity. We justified our actions by stating to one another that it was the Rabbit's fault for not sharing the duties of the trip. Not only was he not contributing to the driving, he wasn't navigating or rolling joints either. He was literally just sitting in the back seat, smoking, sleeping and shitting himself. Silly Rabbit.

Hiroshima

3

The journey to Hiroshima consisted of a pit-stop at Nagoya. We didn't really have time to spare for any real sightseeing and touristy things, but we did get a chance for a little walk around and to see Nagoya Castle. The Rabbit used this pit-stop to stretch his legs and try to clear his mind of the skunk and spice psychosis. The Mohawk and I used this time to smoke more and nap.

Something that Japan has lots of, which the UK doesn't seem to have any more, is internet cafes. These are places where people can just go and hire a booth for however long is needed with a PC and internet access. But these places actually offer so much more in Japan.

Some of the booths don't have a chair, instead they have a completely padded floor area, which allows you to sit and surf the net or snooze for a few hours. It is the norm for Japanese people to sit on the floor at home rather than sofas and chairs. They commonly have large floor cushions known as zabutons strewn around their low coffee tables, allowing the family to sit on the ground while enjoying a beverage, watching TV or whatever. At

Internet cafes they have a decent sized padded floor for people to sleep on, or for two stoners like the Mohawk and I to relax on while we smoked more and then pass out for a while.

There are many places in Japan where you can still smoke indoors. In fact, it's easier to smoke indoors than outdoors in Japan. Outside there are very specific designated smoking areas you have to use or face being fined and receiving many a dirty look from a multitude of unhappy strangers.

It is not unusual in Japan for people to use Internet cafes like hotels. If you've missed the last train home and need a place to crash, hire a booth for a few hours or all night. Don't have a place to live? Move into an Internet cafe – as many do. They also have bathrooms, showers, hair-dryers and even washing machines at many cafes. The staff serve food and drink straight to your booth, 24-seven. For high school students who don't have their own place or even a car, they are used for fucking when a love hotel is too expensive or too far away. Not just students, many a co-worker have slipped into an internet cafe for some private lunchtime shenanigans. For us it was a spot to relax while we continued smoking. We even took advantage of the showers on offer as a way of refreshing ourselves before continuing with the lengthy drive we still had to complete over the course of the long weekend.

Hiroshima

4

Today, the city of Hiroshima looks just like any other major Japanese metropolis. It's only the Hiroshima Peace Memorial that really sticks out to let you know of the horror that once took place there, unless of course you head over to the museum. This is a dark and depressing place for anyone who visits, but when you're as fucked up on weed and spice as we were it can be a very gloomy trip inside one's own mind. I never made it all the way through the museum properly. The drugs enhanced the macabre, my fucked-up imagination took my mind to places where it wasn't happy and my lack of interest in the subject matter prevented me from persevering too hard. I ducked out around halfway through and waited for the other two outside in the park, where there was a festival, stores and sunshine to help bring me back up out of the blackness that my psyche had slipped into while walking around the bleak museum. I agree that it is important to remember the terrible things our species has done to one another and learn from these past actions, but I do not agree with using them as tourist attractions.

Hiroshima was bombed by the US on 6 August 1945 after America had obtained consent from the UK, as required by the Quebec Agreement. It was during the final stages of World War II and many say it ended the conflict. That display of immense power put the fear of God into the whole world, and traditional warfare was forever changed.

Others think that the war was already ending, and that the use of such horrific weapons in both Hiroshima and Nagasaki – with an estimated body count of 75,000 – sped nothing up. It contributed nothing to bringing a swifter end to the killing. Some believe that it was simply a world superpower showing off their new toy and ensuring that the entire planet truly understood who the big dog was.

You couldn't help but think about how this weapon had not been used on Nazi Germany. Where Hitler and his top echelon planned and carried out such atrocities as the Holocaust. Where Albert Einstein claimed the Nazis were in fact developing the same weaponry. Maybe it was because Germany is part of Europe and that tests of other nuclear bombs had shown the superpowers of the world that dropping their new toys in the centre of Europe would have meant dire consequences for everyone on the continent. Whereas Japan, an island off the coast of China, was an ideal target for a worldwide display of arguably the ultimate power. At that time they figured there was no risk of any radioactive fallout getting back to the US or any of its allies. Or it may be because Hitler had already been more or less defeated by traditional warfare and it was only the ongoing fight in the Pacific that posed a threat.

The mainstream theory is that America had two reasons for dropping atomic bombs on Hiroshima and Nagasaki. First, to bring about an end to the war without invading Japan and risking large numbers of American soldier's lives on the ground. Second, to show the Soviet Union what it was capable of. The bombs did both of those things. They stopped World War II, but a consequence of this was the beginning of the Cold War. A war where traditional methods were thrown out and the true age of the spy began.

By the time the Mohawk and Rabbit had finished seeing all that the museum had to offer, I was almost sober and straight-headed again. I had spent my time alone in dark introspection, as well as downing energy drinks and chain-smoking cigarettes. I was ready to take my mind off of the horrific past of the city around me.

Remember the past. Learn from the past. But do not dwell on the past. Live in the now.

When they joined me I was ready to sample the local cuisine so that I could leave on a positive and happy note and not remember the place with negativity.

Hiroshima

5

Japan is one of those countries that has different specialty dishes for different prefectures – areas – and a population of hearty eaters. Despite the typical image of the thin Japanese person only eating sushi and rice, there are in reality a variety of differently sized people, and they all love to eat good food. Japan has a lot of it, and the city we were in was known for its okonomiyaki. This is a savoury pancake cooked on an iron hotplate that can contain all manner of ingredients, depending on where you are and what you're into.

The name comes from 'okonomi', which means 'how you like' or 'what you like', and 'yaki', which means 'cooked'. So it roughly translates in English as 'what you like cooked' or 'cook it how you like it'. This is a pretty good name considering the numerous variations on the dish that exist. Okonomiyaki always contains egg, chopped veggies and either meat or seafood, or sometimes a combination of the two, and then topped off with a savoury-sweet sauce. In Hiroshima it is bulked up by adding either soba or udon noodles. The dish has been described as the 'Japanese pizza' due to the way it looks, but in reality it tastes absolutely nothing like it.

We were in Hiroshima during the right season to have local oysters added as a topping. There are numerous different options that you can chose from depending on the region, city or restaurant that you're eating in. We were at a typical indoor okonomiyaki stall where you sit on tall stools at a horseshoe counter that has the iron hotplate running the length of the entire thing. You sit and watch the chef prepare and cook your dish right there in front of you, and then you eat it straight off the iron.

By the time we were finished stuffing our stoner faces it was time to smoke another J on the road. We decided to cut through the famous cities of Osaka and Kyoto on the way back to Chiba prefecture. We'd all visited these cities before as tourists on foot, and now wanted to experience driving through these historic places while off our nuts on spice and THC.

We took a few wrong turns and wound up driving some pretty narrow and intense roads, some of which even took us through fields used for growing crops and only having tiny concrete tracks running through them originally meant just for pedestrians or cyclists. Of course, the Mohawk and I traversed the tarmac unfit for automobiles like we were professionals and not the two fiends flying by the skin of our teeth like we always did. In the back seat the Rabbit simply gritted his teeth and shut his eyes to the majestic wonder of our natural surroundings. There was lush green all around the car and sticky green being rolled and inhaled within.

The Rabbit, like the White Horse back in Llanelli, was another specimen not built for such travels. The Mohawk and I pushed on regardless.

The Hiroshima road trip had been an interesting and thankfully uneventful experience. By the time we were speeding back into Chiba prefecture the Mohawk and I were running on less fumes than the little 1.3 litre engine that powered the rental. Our eyes told the tale of travellers that hadn't slept enough and had instead relied on narcotics, energy drinks and true grit to see them back home safe and sound. We drove those last miles like maniacs, weaving in and out of the other traffic like something from a Jason Statham movie. There was little interest in the rules of the road or the safety of other drivers, our mission was simple by that point: put your foot down and get us back as quickly as possible so that we can pass out on our beds and sleep for at least a full 12 hours before we had to return to our day jobs.

When the Rabbit departed from us he looked shook up and in need of couch time with a therapist. We looked like we needed a lot of vitamins and rest, but instead I rolled one last J before bed.

Tokyo

16

After several years living in Chiba prefecture and working in Tokyo it was time to leave. My spice addiction had pushed me to looking and feeling like the stereotypical junkie. I never had any money to my name and my complexion was starting to look sallow and worn. Just like when I had been living in London, I had pushed myself close to breaking point and was lucky enough to have the mental faculties to tell me that enough is enough and a new day needed to begin. I never contemplated going back to the UK, as far as I was concerned that was in the past and I was a global citizen now. I needed a new country and new adventures. I also needed money, which is how I came to find out about jobs going in the most unexpected of places.

The Mohawk and I celebrated my departure with copious amounts of spice, as I was completely off the alcohol by that point. The desire to clean my act up had been slowly creeping up on me like a bad memory of something you've forgotten to do. First, I gave up alcohol and then I started exercising again. The spice, however, continued to flow. Like any experienced traveller knows, to truly kick a habit it's best to change locations. This helps you to sever all physical and mental ties to a substance and all that you associate with it.

Moving both in and out of a home in Japan is expensive. When you vacate a rented property you should leave nothing more than the four walls and fixtures. You shouldn't even leave bulbs in the sockets. The country has very strict policies about disposing of rubbish too, so I pissed off the authorities and landlord no end when I departed and left furniture that I couldn't sell in the pad and general rubbish and waste out in the street. I had been living alone for a few years by that point, as the White House had been sold by the company we worked for and subsequently demolished by the new owners. The Mohawk was now in a serious relationship with his girlfriend and had decided to settle down to start a family, so I continued solo.

Now, I was departing properly. After the White House we had lived no more than a 20-minute journey from one another, but after years of spice abuse we were saying fond farewells before I boarded my plane at Narita for a flight that would ultimately land me in one of the most conservative countries on the face of the planet.

Saudi Arabia

Al Khobar

1

"After 24 hour, you call number," the man behind the desk waved his hand at the paper he had just placed in front of me. "Okay? You call."

"And is there a reference number? Should I ask for you by name?"

"Yes, yes, after 24 hour you call." The Saudi customs agent returned to his telephone call as he stretched his legs and placed his shoes on the counter before him. As I didn't speak any Arabic and the only person on duty blatantly wasn't going to take any further action to find my lost suitcase I decided to leave.

It had been a long flight from London, where it had taken months to obtain my new visa to teach English in the desert, and an almost as long a delay to register my arrival at immigration without the added torture of having to wait next to a clapped-out old conveyer belt that never revealed my suitcase – like the most disappointing of game shows that displays an empty box to the unlucky contestant. Between the drive, flight and then a transfer in the shithole known as Istanbul Airport, I had been traveling for around 15 hours. I had then spent a further three and a half hours at immigration, along with close to 200 other weary travellers all waiting for the lazy men dressed in all white to sloppily do their duties between sips of tea or coffee. My time at the side of the luggage belt just felt like that extra kick in the nuts when you're already down on the floor with a broken nose. No sense in starting a fight, be it verbal or with fists, only hours after my arrival into the most conservative country on the planet. Especially not for a suitcase of grubby old clothes.

Time for the next adventure – getting from the airport to my new home. Through the sliding doors was a wall of dark-skinned faces all yelling in foreign dialect. My white skin and lack of robes stood out. As I strolled into the parting at the centre of the waiting crowd I spotted a sign bearing my company's name and logo being loosely held by a dark-skinned man in jeans and a shirt. The man smiled at me, "Hi."

"Hi. You're with the company?"

"Yes, I'm H. Nice to meet you." The sign-bearer smiled widely.

"Nice to—"

"Where are your bags?" H asked as he peered behind me.

"They lost my suitcase. I gotta phone this number tomorrow," I informed him as I held the folded paper out in front of me.

"Okay. The other guy's..." H spun around looking for someone as his sentence trailed off. Amidst the near crowd floated a straw hat. H waved at the hat to come over. As it moved closer I could see the string of the hat ran down the side of the arms of a pair of glasses and then a chubby white face that bottomed out to a huge toad-like chin below pursed lips.

"Pip-pip old chap, how the devil are you?" The Hat clicked his heels together, Dorothy-style, while giving a slight nod. "Found H okay I see."

"He walked straight past me. I found him wandering around just before you came," H informed me as he smiled awkwardly at the man. The Hat was oblivious to the subtle insult. "Okay, shall we go?" H asked rhetorically as he walked away from us and we followed.

"I say old bean, where's your suitcase?"

Al Khobar

2

It was late at night and there was a distinct lack of lighting on the highway that ran from the airport back to civilisation, which prevented me from seeing the country that I would now be calling home. This was no great loss, as when you call the desert your home the view does tend to consist mainly of sand dunes.

H, like all of the other drivers on the highway, drove at high speed and seemed to care little for things like safety and rules of the road. This kind of driving suited me, the only things missing were weed and loud music to make this a more familiar experience. My fellow traveller clearly didn't feel the same way. The Hat clung to the door handle with one hand and dug the fingernails of his other hand into the upholstery, only ever letting go to check the seat belt was still fastened correctly or wipe the sweat from his brow. His fear was blatant, amusing and amplified by the silence that filled the Toyota Fortuner that sped along the dark asphalt in 35 degree heat at three o'clock in the morning.

I sat and pondered whether or not my suitcase actually had been lost or was just kept to be searched by the authorities of this extremely conservative kingdom. I should've probably been worried that they might plug my external hard drive into a computer and see the gigabytes of illegally downloaded music, movies and pornography. I had no idea how long the authorities would be holding my case, or if it was indeed lost how long it would take to be found again.

I came to learn that in this desert kingdom knowing the right person can make all the difference in how long it takes to get anything done or if it ever will be done. In Arabic it is called wasta, which in English is jokingly translated to mean vitamin W. If you know someone somewhere who can get things done for you, then you have vitamin W. If you don't know someone somewhere, then you need to get yourself some vitamin W. I had no wasta at the airport or anywhere else in the Kingdom of Saudi Arabia, and I could only hope that someone at the company employing me did.

The Hat and I were dropped off at different compounds by H and were left with a small welcome pack with instructions to meet a driver at this location early the next morning. And that was that. Dropped outside the big but hardly secure-looking gate of a small compound in the early hours of the morning.

A small Indian man dressed in a shirt and trousers opened a door beside the gate as he looked at me sternly.

"Yes, can I help you sir?"

"I'm moving in?" I said it more as a question than a statement. I'd been given no information. "Please follow me. Your name sir?" The Indian man disappeared back into the compound. I looked up and down the street I was on. There appeared to be some more small compounds next to this one and a hotel on the corner, but other than that there was just dirt, some houses and a highway in the distance. I entered the compound and dealt with the Indian. Thankfully, they were expecting me and the compound was ready for my arrival. My grand welcome consisted of being given my key and told which number I lived in. Nothing else. No being led to my new front door, no tour, no information – just a key and a number. I left the small office situated between the entrance and exit gates of the doughnut-shaped compound. As I walked the palm tree-lined road that circled the compound I tasted the dust in the air of this new and foreign land.

My flat was situated in a small building tucked into the corner of the compound, away from the main circle of the doughnut that consisted of the extremely expensive and large houses that overlooked the outdoor pool and seating area available for residents to use. My duplex flat had one tiny window located at the bottom of the stairs that let hardly any light in at all. This window, combined with my evening working hours and my lack of a desire to spend time outside in the 50-plus desert heat, led to me having a vitamin D deficiency. Bloody typical – in a country renowned for sunshine I couldn't get enough of a vitamin produced by sunlight. If the flat window had been bigger I would have probably had all of the sunshine required and then some, as I spent most of my time sprawled on the couch that was located directly in front of the minuscule glass pane. Lounging on one of the chairs around the picturesque outdoor swimming pool would have been the ideal place to get THC and vitamin D at the same time, but alas not only was cannabis illegal in this part of the desert but they also had a reputation for cutting peoples' heads off for possession of the infamous plant and its various derivatives. This meant that relaxing by the pool and getting high were never to mix.

I spent much of my first night climbing around my new flat trying to find a spot where I could effectively siphon my neighbours' wifi. Fortunately, I had packed my laptop in my hand luggage, so it had not been lost along with all my other belongings. I discovered that if I stood on my bed and held my laptop above my head it would connect to the internet. I set about raising the computer to load pages and then dropping down into a crossed-leg sitting position to do things on the screen, and then immediately bolting upright to raise the laptop aloft again for another connection to the outside world.

I grew up in a time when there was no internet. My generation were the first to really start having it integrated into our daily lives and it being an everyday thing. Despite having spent at least half of my life without having access to it, it is surprising how dependent I had become on the internet. The thought of spending my first night in a new country with no connection to the outside world didn't go down well with me. This led to the ridiculous climbing and walking over everything in my new flat looking for that free connection. After sending some emails I decided to smoke a cigarette. I knew I was living in a conservative country with foreign customs. I knew I was living in accommodation paid for by an employer I hadn't met yet. I knew I was living on a compound that my employer rented a flat in. I did not know whether or not I could smoke in my new home. I decided to go for a walk around the compound to both smoke and also take in my new surroundings and the place that I would be calling home. The small gated community was like a ghost town at that time in the morning, and I would soon come to learn that it was always like that. When I saw the Indian again I asked him if smoking in my flat was permitted and he laughed. I would also come to learn that in this country some rules mean very little.

Al Khobar

3

The first week at the new office was pretty standard. Get to know the ropes and the other staff, don't cause problems, appear to be indispensable whenever possible. The main thing to get used to was the relentless heat. Summers in Japan had been hot, but this was on a whole other level. Summers in Japan had been extremely humid; that first summer in the desert was dry. Dry and in the 50s – centigrade not Fahrenheit. One of my corporate students once played me and a boardroom full of Saudi students a video of one of his friends frying an egg on the bonnet of his Jeep. Yes, it was literally hot enough to fry an egg on the bonnet of a car in the summertime. And this wasn't an extraordinarily hot summer, this was just summer. The whole room found it extremely funny to watch the face of the whitey as he watched the egg fry.

In the Eastern Province summers aren't always dry. Because of its proximity to the gulf coast summers are often humid. A humid desert summer is a whole other beast to deal with in comparison to a humid subtropical summer. You don't have as much water running off your body, but you do have to deal with the dust trapped in the air. The whole city turns into a giant oven where you can literally chew the air that you're breathing. An altogether alien climate for a Welshman.

Something that becomes immediately apparent to British people in this part of the world is the lack of pavements to walk on. The whole country seems to drive everywhere, which seems strange until the summer kicks in. Then the thought of being outside for any reason seems entirely unreasonable. Suddenly you become acutely aware of why there are so few pavements and paths and why everyone drives everywhere in their air-conditioned cars. For me, the only reason not to go walking anywhere was the heat, but for my colleagues there was an entirely different reason: fear.

When I had announced to people that I was going to accept a job offer teaching English in Saudi Arabia everyone said it was the worst idea I had ever had. Every single person I knew (except for the Mohawk) told me that the Kingdom of Saudi Arabia was too dangerous to go to. All of my family, friends and former co-workers informed me of the perils and stupidity of such an idea. I responded the same way to everyone. I would ask two simple questions, knowing full well that the answer to both would be 'no' and more than sufficient as evidence to not heed any warnings from them. My first question: 'Have you ever been to Saudi Arabia?' and my second question: 'Do you know anyone who has been to Saudi Arabia?' The responses to these questions would then lead me to point out that the only reason people had such a negative view of the desert kingdom was because of all the biased negative propaganda spread by the western media. Sure, Saudi has its bad points like any country, but as far as I was concerned there was no reason to believe that living there would result in killing, kidnapping, beheading or any other kind of increased mortal danger. I quickly made the decision to go and see for myself if the kingdom was dangerous or not.

Before the end of my first week I had made the walk from the office to the Corniche, which took a mere 30 minutes at a leisurely stroll. The Corniche is as close to a tourist spot as Saudi really gets, but for Westerners it's just a path running parallel to the sea with a few cafes and restaurants along it. Nothing special. If you like Starbucks and McDonalds it's fine, but other than that it's just a path and a view of the sea – a sea that you can't swim in due to the pollution that officially doesn't exist, but unofficially everyone is aware of. The walk took you along the edge of Khobar central, which was a mixture of American grid-style layout and third world one-way narrow roads lined with shops and the usual things found in a city centre. The whole of the country had adopted the American layout and driving system, which makes things much easier once the streets are numbered and named; this had only recently happened. I came to learn that not even one year before my arrival there had been no street signs or house numbers – there were names for areas and also landmarks. That was it.

By week's end I had explored most of the city centre on foot, and during my first weekend I had got a taxi to drive to the city limits to South Street, which is where all of the Shisha cafes had to be due to the laws imposed upon these businesses by the government, who had declared them illegal within city limits, but not the country.

The taxi driver had to phone his office for directions to South Street as he had never in all his 12 years living and driving in the area been there before. His job on paper was a house driver, but as his sponsor was also the head of the police force for the entire Eastern Province he was also permitted to earn extra cash as a taxi driver for foreign nationals. No expat had ever asked him to take them to this part of the province before.

When we arrived he asked if I really wanted him to drop me off here. The area looked like something from a post-apocalyptic movie. An imitation of a road, which was lined with cafes and surrounded by abandoned vehicles of all makes and models. Some had almost disintegrated due to being left out in the harsh climate for so long, while others had been smashed up and torched. All kinds of rubbish and detritus was scattered across the sand. The driver tried to convince me that it would be better not to be here alone, and that I should return another day with friends. I paid the fare and informed him I'd call when I was ready to leave.

I stepped out of the car into this end-of-the-world environment and made my way to the nearest cafe. A giant neon sign bore the shape of a hookah and the name of the place in Arabic. The taxi slowly crawled away, the Indian driver's gaze fixed on me with a look of horror in his eyes.

I strode confidently into the fine establishment with walls lined with plasma televisions, large plush chairs and extremely attentive staff who all spoke great English. I ordered the most expensive flavour shisha they had – double apple – and a coffee. The two were delicious. I connected to the free wifi, breathed giant mouthfuls of sweet-scented smoke and drank a lot of Arabic coffee while Skyping friends and surfing the net. After several hours I called the Indian taxi driver to fetch me. Upon arrival he immediately asked, "Are you okay sir?"

Al Khobar

4

The weeks rolled by and I learned more and more about both the city I lived in and the country it was situated in. Something that stood out to me immediately were the roads, and what a contrast people's attitudes when driving were to when they were on foot. Every single journey I went on I saw crazy, aggressive driving that had an insane Mad Max feel to it, made all the more real because of the sand and sun. People would immediately begin smashing their palms on the horns of their cars the instant a traffic signal turned green, regardless of whether or not the cars in front had started moving. Traffic tore down hard shoulders, inside lanes and every other route at top speed everywhere you looked, occasionally in the wrong direction. Speed cameras flashed with an almost strobe-like effect along the highways. There were car crashes every time you were on the road – vehicles would constantly cut each other up and there's the never-ending sound of horns blasted at each other. Driving was considered extremely stressful by most expats and something that was to be avoided by most sensible people.

The largest oil company in the kingdom is called Aramco, and they funded and released a short but extremely informative video stating the statistics of road deaths in the country and comparing them to the death tolls of all of the military conflicts that were occurring in the Middle-East. The number of people who had died on asphalt in Saudi Arabia far exceeded the number of people who had died in wars and theatres of combat by a long margin.

In the kingdom there are three flavours of piggies – the regular police, the religious police and the traffic police. The regular mob have a reputation for what they may do to criminals that get on their bad side by way of a saying that roughly translates to English as 'being buried behind the Sun'. What this means in less prosaic terms is that the police bury bodies in the desert and you'll never be found.

The religious police have a reputation for being miserable old fuckers who consider everything except praying to be bad and worthy of a beating with a wooden stick that they handily carry. These guys are the reason Saudi has the poor reputation that it has in foreign countries. Whenever you hear of inhumane acts, fevered anti-western rhetoric and extreme violence, it's almost always related to these fossils. By the time I visited the kingdom they had been stripped of any kind of real authority and were seldom seen in public places. They were no longer allowed to carry sticks and megaphones, no longer permitted to interact with the public and were more or less confined to mosques and other secluded places to be alone in their religious devotion.

The traffic police stand in stark contrast to their fellow brothers of law enforcement. The traffic pigs have a reputation for being the most lazy and corrupt police force ever squeezed into a uniform. I have seen countless boy racers speed past traffic police and not so much as cause the officer to look up from his phone. The few stories I did hear of traffic police actually stopping someone always ended in the officer taking a bribe and sending the offender on their merry way. This is why there is little to no crime in Saudi Arabia, although their roads are covered in more blood than your average war zone.

Over time I would ask natives why they drove like cunts, and yet when on foot they were some of the most docile and polite people on the planet. The contrast between a Saudi in person and when they get behind the wheel of a car is only believable when seen with your own eyes. It is like night and day. They would only ever answer my questions with a smile and a laugh, sometimes with an 'I don't know. My people are crazy', followed by a loud 'Ha-ha-ha-ha-ha.'

While many Saudis own and drive large Japanese and American 4x4s due to the awful conditions of the tarmac and their love of going off-road into the desert, the Eastern Province is famous for other vehicles. Dammam, Dhahran and Khobar are known for speed and muscle. If you want to buy a Dodge Charger, you go to the East. If you want to buy a Lamborghini, you visit the East. Not five minutes from the compound I lived in there was a road lined with car dealers. Outside the dealerships you could see all manner of shiny metal beasts just begging to be bought and manhandled like a teen porn star who had signed an airtight clause in a contract. For a young man from Wales, the idea of owning an American muscle car is considered a fool's dream. But for a young man living on the East coast of Saudi Arabia, the idea is easily turned into a reality.

In less than two months I was tearing up the tarmac in my very own bullet-grey, twin big bore exhaust, limited edition GT 2004 Ford Mustang. It was a beast of the most ferocious kind. A V8 that shook the windows in the flats around where I parked it inside the compound. Its 4.6-litre engine went through guzzoline like a Welshman goes through beer on a stag-do. Its 260-horsepower vibrated its surroundings like there actually were 260 mustangs charging past. And this is what I would use to pick up and transport hashish in.

Al Khobar

5

In the Old World the Arabs didn't have tobacco to roll joints with, so hashish was simply eaten – the world's first edible. It wasn't until the 1500s that tobacco came about and Arabs could blaze a joint properly. Its production and use has been traced as far back as Ancient Persia where it was used for ceremonial reasons for many centuries. Some believe it was the Mongols who brought it with them on horseback from India where it was known as charas, before the 1206–1227 ad reign of Genghis Khan.

Today it is smuggled by numerous people, usually by boats across the Gulf of Oman, the Arabian Sea and the Gulf of Aden. It starts its journey in either Afghanistan, Pakistan or India, where it is transported in 4x4s due to the harsh driving conditions of the mountains where the plants grow.

Local farmers harvest their crops and then undergo the process of extracting and packing the resin before sending it, and the buds, off to all parts of the world, including their domestic market where it is very, very popular.

When the Saudis went to war with Yemen in 2015 the amount of hashish in the kingdom dropped to almost nothing. This had been the long-time favourite route for smugglers to bring hash across the water to the smoker. Most smugglers wouldn't bother trying to sail through the Gulf of Aden and on to the Red Sea, where they would have direct access to the kingdom. Instead, it was easier to step onto the dry and dusty land in Yemen and then transport it in Jeeps across the damn-near open border and then to anywhere in Saudi you wanted to sell it. Of course, other routes were eventually found that didn't involve the danger of a bomb dropping on your head from the Saudi forces. First, the gear came back low in quality and high in price, but eventually things evened out again.

For people outside of the kingdom, Westerners in particular, it is almost impossible to believe that hash is so widely available – and popular – in this most conservative of countries. But for the right kind of traveller with his or her eyes open it's here to be found, purchased and smoked in large amounts. For the average Westerner, the only tales of hash in the Middle East they have ever heard of is that of the infamous Hashashin – the holy sect of Islamic extremists made popular through entertainment such as video games and movies.

Al Khobar

6

The Hashashins were assassins who came about sometime around 1090 and were eventually driven underground by the Mongols in about 1256. They were a cult-like group who were formed in most part to contend with the invading whities during the Crusades. Their tactics and skills ensured their name would live on for centuries. They were one of the most feared bands of killers to have ever existed anywhere in the world.

A popular Muslim by the name of Hassan-i Sabbāh from Persia gathered followers who were vehemently religious, and he taught them how to hide, disguise themselves, fight and kill. He taught them all the tricks of the espionage trade, starting with know your target inside-out, be able to blend in anywhere and always gather as much intelligence as you can before carrying out your attack. He taught them how to use a multitude of weapons as well as how to fight with their bare hands, but they became famous for their use of the dagger. Hassan-i Sabbāh used his small army of highly skilled killers to manipulate politics, economy, the direction of religion and the outcome of the Holy War raging across Jerusalem known as the Crusades.

His troops, or assassins, were called Fida'i, which translates roughly as 'self-sacrificing agent'. The reason behind this name was because the assassin would always stick around and fight to the death after they had killed their target. They would kill royalty and high ranking members of society out in the open, and then stand and fight the soldiers, guards and whoever else rushed to the aid of the fallen target. The Hashashins never lived to tell their tales. They killed their targets and then fought to their own bloody and brutal deaths. If there was nobody there to fight then they took their own lives. These men sometimes spent years living and working for their targets like sleeper agents before taking them out and meeting their own demise. They would try to ensure that they never got arrested by fighting fiercely and killing anyone who approached, so that those who remained only had the one choice of taking the assassin out. There were some who didn't manage to end their own lives after their mission was complete, but extremely few.

Some say the name Hashashins came about because of Hassan-i Sabbāh's use of hash. He didn't eat it to chill out of an evening in his castle fortress in Alamut, Persia. No, he would slip it to the young men who he had almost convinced to join his deadly cult. While they were knocked out on hash he would take them to a luscious green garden, complete with waterfalls and a little river, where they would be surrounded by cool air, bountiful food and water as well as a bunch of scantily clad prostitutes up for anything. Hassan would tell the young man that they were in heaven, and that if he ever wished to return here he would have to obey Hassan, be a devout Hashashin and die carrying out a successful assassination. Of course, for some young Arab dude whose entire life had been spent in the harsh climate of the Middle Eastern desert surrounded by sand and other men, this was a paradise too good to give up. They would devote themselves 100% to Hassan in the hopes of returning to eternal paradise in death for the order of the Hashashin.

Others say that the word 'hashishi' came about as a derogatory term to use against the Syrian Nizari Ismailis, who were Shi'i Muslims. It was used as a term to denote someone as no good because they ate hashish.

Others think that it derived from a misunderstanding of a similar sounding word in Arabic to denote Hassan'i Sabbah's title as a leader. Some historians believe that Marco Polo, and the Crusaders, misunderstood some pronunciation and then rumours spread as far and wide as Europe with the returning knights of Arabs using hashishi.

In the 21st century, it was still young men who were consuming hash. But now we were heating it up, dropping it into a pile of tobacco, mixing it up – much like you make a mix for a bong in the UK – and then rolling it in a Rizla. We weren't being fooled with false paradises, just getting a mellow buzz on to go about the day and night in the real world.

Al Khobar

7

In modern-day Saudi, getting caught with rolling papers is no different to getting caught with hashish itself. You can't buy rolling papers or rolling tobacco in the kingdom, only packets of cigarettes. To purchase papers you have to find a little market or corner store, preferably run by Pakistanis, and then discreetly ask them for papers and make the internationally recognised hand gesture for rolling a J. If they sell them, and there are no other customers around, you'll get the small but wide papers that you need. If you are caught with papers or puff, then prison is probable. You may be lucky and get a piggy who can be bribed, but only if you can communicate well enough.

The way the judicial system works in the kingdom is that punishments are always done in threes. They still have capital punishment, but you have to be convicted of the same crime three times to earn a decapitation. If a death sentence is not warranted there is always the option of hacking off a limb. For hashish, you get an automatic seven year sentence the first time that you are caught with it, and that is doubled to 14 years should you be unlucky enough to get caught a second time. Get caught a third time and it's off with your head in public at the now infamous 'chop-chop square' in the country's capital city. In many countries around the world today it is a decriminalised or legal substance, but in the desert you can still go down for many, many years or even lose your head for just having a few grams in your pocket.

Al Khobar

8

The Fox had been a student of mine. His English was already advanced, but his company wanted him to be as fluent as possible so they sent him for night classes with us. We both smoked cigarettes and got to know each other standing outside and enjoying a smoke with a cup of coffee during the break between lessons. At some point I had mentioned that it didn't bother me living without alcohol in Saudi Arabia because I had quit drinking alcohol before coming to live and work in the desert. Like all Muslims he nodded approvingly and said this was a good thing, despite the fact that he regularly enjoyed a drink at the weekends over in the Kingdom of Bahrain, an island state in the Persian Gulf and Saudi's equivalent of Las Vegas.

Our friendship developed and it was the Fox who offered to help me buy the muscle car I yearned for. I'd mentioned weeks earlier that I was in the market to buy one but was just waiting for my money to come through as I had already received my driver's license. The Fox was kind enough to drive me around to check various cars that were for sale, as well as take a look at them with me; his knowledge of motors being far better than mine as well as his ability to speak Arabic to the sellers.

One day while out checking a less than attractive car I mentioned in passing how I would be going to Amsterdam that summer for a friend's stag party. He asked me why I would go to such a party if I didn't drink alcohol – he had heard that these were messy affairs that involved huge volumes of liquor being consumed. Seems like the British's reputation for hard drinking is known even in the most conservative of nations. I shrugged and said that I didn't have to drink to enjoy my time with my friends.

"Maybe you will do other things, no?" he said with a sly smile and rise of an eyebrow.

I laughed.

I trusted the Fox but hadn't known him that long. I was in a country that I believed killed people for smoking weed, so I wasn't going to make it a topic of casual conversation.

"Come on man," he said, still smiling, but now holding back the laughter.

"What?"

"What? You know what. Amsterdam, man."

"Like I said, I don't have to drink to have a good time."

"So what will you do?"

"There are more ways to have fun in Amsterdam than just drinking, dude."

We both laughed. It was obvious we knew that the other smoked weed. However, we were both being cautious not to say anything too incriminating for fear of reading the situation wrongly and paying a hefty toll.

"So, you...?" He smiled broadly and made a joint rolling motion with his free hand, the other still resting on the steering wheel of his Toyota as we cruised through the city.

"That's illegal here, no?" I said with a sly smile. We both laughed hard.

"Fuck it," the Fox said before raising the arm rest between us to reveal a small compartment behind the handbrake. From within he retrieved a small lump of hashish. "So, you...?" he laughed.

I hooted loudly at this latest revelation. I had officially met my first weed smoker in the desert. Things were about to get interesting.

I learnt over the next few months just how rife hashish is in the kingdom. They love it in the desert. Maybe it's the lack of entertainment and things to do, maybe it's a desire to express their wilder sides, who knows? But one thing is for sure – there is a lot of hashish going into the desert kingdom and being smoked, particularly by young males. I was once told that if I wanted to score some puff I should just ask the first teenager that I saw.

Of course, like everywhere in the world price and quality can vary greatly. Fortunately for me, the Fox was a connoisseur of the sticky black bricks and only bought top-quality smoke.

The hash smelled amazing, both before and after heating it up. Unlike soap bar, this had a bluish haze to the smoke as a genuine signal of the real potency of the puff. It had a very heavy head to it and would numb you for hours at a time. I spent many a weekend in those days flat on the couch, staring glassy eyed at the large TV screen opposite me, not speaking, watching, listening or thinking; just being and working on my vitamin D deficiency.

I thought paranoia would ruin the high for me the first few times that I smoked alone in my flat. The fear of being in a country known for decapitating recidivist drug users would be enough to give any toker the fear, and yet it didn't happen. I stood at the single, tiny window in my flat on the third floor facing a quiet road, blowing the sweetly scented smoke out into the desert air unnoticed and uninterrupted both day and night.

The weekends are not Saturday and Sunday in the desert. When I was there, the weekend was Friday and Saturday. It had only changed months before I arrived. The previous way of having the weekend on Thursday and Friday had been causing international business too much trouble, as it meant they were unable to do any trading four days a week. Eventually the king made the decision to change the days, and without any prior warning or notification he woke up and announced to the whole nation that the weekend was now changing to Friday and Saturday effective immediately.

For Muslims, Friday is a holy day, much like Sunday is for Christians. Nothing is open before 4.00 pm except maybe for some small local stores. Most of the country stays in bed or relaxing at home. The roads and highways are damn near deserted on Fridays until around two or three in the afternoon. This meant I had no fear of being seen or caught puffing out of my window or walking around outside baked physically and mentally, both in the midday sun and by the THC. There were no workers around, in fact there was no one around. The cities were silent and deserted. Sometimes I would go and smoke on the roof of my building. At night it was a very safe thing to do so, as there were no workers or staff to see or catch you, but during the day it was a completely foolish idea... except on Fridays. Standing on the roof, staring over a city in the desert while stoned out of my brain was a surreal experience. Smoking for so many years in Wales it would have been hard to imagine getting stoned while looking out over the sand and feeling the hot sun on your face. And yet there I stood and smoked. I'd grown up in Wales in a working class family, dropped in and out of the drug game and now stood in the desert sun smoking a fat joint of hash looking out over the rooftops of a compound and at the tower blocks that mingled with mosques that represented a religion known for its Draconian measures against people who smoke joints.

When you're in the birthplace of a religion you can't help but think about the topic of theology, the various religious texts and even the extremists that represent the various faiths. Sure, I'd turned my back on all such delusions decades earlier, but standing there in the sun stoned out of my mind it was hard not to think about the topic as the sand blew against my skin. How had I arrived at that place? Fate? Devine intervention? Freewill and dumb luck? Was there more to religion than I had been giving it credit for? The fact that so many vehemently believe in one faith or another – approximately 75% of the world's population according to some figures – and that the holy texts have all been around for so long and read by so many meant that it had to mean something, no? Carl Gustav Jung said something along the lines of the Old and New Testaments being representations of the times they were written in. They were both literal and metaphorical in their depictions of the world and the times the writers of the text were alive. This is why the Old Testament God is harsh and cruel: he represents how the writers viewed life and their world at that time – a difficult and unforgiving place where a fuck-up would mean you pay the ultimate price. The New Testament granted more powers to the king, a sign of a shift in power. Islam was the youngest of the major religions, and according to the author Christopher Hitchens it copied extensively from the older texts. The young faith taught that nothing happens without the will of the creator, which is terrifying when you consider all of the evils of this world. Sure, it would have been an easy way to deny responsibility for my act of standing on the rooftop smoking a joint, but deep down I knew differently. I was stood there enjoying that sweet smoke because I fucking loved it. I and me alone put me there with that fat biff between my dry lips.

Al Khobar

9

As usual, things started out small. I'd buy a little for the weekend and then stay straight-headed for work during the week. It wasn't long before I was rolling my breakfast and consuming it on the way to the office. When the Fox realised how much I could smoke, and the fact that I had the balls to drive around with a brick of hashish in my car, he spoke to me about stepping up to the next tier. The conversation started in an unusual way.

"I have to ask you something, man," the Fox said to me one evening as we cruised the city smoking in his 4x4. "You really a teacher?"

I didn't know how to answer that at first. My initial thought was that he was having a laugh, making a joke about my style of teaching or the fact that I puffed – fair enough, it's not something most people associate with teachers.

"What do you mean?" I had to ask.

"You don't do some other kind of business?"

"Like what?"

"Come on man. Just answer the question, this is serious."

"I'm just an English teacher, dude."

"Really? That's it?"

I nodded confirmation and observed my companion with curious eyes. He went on to tell me stories he had heard about the British government using the role of a teacher as a cover for their spies. It's true that in Russia in 2008 British Council employees had been accused of espionage, but to the best of my knowledge that had been a one-off. The whole idea made me laugh hard. A dope fiend such as myself being a respected language teacher for a reputable firm was one thing, but to be mistaken for double-oh-seven... very amusing. There are foreign governments that still believe that some language schools are actually fronts for spy agencies. Some more tyrannical countries of the world even have stricter and harsher administrative applications for Westerners applying for visas as English teachers, due to firm beliefs that they would eventually turn out to be spies. It's true that English language teaching had originally started out as part of the foreign office of the British government, but for completely different reasons to spying. The correct word was slavery. Well, slavery in the guise of colonialism at least. The UK discovered that it made far more sense to have conquered natives understand your commands rather than constantly having to beat and kill them because of a lack of compliance, which was ignorantly first thought of as resistance rather than a language barrier. So the easy choice had to be made – learn the foreigners' languages or teach them English. And so the world of English as a Foreign Language was created.

"So you are not scared to drive around my city with the stuff?" he asked with a sly smile.

"Do I look scared?"

"That's good. But you know your car is very..." he trailed off, looking for the right words. "How do you say? The fucking police like to stop your kind of car man. It's fast, it's loud, they love to fuck with powerful cars in my city."

"Yeah, it stands out a bit."

"Exactly." He nodded confirmation that we understood each other. "What would you do if they stop you?"

"Just speak English at them," I said with a knowing grin, "and put a fake posh English accent on, as thick as I possibly can. That shit always works."

"What do you mean?" the Fox asked, puzzled.

I explained to him that when a traveller such as I is in foreign lands and has to deal with the law, particularly when infringing it, that the best thing to do was be as British as possible. I spoke a little Arabic, sure, but the police wouldn't know that. The vast majority of police in the kingdom spoke zero English, and I knew that. So I would use the language barrier to my advantage. Whenever dealing with foreign authorities that you know to be lazy and unable to understand you, speak more. Speak long and speak fast. Speak gibberish. Repeat yourself. Just keep talking. Maybe add in some Welsh. Whenever they speak to you simply state, "Sorry old chap, but I don't speak the lingo I'm afraid."

With a smile and confidence that says, 'hey man, I'm innocent and you're just wasting your time and testing your own patience fucking with me today', it won't take long for the foreign piggy to get bored and decide that it's better to wave you on and go about his day; at least that was always my experience in those situations.

The Fox laughed long and hard before acknowledging that it was a good tactic, and one that he would have to remember for when he travelled.

I was introduced to some of his close friends. Between them they were buying bricks from whoever had the best quality and then punting it out in smaller measures to the general smoker. They agreed to bring me in as a driver, all acknowledging that I stood less chance of being stopped and searched than they did due to the traffic police not wanting to start any international disagreements during a time when the UK government was selling weapons to the Saudis. Sure, my car was a magnet for attention from pig and public alike, but my white skin was a game changer. I wouldn't be able to do the buying by myself as I didn't speak fluent Arabic and the smugglers spoke no English. The Fox also thought that the smugglers may get jittery if dealing with a white face, as none of them had ever done so before. Their first suspicion would probably be along the lines of this fucker must be CIA or some other foreign agency with designs on incarcerating or killing them.

We decided that the best plan would be for the Fox and another friend to do the wholesale purchasing somewhere deep in the desert, and then I wait for them on the outskirts of the sand where we could shift the gear into my car for the drive back to the city. This plan worked smoothly and without so much as a single pull for months. Travelling as a convoy of cars always limited the chances of the hot car being pulled over, but not once did any of the vehicles see berries and cherries in their rear-view mirror.

Now that I was a part of the operation I was no longer spending huge sums of cash on hashish. I was effectively getting paid to smoke it.

The Desert

1

We flew along the highway at 100-plus, the battered Toyota Hilux growling. The Bedouin chatted casually to me as he steered the once white hunk of metal down the dusty asphalt.

"Is good you come. Welcome my friend!" He smiled widely and warmly as he looked in my eyes and not at the road.

This was the typical reception I had come to receive from Saudis. Most that I had met welcomed me warmly to their country and hoped that I enjoyed my time there – good hospitality is an important part of Saudi culture, be it their home, hometown or homeland. He nodded and smiled to himself as he returned his attention to the highway ahead.

"Thank you dude," I replied while taking in the surrounding countryside.

Sand. Lots of fucking sand. Sand as far as the eye could see. The highway was a grey snake that ran through the unrelenting desert, occasionally looking injured where patches of the asphalt were covered in dust and drifts. We headed out to my companion's farm.

For a guy from Wales, farms are green and smell of cow shit. But in the desert they are different. After about an hour or so of highway we suddenly cut left across the central reservation and tore across the four lanes that ran parallel to the edge of the highway, weaving between the oncoming traffic to surprisingly few horn blasts. The Bedu stopped the truck and stared at the embankment alongside us. We crawled forward slowly as he searched for something amongst the dead bushes that lined the steep slope. After a few moments he smiled and stepped on the accelerator. We drove along a semi-visible dirt road, which climbed the embankment and led to a gap in a barbed fence that ran the perimeter of the desert that we were now entering. The Hilux followed tracks in the sand, which had been made by countless vehicles using the same entrance for a long time. The 4x4 bounced around like the needle of a polygraph machine while questioning a politician. In the distance shapes began to appear.

"You see? Many farms here. Police want stop. They come break everything down, make fire," the Bedu said, explaining our surroundings.

We were now approaching a large area with multiple wood shacks and fenced areas scattered around and loosely connected by tracks in the sand.

"But nobody care. They come back. See, many times." He laughed as he pointed to the shack-farms. "We Saudis are crazy," he said as he laughed harder.

Some of the shacks were for people, some were

for animals. Namely camels and sheep. Some of the farms also had giant tents for the owners to stay in. The Bedu's farm was big and the whole area was cordoned off with a barbed-wire fence. The entrance was marked with two giant wooden posts reaching high into the sky. Beyond them was a giant tent that could even be described as a marquee, a huge pen made from sheet metal and planks of wood holding around 70 sheep, a few smaller huts and a huge open hanger that acted as shelter for the camels who feasted on gigantic bales of hay. It was difficult to get any kind of bearings at first. The multiple huts and roped-off areas had no identifiable order and I wondered how the Bedu ever remembered his way around or the way into this place. Even on the highway there had been no real identifying sign that this was the point along the road with an entrance to the desert. The grid structure of the surrounding farms had been slightly visible, but at night would be impossible to spot by an outsider. The farm itself would take some wandering around to get used to, but it was overwhelming when first taking it in. An illegal camel farm in the middle of the desert was not something you stumbled across every day if you're from Wales.

As we strode from the truck toward the camels a quad came roaring up to us ridden by two children. They were less than 10 years old and handled the quad like they'd been born on it. The Bedu and children exchanged some words before they all laughed and the quad sped off into the desert. The farm belonged to the Bedu and his brothers. They were six in total, but one of them lived in the capital so the farm was run by the remaining five equally. This meant that there were always people coming and going – all family members, friends, extended parties or guests of the tribe. The farm itself was also home to several Sudanese farmers. They had entered the kingdom illegally and were now living on the illegal camel farm, working for food and shelter. They were paid a little cash too, but not much. This was fine for the farmers though, they had fled war and death so keeping a small sheep and camel farm while occasionally acting as servants to the Saudi tribe was easy in comparison.

Most of the afternoon was taken up with drinking tea, smoking cigarettes and being introduced to all of the different men that came and went from the Bedu's farm.

At one point we had gone for a drive around the area, kind of like a mini-tour, but the only sights were more shacks and more sand. Occasionally we would see other 4x4s tearing through the sand, which was a common thing to do at the weekend in Saudi Arabia for young men with nothing better to do with their free time. The Bedu stopped the Hilux and relaxed in the driver's seat. "I love this place," he said with a smile and a nod. "Is home for Saudis. City is no good. Too much stress and work and..." he trailed off and flicked his wrist as if swatting a fly away. "You will like the desert, is very good. You are my guest, you are welcome," he said proudly with a big smile that revealed his terrible teeth.

The Desert

2

Being British, you come to learn that other
countries, particularly the Americans, mock our
dental hygiene, or lack thereof. The teeth of the
typical Brit are a sorry, mangled state in
comparison to the standard pearly white, straight
and even display of your average Yank. I have never
denied that my own teeth are in poor condition, but
in comparison to the average Saudi mine were
impeccable.

British people don't brush thoroughly or often
enough, but many Saudis tend not to brush at all.
Some, like many from the Middle East, prefer to
use what is known in Arabic as arak. This is a
chewing stick from the fibrous Salvadora persica
tree, more commonly known as miswak. It is
almost unheard of in the West but it is encouraged
in Arab countries by many dentists. The trees are
indigenous to arid regions and the planting of them
has been known to reduce desertification in areas
where nothing else can grow. By chewing on the
stick, or root, fresh sap and silica is released that
acts like a Brillo pad to remove stains and also
clean the teeth. If you research findings and studies

made by Islamic doctors and scientists, they will all tell you that the use of miswak is better than brushing with paste, as is done in the West. But go to any country, city or community where the use of miswak is prevalent, and your eyes and nose will soon tell an entirely different tale. Dentistry was still on the rise as a money-making business during my time in Saudi, closely followed by the health industry. Both had recently become booming industries due to the lack of knowledge in this part of the world of diet and dental hygiene, among other things.

It was announced shortly after my arrival in the kingdom that diabetes was now a major problem thanks to the introduction of American fast food. Go to any town or city on the Eastern Province and you will almost go blind from all of the bright lights enticing you into some fried food establishment, where for only a few riyals you can stuff your face with all manner of fatty and sugary delights. It was extremely enticing for families who had only known rice and meat with a few spices for most of their lives.

The Desert

3

We spent some more time driving around the almost invisible network of tracks carved into the sand by 4x4s, which criss-crossed through multiple farms of various sizes. In Saudi, particularly the desert, nobody really cares about rules and laws, least of all those who are paid to enforce them.

That evening, more than 20 of us gathered in the main tent. All men, all Saudi Bedouin – except for me. I was the only white face in the tent, and most probably that area of the desert that evening. And I was the only one not wearing white. All of the Bedouin wore the traditional white thobe, while I was kitted out in jeans and a hoodie. We all sat on the carpeted floor around giant silver plates, four or five men to a serving, and dined on a traditional Saudi rice and lamb dish known as kabsa.

I'd eaten in public enough times by then not to feel embarrassed about eating in the traditional Arab way, but I had never tried to rip chunks of piping hot lamb off the bone before. In the kingdom of Saudi Arabia, you eat only with your right hand. To tear red-hot meat from its bone with only the bare flesh of one hand needs practice.

Fortunately, my friend knew I would struggle and being the impeccable host that he was, he proceeded to pile chunk after chunk of lamb in front of me. Eating rice was no problem by this point for me; I'd mastered the art of clumping it together inside my fist and then using the upper front half of my thumb to push it into my mouth. What I hadn't mastered was getting it all into my mouth. It is accepted in Saudi that when eating some of it's going to be spilled, especially when eating with children and foreigners, so nobody thought anything of the slowly rising pile of rice forming directly in front of me on the plastic sheet that had been spread out on top of the carpet.

After the meal, of which I ate a lot, we went outside and washed our hands. In Arab culture, particularly the kingdom, smelling nice is a very important thing. It would not do to spend the rest of the evening with your hand smelling of lamb or whatever else you have eaten, and so after washing your hands you spray cologne on them.

In Saudi, bad smells are associated with evil. In your home, at the end of the evening after you have finished your main meal, you should empty the bins and take them outside. They believe that leaving rubbish, or more precisely the bad smell created by it, can attract evil spirits into your home. These evil spirits are referred to as Jin in the Middle East and Demons in the West.

The Bedu and I strolled around his farm, spending time with the camels and emptying our full stomachs of our own evil smells. Even in a country as conservative as the kingdom, some people are just as amused by farting as the Brits. They're just not as open about it.

That is a big part of the Arab mindset, and the Saudis in particular. Never really show what is going on or what you are really thinking. It is better to say a positive lie than a negative truth. You should always help your fellow brother in order to learn when he is vulnerable and needy.

The Desert

4

Over the months I continued to accept invitations
from the Bedouin to join him at the camel farm in
the desert. I would be careful how much hashish I
smoked before meeting him as it had been a subject
neither of us had brought up, and so I didn't know
his feelings about the practice of puffing. I knew
that he occasionally liked a sip of Chivas when in
Bahrain, but I also knew that he prayed five times a
day and that the Bedouin were the old school
Saudis. These were the guys who tenaciously clung
to their culture and traditions, usually very
reluctant to move forwards with the times.

There had been little in the way of signs or
evidence that anything untoward happened at the
camel farm. Other than the Sudanese farmhands
living illegally in the country and doing essentially
what could be classed as slave labour, it was just a
spot for men to hang out at weekends. Some of the
younger guys did look a little out of it when they
came, but then you can't judge someone by the way
their jaw hangs limply.

It came as a huge shock to me, and almost as
shocking to the Bedouin, when late one Friday

evening I walked past the wrong sheep enclosure at the wrong time while on my way to the portable toilet that everyone shared. Inside, one of the younger Bedouin, aided by one of the Sudanese farmers, was packing a sack with small brown bricks. Usually not one to let my guard or mental faculties slip, I would have kept on stepping lightly and ensured my presence went unnoticed, but that one time things went differently.

"Waaaawwww..." was the sound that passed out of my open mouth and to the ears of the guys bagging up the hashish. It wasn't my fault really, there was a lot of hash and I was in the mood for a smoke after filling my belly with rice and meat. What's a dude to do when he unexpectedly sees a giant sack of beautiful brown hash right there in front of him? It's only natural to be impressed and start dribbling on the sand.

Things went a little sideways after that.

The young Bedouin man immediately took out a dagger while yelling at the top of his lungs in his native tongue, and the farmer leapt at me to try to stop me from going anywhere and telling anyone what I had seen. The farmer was a fool and got slapped hard by me for his efforts and lack of grey matter. My hand collided hard with the side of his head and sent him face first into the sand. I then stepped back and into a more suitable stance to take on the guy with the blade, but by then others had come running to see what all the noise was about.

My friend spoke to the young knife fighter in

Arabic, and the two exchanged a lot of angry words before I was brought up to speed. The Bedu informed me that his nephew was not happy that I'd seen what I'd seen and was insisting that the tribe not take any chances by allowing me to return home and possibly run my mouth to the authorities. The Bedu explained that this was an awkward and dangerous situation for him, as blood was thicker than anything and everything – except God – for him and his people.

I did the only thing I could in that situation. Running for my life into the desert night would have been stupid and a certain end of it. Trying to fight the entire tribe would have been painful and ended with my swift death. So, I simply asked the Bedu to open one of the bricks and roll a joint for me.

You could have stuck an 18-inch cock in the Bedu's mouth it dropped so far open in shock.

"You know this?" he asked, pointing to the pile of hashish in the enclosure.

"Know it? Shit, I'm it's biggest fan," I said with a smile and a nod.

The other Bedouin were confused and the Bedu had to explain it to them in Arabic. They were very reluctant to believe that this pale face was a stoner and would be up for rolling and blazing a J here and now in the moonlit desert. I insisted they give me a piece of gear and a rolling paper or two, or as many as I could get my greedy paws on. They told my friend not to take the risk. Simply cut my throat and bury me somewhere in the sand deep in the desert.

The Desert

5

An hour later most of us were very high and very mellow. There was no more talk about cutting throats and digging graves. The Bedouin had good gear, and I started my enquiries about a deal being struck that the Fox and I could use to our advantage.

The Bedu explained how his tribe had been involved in smuggling hashish for many generations, and that it was something of a family trade. I couldn't believe it. Two of my students here in this most conservative of kingdoms had turned out to be deep into the drug game, and I was about to take full advantage. I let my friend know that I was also involved in moving bricks from one place to another as well as smoking as much of it as I could, and that we should look at possibly working together. He liked this idea, although some of the other members of the tribe were not happy about it. I was an outsider and should be left as one. Be friends, sure. Visit the camp and hangout with the tribe, no problem. Eat their food and drink their tea, of course you're welcome. But get involved with the illegal smuggling and selling of narcotics?

Think again.

My friend had made up his mind and he spent the next several weeks convincing his brothers that as I was already in the hashish business it made sense to keep me close and do business with me.

I spoke to the Fox, but he was not happy. From minute one, day one, he had stated that under no circumstances should I tell anyone about my involvement with hash in any way, shape or form. Now here I was telling him that I had made contact with a Bedouin tribe who were moving it in bulk in far larger quantities than we were doing. I set about persuading him that we should stop buying our gear from other suppliers and just start getting it from my friend the Bedu. The Fox took a lot of convincing. He said it made more sense to keep buying from different suppliers; use different people at different locations in order to not create any trends or patterns that the authorities could follow or use to lay traps to catch us. He made a good point, but I put up the counter argument that many of the smugglers he was dealing with were complete strangers and he was therefore increasing the chances of getting fucked over or being caught in a sting by undercovers posing as traffickers. As far as I was concerned the Bedu was a friend and worthy of my trust.

After a lot of going back and forth by both me and the Bedu, we eventually managed to convince all parties concerned that we should start doing business together. For the Bedu, it was business as usual. Someone (me) came to his camp and bought the gear. For the Fox and I things were now a little different. He had been convinced to buy from the Bedu, but he still didn't want to meet him or his tribe. As far as he was concerned, the Bedu was my contact so I should be the one to deal with him. This was fine by me. So now I went into the desert on a regular basis and loaded up on hashish that I then drove back to the Fox's place.

So as not to raise any suspicions, the Bedu and I kept to the same routine as before. I would spend most if not all of the day at the camp. We would hang out, eat, drink and smoke. They did, however, have a strict rule of not smoking hash at the camp. Cigarettes only so as not to attract any unwanted attention or cause panic should a random military or police patrol decide to come calling.

The only slight danger we faced was my vehicle's lack of four-wheel drive. To get from the highway to the camel farm, you had to drive across some real desert. Not just a little sand, but proper desert. These are not the kind of driving conditions an American muscle car is made for, especially one sitting about an inch off the ground. My only choice was to drive to where the hole had been cut in the fence at the side of the highway, phone the Bedu to collect me and then leave my car there. If I had been driving something regular like a Toyota Camry, an extremely common car in the kingdom, then it would not have looked suspicious. But to leave a beast like my Mustang sitting alone at the side of the highway would stand out to even the most lazy piggy or car thief. The Fox and I decided that the weekends I went to pick up he would swap his Jeep for my car seeing as I was delivering all of the gear to his pad anyway, it made no difference to exchange vehicles for the day. We made the necessary adjustments to the paperwork in case there ever were any stops, but we foresaw no danger with this arrangement.

The months rolled on, and our operation ticked along like clockwork. Nobody had any problems, there was never any fuss and the hashish tasted amazing. That was until the following summer.

The Desert

6

I made my usual drive to the camel farm but was met by an unhappy Bedu on crutches. His right leg was in plaster and he had some cuts and bruising on his face. He explained to me that he had been in a pretty bad car crash a few days earlier. To make matters worse, all of his brothers were away for various reasons and unable to return to the eastern province for at least a couple more weeks. As a result of all this, he had been unable to go and pick up their supply of hash, which meant they couldn't fulfil our order. The Bedu then asked if I would be able to accompany his nephew on the run to pick up the gear from very, very deep in the desert. They needed two trucks to collect the vast amount that they moved, and everyone else that they trusted was unavailable. Their contact had already been waiting longer than they were happy about, and the whole operation was now in danger of coming undone.

The Fox had already warned me multiple times that I should never ever go deep into the desert. He always told me that it was easy to get lost and you never knew what would happen next. It was too easy for something to go wrong with your vehicle, like getting stuck in sand or the heat causing something to blow. And there were too many crazy people residing in the depths of the sun-drenched plains.

He had told me about the old lunatics who survived out in the wilderness, never going to built-up areas. The ones who dealt in black magic, drank strange potions and were able to walk through fire and not so much as singe a hair on their heads. I believed none of it and had insisted whenever he mention such bullshit to take me to them so that I may see it all with my own eyes. We never went as he always said it was too dangerous and that he was too afraid to be around them. He also believed that deep in the desert is where the Jin resided. I found the Fox to be an intelligent and sharp guy, but sometimes this kind of talk would make me question my assessment of his mental faculties.

A more realistic danger he warned me of were the actual drug smugglers themselves. Apparently, most of the gear was transported through the heart of the desert by the real old Bedouin tribes who still clung to a system of warlords and chiefs, not giving a fuck about modern society and the royal family who controlled the country. He said that they would probably shoot a pale face like me on sight or try to sell me to some terrorist outfit at one of the borders. I had no idea how serious he was about these warnings, as he joked about me becoming famous online in a video displaying my beheading to the entire world. Dark humour, which now made me think twice about helping the Bedu to get the shipment of hashish.

"Please, my brother," came the request from my fat friend with only one working leg.

In Saudi culture it is considered very rude to decline a request for help, particularly from a family member or a friend. To say no to a stranger's request is bad, as their religion teaches them that you should always help people. Despite the dangers and my common sense I agreed to help. Even his nephew was reluctant to go along with the plan. He was young and had only been a driver himself when dealing with the smugglers. He had never had to take the lead when making a buy. And now he was about to not only take the lead, but do it with only a white faced, non-Arab and non-Arabic speaker as his backup. To say the idea was sketchy would be far more than an ignorant understatement. We were being downright foolish and we all knew it. The problem was we wanted that hashish and this was the only way to get it.

The only thing to compare being deep in the desert to is when you are far out to sea. You are surrounded in all directions by one thing, and it gives you no real indication of where you are or where you're headed. You just have to keep travelling in the direction that you think you are travelling in and rely on more than just your eyes and surroundings. It can be very disorientating, confusing and frightening if you allow it to be. You can drive past a sand dune, turn around and already be lost and headed in the wrong direction.

We drove for hours, deeper and deeper into the desert and the baking heat. As the car's air conditioner blasted cold and recirculated air into my face and the interior of the car I wandered how people had survived here without it for so long. How the fuck had the Arabs stayed here for so many thousands of years, living, working and flourishing? I thought about what it would have been like to travel across the sea of sand I moved across but on a camel rather than in a 4x4. Fuck that. It didn't bear thinking about, and just sent a hot shiver down my spine. There was no station for the Hilux's radio to pick up signals from out here and no CD player or port to hook up my phone, so I had to do the entire journey with nothing but the sounds of the engine and occasional gust of wind. It's ball-shrinking to say the least when you are driving through still desert air and suddenly a strong burst of wind hits the side of your vehicle out of nowhere. It helps keep you alert and focused with both hands on the wheel. I never drove with both hands on the wheel, I always had that one handed casual grip with pimp-like posture. Not in the desert. There I was sat upright with both hands knuckle white on the wheel for the entire duration of the drive into the heart of heat.

How the Bedu's nephew knew where to go was completely beyond me. I simply followed his Jeep and prayed to science that I never lost sight of it. We drove at high speeds all the way until hours later when we eventually saw a small gathering of vehicles waiting in the hot sun. Simply sitting there in the middle of nowhere, waiting for us to arrive.

When we stopped in front of the other vehicles I opted to stay in the Toyota until beckoned out. I watched the nephew greet the smugglers with the traditional handshakes and rubbing of the nose or three kisses back and forth to the air by the cheeks. It all seemed pleasant enough, but after the formal greetings came the raised voices and wild hand gestures. I figured the smugglers were busting the nephew's balls about how long they had had to wait for us here in the middle of the desert, burning up under the searing sun. I watched and waited until the nephew had done his best to calm them down. He made many hand gestures, most of which were to indicate to slow down or calm down, and then he showed them the fat bags of cash he had brought them. For reasons I couldn't comprehend this managed to anger them more. The voices got louder and turned into angry barks. The nephew tried to shove the cash into the head smuggler's chest, like he was insisting that he accept something he didn't want to take. I was even more confused – surely the smugglers wanted the money?

My confusion was suddenly shattered by the sound of a single bang. Right there before my eyes I saw the side of my friend's nephew's head explode out over the sand. The smuggler's right-hand man, smoking revolver still gripped tightly, stood over the dead boy and fired several more shots into his torso turning his traditional white thobe crimson. Without thinking, I simply fired up the Hilux's engine and stuck the stick into reverse. I put my foot down, as well as my head, as I drove backwards and away from the smugglers as fast as I could. I contemplated sneaking a peak over the steering wheel to see if they were giving chase, I thought about turning the vehicle around so that I could drive forwards at a faster speed, and then I heard an almighty crack and smash as the windscreen exploded over me. The bullet went straight through and caused the same explosion to occur in the small back window. I screamed aloud to the sound of roaring and knew that...

The Desert

7

Blackness.
Silence.
Nothing.

The Desert

8

When I woke, I found myself still inside the Hilux.
Only now I was slumped on my back, with my legs
being held above me by the steering wheel. There
was a ringing in my ears and a pounding in my
head. I slowly regained consciousness and took in
my surroundings. The 4x4 was clearly upside down,
with me strapped inside it. There was still a lot of
sunlight burning into my eyes, despite the fact it
wasn't shining directly on me. And there was a
harsh smell of burning.

I painfully and awkwardly undid the seat belt
and lowered myself onto the roof of the Hilux. I
crawled out onto the sand without thinking, which
caused me to recoil in pain. The heat of the sand
burning my pale palms and reminding me of where
I was. After a few moments my mind started to
catch up with my body. I was now asking myself
what had happened and answering myself with the
only possibility I could think of. The smugglers had
fired some kind of RPG at me and were now headed
over to the flipped 4x4 to finish me off. There were,
however, no sounds coming from outside. At first I
thought I might be deaf from the explosion, but

then realised I could hear the desert breeze mixed with the ringing in my ears. I lowered my head and gazed out through the empty window.

Behind the Toyota I could see what is best described as a giant fuck-off crater in the sand, black smoke still rising from it. Had someone dropped a bomb on the smugglers? Had the CIA been watching us and decided to attack by drone strike? I had no idea. All I knew is what my eyes could see. A hole where the smuggler's vehicles had once been. And a lot of black smoke. There was still some wreckage left strewn around the big hole – the leftovers of the vehicles used by the smugglers.

I turned my aching body and crawled backwards out of the flipped pickup so as not to touch the hot sand with my naked flesh. The sunlight was almost blinding once I was out of the shelter of the vehicle, and it took me a while to see properly through squinted eyes. Walking took a little longer to master as my legs were jelly-like from the ordeal I had just been through. The long drive into the desert before the explosion probably hadn't helped them either.

Once I was mobile enough, I approached the smouldering hole. Inside was a big black rock, which still gave off smoke and steam from the immense heat of the thing about the size of a bowling ball. I couldn't believe my eyes and at first figured I must be dead or unconscious in the flipped vehicle, dreaming some crazy shit about a rock falling from the sky. It was only the pain that really made me aware that I was in fact awake and really seeing what I could see. A fucking big black rock laying in a crater-sized hole where the smugglers had once stood when trying to kill me. What were the odds? I couldn't believe it. A fucking meteor had saved me.

I slowly staggered away from the rock and tried to look for any signs of life or shelter in the sea of sand that surrounded me. Just dunes and sunlight as far as the eye could see. I was fucked. I took shelter inside the flipped Toyota and considered my extremely limited options.

1. Stay and get baked alive in the hot desert sun.

2. Walk and get burned alive in the hot desert sun.

Neither option was particularly appealing.

I remembered something about the best way to survive in the desert is to travel at night when there is no sun in the sky to cook your lily-white flesh. This could have been some bullshit I'd seen in a movie, as I also recalled something about the desert being dangerous to walk across at night due to the huge drop in temperature and the camel spiders.

Camel spiders are what appear to be the main inspiration for H.R. Giger's designs for the alien face huggers. Large spiders with long legs. They are nasty fuckers that live in the desert and get their name from feeding off camels. They have an anaesthetic in their bite, which allows them to numb an area that they then devour. Foreign soldiers in the desert have apparently woken up with giant chunks of their legs or arse missing from where one of these horrible beasties has feasted on them in the middle of the night. They don't kill you, they just eat a large part of you.

I decided to just go for it as the sun was already close to setting anyway. I stripped the inside of the vehicle of any and all cloth that I could tear away, and then proceeded to wrap myself like a living mummy to protect my skin from the desert sun. I pointed my nose in the direction I figured we had come from based on the tire marks and location of the big hole in the sand. Then I set to walking. With no water and no clue, I started walking in what I hoped was the right direction back to civilisation.

The Desert

9

It was only a matter of hours before the sun had set and I was walking in the dark. Out in the desert, provided there is no cloud cover the sky is huge in the way you imagine infinity is. The stars are endless and the moon is gigantic. The entire thing feels like it is crushing down on top of you. The vastness of space and all that resides there makes for a lot of light when there is no light pollution from the cities and no rain clouds to hide it from you. I staggered onwards for as long as I could, hoping I would come across some kind of shelter to use as a rest area, but there was nothing except sand and stars. The blanket above me was overwhelming when looked at for too long. It reminded you of just how small you are in the universe and made you feel somewhat insignificant. Nobody likes to feel insignificant, and it's hard to believe that we, as a species and planet, really are inconsequential. We represent conscious life and for all we know we're the only one of our kind – that means something even if we are just star dust.

Sand and stars were all I had for a long time, and then it changed to sand and sun. The sunrise was foreboding and made me regret ever leaving the shelter of the flipped Hilux. I trudged onwards, feeling the sweat start to trickle and then pour from my pores. It wasn't long before the bits of cloth I had wrapped around me were damp and sticking to my flesh before becoming so wet that they started to slide off me and drop to the baking sands beneath my boots.

I walked for as long as I could. Willing my feet forwards through the heat and torture of the desert landscape, but the inevitable happened and my legs eventually gave way beneath me. I dropped down onto the sand and let out a dry and coarse wail from my parched throat at the burning sensation I felt on the bare parts of skin that were exposed to the hotplate-like sand I now lay pressed against. Even the parts of me that were covered felt the increase in heat from the ground beneath me that had endured millennia of sun beating upon it.

I figured that I probably looked something like Clint Eastwood's character Blondie from the classic The Good, the Bad and the Ugly when he was made to walk through the desert by Tuco. These thoughts didn't last long. All I could really think about was death. My mind flooded and overflowed with the knowledge that I was going to die in the desert, burned, dehydrated and starved. A horrible way to go. I pictured my blistered and peeling corpse being found by some nomadic Bedouin travelling through this way in months to come, and then wondered if they would even bother to stop and stare at it yet alone pick it up and take it to the authorities.

Maybe there would be nothing left to find, my bones being covered by the sand after the camel spiders had had their fill of my dead meat.

I closed my eyes and thought about my life and whether or not I deserved such a horrible death. Had I really been such a bad person? Did it even matter? Was there such a thing as karma or an omnipotent being, and did it actually give a fuck how we behaved? I knew that I would never learn the answers to these questions and I didn't really care. All I really wanted was water, not information or insight or enlightenment – just water. And possibly a spliff. But only after my thirst had been quenched.

I started to wonder if my participation in drug crimes had been my downfall. I'd gotten deeper and deeper into the game as the years rolled merrily along until I found myself in the situation of purchasing and smuggling vast quantities in foreign lands. Was this the reason why I lay on the hot sand, red skinned and red eyed? The law had never caught up with me and so fate had intervened and punished me instead.

Cosmic karma of the cuntiest kind.

It was just a little puff, nothing heavy dude...

The Desert

10

I opened my eyes at the sound. The white burned into my retinas and the movement of my seared eyelids caused me to try to scream in agony, but my throat was too parched to allow sound to pass.

The engine roared loud in the distance and was definitely heading my way. I forced my upper torso to move and used every ounce of my willpower to sit upright. My movements must have made me look like Nosferatu when he sits up in his coffin at sunset, slow, stiff and rigid. I couldn't have looked much prettier than that either. I almost cried through the pain of turning my head in the direction of the rumbling that drew ever closer and for a fleeting moment I allowed myself to hope a little. Maybe I wouldn't die here on the desert sand.

The small white dot in the distance grew larger and my heart sank a little at the sight of the heat waves rising from the ground. Those wavy lines that look like water caused me to start to believe that maybe this was just an illusion, a mirage like I saw happen to people in the movies who got into this kind of shit. They rippled back and forth, causing the approaching dot to move with them and I thought I would cry, but there wasn't enough fluid left in my body to shed any tears of fear or joy. I raised a hand and managed to wave it a few times before collapsing back down flat onto the baking sand where I struggled to remain conscious. The approaching sound was like fuel for my willpower, urging me to stay awake long enough to ensure I got rescued.

By the time the Jeep arrived it was all I could do to keep a single slit open on my scorched face that had almost no skin left on it to burn. The driver stopped, lowered his window and peered down at me. And then I heard him say "Fuck me! You alive mate?"

I lifted a shaky hand up enough to indicate that I wasn't a corpse, but didn't bother to try to speak.

"You look dead to me," he said before sitting back inside the comfort of the air conditioned 4x4 and starting to close the electric window. The sound of the glass sliding back up shut again terrified me to my core.

"Wait!" I managed to blurt out between my cracked and bleeding lips. He paused and then half leaned back out of the window, just in time to witness me push myself back up into a sitting position, "I'm alive!"

"So?" came the gruff Australian response.

"Help..."

"Fuck that. What use are you to me?"

It was then that I realised something. I knew that voice. Sure, I'd heard plenty of Aussie accents over the course of my life, I'd grown up during the heydays of both Neighbours and Home and Away, but this was a voice I'd heard face-to-face in the real world. I racked my almost dead brain for the memory, I pushed through decades of drug abuse and debauchery until eventually it came back to me, just as I saw his window fully close again. "Rocks!" I yelled as loud as I could. The Jeep jerked forwards and then stopped with a jolt. There was a pause before the window lowered again and his head peered out. He had a short beard and sunglasses on now, but I remembered his face. I remembered that mean voice and surly attitude. It had been several years, but I still remembered our brief encounter at the bar in Vietnam. I still remembered that he was a meteorite dealer.

"Did you say *rocks*?"

"Yeah..." I managed to say as I collapsed back to the sand again.

"What fucking rocks?"

"A meteorite..." I managed, "...as big as..."

I passed out.

The Desert

11

I woke to cool air and cold water against my burned and haggard face. The Australian was gently patting my forehead with a wet rag now that he had moved me inside the Jeep and had me laying across the backseat.

"It's about time you woke up. You best start telling me about these rocks before I kick your arse back to the sand."

I slowly raised a single index finger.

"One? One what? One rock? You gotta be shitting me!" the surly man said before leaning over me and opening the Jeep door, clearly intending on dumping me back out onto the desert to die. I held up both hands and indicated how big the meteorite I'd seen was.

"Are you fucking sure?" he barked.

I nodded my head yes before starting to drift back into unconsciousness.

"Where, you cunt?!" He shook me hard.

I pointed in the direction I had been walking from and passed out again.

The Desert

12

The thud and sudden heat woke me with a jolt, and I sprang upright with my hands flailing. Then I was on my back and being dragged across the burning sand by my ankles until I was a few metres away from the Australian's 4x4.

"In-fucking-credible!" He said with a smile and nod of his head. "You weren't fucking kidding you limey cunt. It's huge, probably the biggest fall yet unfortunately for you."

"What?" I croaked.

"Not enough room in the Jeep for me, you and the meteorite. And, let's face it mate, I weren't driving around the fucking desert looking for half-dead cunts now was I?" He grinned like a psycho about to slash his next victim.

"Cunt," was all I could utter.

The Australian chuckled as he started preparing straps and tools to recover the meteorite, most likely still burning hot, out of the crater it had created for itself upon impact with the desert.

The sun was low and the air was slightly cooler, which meant I had been asleep for hours. This had allowed me to regain some strength and move

closer to being classed as alive rather than dead. I
was still very far from 100%, but I now had fresh
motivation to fight for my life. In front of me was a
perfectly working vehicle, complete with air
conditioning, drinking water and a GPS that could
get me back to civilisation. All I had to do was ditch
the bastard who was in possession of these things.
Sure, this would probably mean killing him, but
then what happens in the desert stays in the desert,
much like the woods. I bided my time, playing
possum and allowing him to do all of the heavy
lifting. I figured that if I took care of the Aussie
after he'd loaded the meteorite into the Jeep then
not only could I save myself, but I could possibly
get a giant payday too.

Meteorites are worth a lot of money. Sure,
technically they're just bits of debris. But they're
debris from comets, asteroids or meteors that
originate in outer space and have survived passing
through the Earth's atmosphere. They've survived
not only the dangers and cold of space, but also the
friction, pressure and chemical interactions with
the atmospheric gasses of our planet's atmosphere
that heats them up enough to radiate energy and
turn them into fireballs, more commonly called
shooting stars by those who witness them. The one
like the Aussie was currently wrapping straps
around was classed as a meteorite fall, the other
kind being meteorite finds. Falls are observed and
are far more rare. There are roughly only five to 10
falls recovered a year.

Until the late 1980s and early 1990s, most

meteorites were given to or purchased by museums or similar institutions in the name of science, but then the commercial market started to boom, particularly in Morocco, with an increase in private collectors from the West. Some collect them for the glory and prestige, others use the minerals to create new things. There's one guy in the US who even uses the iron-nickel contained in meteorites to make spectacular and intricately designed knives that sell for stupendous amounts at auction.

Not too far from where I lay in the burning sun in Oman, the recovery of meteorites had been banned and they have been classified as national treasures. This, I figured, was why the Aussie was currently in Saudi. Even after Oman had made it illegal to move any meteorites from within their borders, some hunters – mostly Russian – had continued to do so and had quickly found themselves locked up in prison for it. From what I've been told, Middle Eastern prisons are no joke, especially if you are neither Arab or Muslim.

Until now the biggest meteorite recovered had been half a kilo in weight, and that too had been recovered from the desert of Saudi Arabia. Some believe that the black stone set into the wall of the Kaaba is a meteorite, but that has never been proven and probably never will be. This time it was laying in the Saudi desert, but it was heavier than half a kilogram. I guessed that the rock was closer to 10 kilos, but I was no expert just someone who had watched a lot of YouTube videos when high and up alone at night.

I lay still, thinking about not only the rock, not only recovering my strength, but also plotting. How would I dispose of my soon-to-be attempted murderer without him overpowering me? I was far weaker than him in my present state and I was also unarmed. He, on the other hand, had a giant knife stuck in a leather sheath on his belt and looked like he was in prime physical condition and not afraid to use it. Actually, he looked like he would enjoy using it on me and may even have been planning to.

Fortunately for me, but unfortunately for him, my previous training in martial arts came in very useful when he was foolish enough to step close and bend down to insult and thank me before announcing it was time we parted ways. I quickly wrapped my legs around his waist and pulled him down on top of me, before hooking one arm behind his neck and using my other hand to slide his own knife out of its sheath and into his side. I forced the blade in and across as far as I was physically able to, which happened to be a lot more than I previously thought I would. It's amazing how much strength and endurance the human body can produce when under the right strenuous circumstances. It didn't take long for the Aussie to stop struggling and die there on top of me on the hot Saudi sands. I had twisted, dragged and pushed the blade enough to open him up wide, which caused him to bleed out quickly. I'm pretty sure that I ruined some of his internal organs too, but then again I'm no expert on human anatomy. Once I was sure that he was dead I pushed his corpse off of me and then tried to sit upright, but I found I no longer had the strength. I collapsed, covered in blood, crimson blade still in hand and struggled to breath.

Faust's Mephistopheles believed that the world and existence was chaotic misery and suffering that would be better off not existing, but laying on the hot sand dying I had to disagree.

CPSIA information can be obtained
at www.ICGtesting.com
Printed in the USA
BVHW071723281222
655161BV00004B/75

9 781916 050358